Fortuity's Arrangement

Seven Unsuitable Sisters
Book 2

BY MAEVE GREYSON

ARE YOU SIGNED UP FOR DRAGONBLADE'S BLOG?

You'll get the latest news and information on exclusive giveaways, exclusive excerpts, coming releases, sales, free books, cover reveals and more.

Check out our complete list of authors, too!

No spam, no junk. That's a promise!

Sign Up Here

www.dragonbladepublishing.com

Dearest Reader;

Thank you for your support of a small press. At Dragonblade Publishing, we strive to bring you the highest quality Historical Romance from some of the best authors in the business. Without your support, there is no 'us', so we sincerely hope you adore these stories and find some new favorite authors along the way.

Happy Reading!

CEO, Dragonblade Publishing

Additional Dragonblade books by Author Maeve Greyson

Seven Unsuitable Sisters Series
Blessing's Baron (Book 1)
Fortuity's Arrangement (Book 2)

The Sisterhood of Independent Ladies Series
To Steal a Duke (Book 1)
To Steal a Marquess (Book 2)
To Steal an Earl (Book 3)

Once Upon a Scot Series
A Scot of Her Own (Book 1)
A Scot to Have and to Hold (Book 2)
A Scot To Love and Protect (Book 3)

Time to Love a Highlander Series
Loving Her Highland Thief (Book 1)
Taming Her Highland Legend (Book 2)
Winning Her Highland Warrior (Book 3)
Capturing Her Highland Keeper (Book 4)
Saving Her Highland Traitor (Book 5)
Loving Her Lonely Highlander (Book 6)
Delighting Her Highland Devil (Book 7)
When the Midnight Bell Tolls (Novella)

Highland Heroes Series
The Guardian (Book 1)
The Warrior (Book 2)
The Judge (Book 3)
The Dreamer (Book 4)
The Bard (Book 5)
The Ghost (Book 6)

A Yuletide Yearning (Novella)
Love's Charity (Novella)

Also from Maeve Greyson
Guardian of Midnight Manor (Novella)
Once Upon a Haunted Highland Mist (Novella)

Chapter One

Lady Atterley's Masquerade Ball
Mayfair London
February 7, 1821

GENTLEMEN TRAVEL IN *packs, behaving like wolves on the hunt for the weakest of the debutante herd,* wrote Lady Fortuity Abarough, third sister to the Duke of Broadmere—at least, third as far as birth order was concerned, since the duke had seven sisters in total. She wriggled her nose to relieve the terrible itch caused by the feathers on her crimson mask, huffing at the annoying plumage tickling her face. While doing so, she spied her brother Chance, fifth Duke of Broadmere, politely removing himself from the clutches of an older miss she recalled seeing last Season. She made an addition to her notes: *At times the gentleman becomes the hunted, chased with great enthusiasm and desperation by those ladies experiencing their second or even third Season.*

"Such cutting words," said a familiar voice from behind her. "You surprise me, Fortuity. Might I ask what this study is for?"

She folded the paper and stuffed it into her feathery reticule that matched the deep ruby shade of her gown adorned with the same infernal swath of plumage besieging her nose. What on earth had the modiste thought by suggesting this birdlike creation, and why had she agreed to it? Without a glance back at the owner of the voice, she lifted her chin and kept her focus locked on the participants of the Marriage Mart circling one another on the dance floor.

"It is most rude to poke one's nose where it does not belong, Lord Ravenglass." She kept her voice low even though they stood off to themselves beside an overwhelming froth of bright red tulle cascading down from the gilded bow and arrow of an elaborate white cupid bearing a somewhat demonic expression. "And yes, you may ask about my study, but do not expect an answer."

He chuckled softly. "*Lord Ravenglass?* I can always tell when I've piqued your ire because you resort to formal address. Are we not friends, Fortuity? Allies, even? Especially after last year? Why, even your sister Blessing said she thinks of me as a second brother."

"Knowing my sister, she did not mean that as a compliment." Fortuity turned and looked up at him, even though she knew it to be a mistake. Viscount Matthew Ravenglass was by far the most exquisite man she had ever met, and the handsome fool probably knew she thought that.

Mischief danced in his flinty gray eyes set off by a dashing black mask that convinced her that perhaps the next romantic story she wrote needed a dark-haired hero who stole the heroine's heart at a masked ball. "And yes, we are friends and allies, but that does not mean we are confidants."

His boyish smile made her heart beat faster as he dramatically pressed a hand to his chest. "You wound me, my lady."

She struggled for a witty response, distracted by the observation that his black evening coat required no stuffing or special tailoring to make him appear as powerful and broad-shouldered as a Greek god, as the mighty Zeus, even. He just looked that way because he was and would undoubtedly look even better stripped naked. Her cheeks burned hot at that scandalous thought, and Mama was surely frowning down at her from heaven.

She tossed her head and huffed at the annoying feathers again before returning her attention to the dance floor. "Methinks your wounds are contrived, my lord."

He leaned in so close that his clean, warm scent of citrus and sandalwood wafted across her, making her inhale deeper to savor it. The familiar fragrance reminded her of his wonderful parlor, filled with the books she had itched to peruse when she and her siblings had first visited him last year while attempting to save her sister Blessing's husband.

"Fortuity?" he said, his voice deep and coaxing.

She swallowed hard and tensed every muscle to keep from betraying herself with a reaction to his nearness. "Yes, Matthew?"

"You know you can trust me. Do you not?"

"I suppose."

"What are your scribblings for?" he asked ever so softly, his breath tickling her ear. "I remember your doing the very same thing last year the first time I saw you." He rumbled with amusement, the sound as warm and rich as a sip of the finest chocolate. "You were a most studious little thing, hiding in the shadows of the drapery that night, scratching away at your scraps of paper."

"*A most studious little thing.* Why thank you, Lord Ravenglass. What a lovely compliment. With such charm and wit, I cannot believe there is not a pile of ladies fainted dead away at your feet." She tightened her hold on her reticule and fanned herself with an obscenely feathered accessory that made her eyes water with the need to sneeze. "Why are you so inquisitive?"

"Because you intrigue me."

She gave an indignant huff. "I do not intrigue anyone, my lord. Least of all you." She tipped a nod at the other side of the dance floor. "Did I not just witness you *intrigued* by not one but three of those ladies currently smiling at you and glaring at me?"

"Do I detect a hint of jealousy?"

She snorted again. "You detect my ability to take notice of the obvious, nothing else." She turned, snapped the plumage of her fan shut, and tapped his chest with the feathery thing. "You are hiding from them. Aren't you?"

The muscles in his chiseled jaw rippled. A sure sign she had hit the mark.

"Were they truly so forward you felt compelled to seek cover in the land of the wallflowers?"

"You are safe, Fortuity." He glanced up and down the room and eased deeper into the shadows behind her.

"Safe? Why, thank you again, my lord." No woman wished to be called *safe* or *a studious little thing*, but she supposed that was better than some of the criticisms she had overheard from those who found her lacking when comparing her to her beautiful sisters. "You do realize that I am neither tall enough nor broad enough to hide you from view?" She stretched up on tiptoe to see the refreshment table. "Where are your cousins? The two of them might conceal you better than the one of me."

"Eleanor is working through her dance card, and I believe her mother is hiding in the ladies' retiring room once again."

Genuine sympathy for his older cousin, Mrs. Agnus Sykesbury, filled Fortuity. "I am sorry. By the cheerfulness of her gown, I thought your cousin much improved." Poor woman. The pair had come to live with the viscount after Mr. Sykesbury's death and a complicated unpleasantness with his family in India. Even though they were well over two years past the usual period of mourning, Mrs. Sykesbury still wrestled with paralyzing bouts of grief. Her daughter Eleanor suffered no such incapacities. "Do you think you should take her home?"

"I offered, but Eleanor fussed enough to compel her mother to stay." He grumbled—or growled. Fortuity couldn't decide how she would describe his disgruntled sound if she were to write it. "You know Agnus never denies her daughter anything."

"Yes. I am aware." Fortuity was very much aware. None of the Broadmere sisters liked Miss Eleanor Sykesbury after she attempted to cause problems between Blessing and Thorne before they married. The conniving little chit thrived on stirring trouble. Her mother, Mrs. Sykesbury, was kindness itself. Eleanor was an insufferable cow.

"Lord Ravenglass," said Fortuity's eldest sister Serendipity with well-aimed shrewishness as she joined them. "How are you this evening?"

"Weapons down, Seri," Fortuity said. "He is here because he is hiding from his admirers, not attempting to ruin me." She fluttered her fan at the trio of ladies slowly making their way around the edge of the dance floor. "Perhaps you should run, my lord. Your huntresses are on the move. They approach their prey."

With a mischievous wink, Matthew positioned himself between her and Serendipity. "Surely I am quite safe while flanked by the esteemed Broadmere sisters."

"Yes," Serendipity said, sounding distracted as she gazed around the room. "Speaking of which, where are Grace, Joy, Felicity, and Merry? Have either of you seen them?"

Serendipity had promised Mama she would look after her six sisters and not marry until each had found love and happily settled down with a husband. Even though it was rather against the usual for the eldest to marry last, nothing about the Broadmere family and their beliefs had ever been orthodox or usual. That knowledge made Fortuity smile. She took great pride in their eccentricities and the rare way Mama and Papa had raised them.

"I have not seen them since we arrived," she told her sister. And she hadn't. If she had, she would point Serendipity in their direction to save herself from being forced to dance and interact with those she would much rather observe from the safety of the shadows. After all, as her siblings had so indelicately put it, she was next on the chopping block, since Blessing had married. Their brother couldn't come into the full of his inheritance until all seven sisters had found the bliss of love matches. As far as Chance was concerned, the tally was one down, six to go, and he couldn't get them settled fast enough, since his monthly stipend was less than what he considered adequate. He wanted access to the entirety of the family's vast coffers, and he wanted it now.

"What about you, Matthew? Have you seen them?" Serendipity craned her neck and continued scanning the crowded room.

"This is a masked ball, my lady," he said, gentling the reminder with a lowered voice.

"You found me easily enough," Fortuity retorted.

"You were unmistakable to me."

The smug slant of his smile and the exciting wickedness smoldering in his eyes made her catch her breath, but she refused to let him know how he affected her. After all, they were friends. Nothing more. He had often said so himself. "Ah yes, my fervent scribbling in the shadows of the draperies. I gave my studious little self away, didn't I?"

"Well, I must find them," Serendipity said, then gave Matthew a stony glare before turning to Fortuity. "You should come with me, Tutie."

"I will not." With a broad wave of her feathery fan, Fortuity encompassed the large ballroom. "I am far from unchaperoned in this crush, have yet to finish my observations, and Blessing is just over there. She will watch me to maintain all proprieties." Fortuity couldn't resist a gleeful smirk at the viscount. "After all, I must protect our dear friend here from the beasties headed his way. I am sure they have their claws out."

"Indeed, they do," Matthew told Serendipity with mock seriousness.

Serendipity looked past him and perked like a hound catching the scent of a fox. "I believe that's Gracie over there. Do excuse me." Before she charged through a cluster of lords and ladies, she pointed her fan at Fortuity. "Please join Blessing and make sure she does not overdo. You know how impossible she has become."

Fortuity nodded and shooed her onward, even though she had no intention of plowing through the guests to reach her sister Blessing's side. Thorne would watch over his wife and ensure nothing endangered her or their unborn child. Their presence at the ball had surprised Fortuity because none of the Broadmere sisters had ever cared overly much for such functions, and

Blessing could have used her condition as an excuse even though she was barely rounding in the middle. All became clear when her sister explained that Lady Atterley's husband had proposed a lucrative business venture to Thorne that required the expediency of discussing it tonight rather than waiting for a more suitable moment.

"May I have this dance?" Matthew asked with surprising urgency.

"Why?" Fortuity turned back to him. "Are more lovelies headed your way?"

With a pointed look over her head, he stared at something behind her. "This waltz will save us both, my lady. Is that not your favorite marquess coming toward us?"

She turned and allowed herself a groan. "Oh dear, the malodorous Lord Smellington." She flinched. "Beg pardon. I should not have said that."

Matthew threw back his head and laughed as he swept her out onto the dance floor before the man reached them. "Your sister always called Lord Pellington the Marquess of Debt, but I believe your moniker for him is more accurate."

"Last season his stench caused poor Merry to gag on her lemonade and spew it all over him." Fortuity shuddered.

"He believes bathing causes illness."

"His lack of bathing causes illness. I nearly retch whenever he is near." She struggled to concentrate on the steps after treading on Matthew's foot yet again. "I am so sorry. Now you know another reason why I keep to the shadows with my scribbling."

"You have yet to tell me the first reason, my lady." He smiled down at her, making her heart flutter in a manner that made her breathless. "Since I rescued you from Lord Smellington, should I not be rewarded with an elevation in status from friend to confidant?"

"You are more tenacious than one of Gracie's dogs with a favorite bone."

"I shall take that as a compliment." He lowered his head and looked into her eyes as if she entranced him while they spun to the music. "Tenacity is an honorable trait. Denotes patience. Perseverance. I always get what I want, my lady."

Of that, she had no doubt. "One might also call it stubbornness, my lord," she told him with her most blinding smile. "A trait rampant among toddlers and spoiled children who think they should always get their way."

"I am hurt you do not trust me, Fortuity."

"A shift in tactics, my lord? You almost sounded sincere." She curtsied as the music ended, then stared at him in surprise when he didn't bow. He just stood there, glaring at her. Was the man pouting like a sullen child?

Behind the mask, his gray eyes had shifted to a flintier shade, and he did not smile as he offered his hand. "Shall I escort you to Blessing?"

"Yes. Thank you." She *had* hurt his feelings. It echoed in his tone. She slid her gloved hand back into his, the same hand that had tingled from his touch as they danced. "I trust you, Matthew. I simply do not wish to be laughed at to my face or behind my back."

He tucked her hand into the crook of his arm and marched them off the dance floor at a quicker pace, not to her sister, but toward the double doors thrown open to an expansive conservatory of leafy plants and flowers that provided the illusion of a summery retreat for the chilly February evening.

"I would never laugh at you," he said. "I might tease or jest to coax a smile from you, but I would never make amusement at your expense." Just inside the conservatory doors and still within view of the guests, he halted and frowned down at her. "I would have thought you knew that about me by now, considering how observant you are, my fair, quiet watcher of every social gathering in Mayfair."

She had not only hurt his feelings but angered him as well. Perhaps it was time to show him she was not the helpless wallflower, the plain Broadmere sister no one ever noticed or gave a second thought to. She was—dauntless. Somewhat. "How dare you."

"How dare I?"

"Yes, how dare you attempt to make me feel guilty about protecting myself from Society's cruel barbs. Do you think I am deaf to what they say about me? How I am the plain one? How my hair is not the angelic blonde of my sisters but more like tarnished gold? How I barely possess enough curves to prove I am female even though I have reached the ripe old age of one and twenty? That my intelligence must be lacking because my tongue becomes tied more often than not when I find myself among those who disconcert me?"

He shifted with a deep intake of air, his mouth tightening with displeasure before he bowed his head. His arm flexed beneath her fingers, then he covered her hand with his. "This conversation has taken an unseemly turn, my lady, and I must beg your pardon." He leaned toward her, aligning his eyes with hers to prevent her from looking away. "Contrary to what you have heard or experienced in the past, you are not the *plain one.*" His gaze swept across her, making her catch her breath as he raked it down her body. "Your hair is the warm, rich color of ripened wheat, and your eyes the blue of a stormy sky after the rain has ceased." He boldly swept his focus across her again. "There is no doubt in my mind that you are a woman, and I daresay your tongue has been loose at both ends this evening."

He took her hand from his arm and cradled it between both of his. "I consider you a friend, Fortuity. One of the very few people I place in that exclusive category." He stared down at their joined hands. "I will not trouble you again with my questions. As I said earlier, you and your scribblings merely intrigued me." He nodded and tucked her hand back into the crook of his arm. "And now that I have made myself clear, I shall escort you to your sister."

"No, you shall not." She planted both feet and refused to budge. "Not until I have made myself clear."

He stared down at her. A faint, unreadable smile tugged at that mouth of his that she had committed to memory and envisioned on every hero she had written since meeting him. He released her hand and gave her a proper bow. "By all means, my lady, make yourself clear."

She stared up into his dark gray eyes and braced herself for his cruel laughter and disbelief that would surely come when she told him about her passion, her life's work, her stories. She had never known him to be cruel before, but in this, she had no doubt he would be like everyone else.

Well, not exactly like everyone else. Mama and Papa had supported her dreams because they loved her and had to support her. They were her parents. Her siblings didn't understand her need to write, but since she accepted their eccentricities, they accepted hers. Her sisters did, that was. Chance had been a complete toad about her stories. But Matthew fell into none of the categories that required him to be nice and understand her penchant for writing fiction.

"My lady?" he gently prompted her.

"My observations at all of Mayfair's social gatherings help give my characters more realism."

"Your characters?"

"Yes, if you must know, the characters in my stories that I mean to publish someday. Under my own name. Not some male pseudonym or anonymous labeling. *Written by Fortuity Abarough* will be on the title page of my books when the world receives them." She backed up a step, clenching her fan and reticule to her middle as if they were her shields. She waited, staring at him for what felt like forever. When he remained silent, she stamped her foot. "Well?"

"Well, what?"

She wished he would take off that bloody mask so she could better read his expression. "Well, go ahead and laugh like my brother did when he found out." She jutted her chin higher. "Blessing filled his bed with frogs when he was so mean to me that day."

"Why would I laugh?" he asked quietly, seeming genuinely befuddled.

"Because women are to marry, manage households for their husbands, and give them children. They do not write books and publish them—as women with their real names. Or, at least, most don't if they wish to be successful authors and not have Society label them as pitiful oddities. And my wish to do so, to write something other than gossip sheets, and have my books receive acclaim, is like hoping for lightning to strike me in the middle of a cloudless day."

"You are aware of my love of the written word? My fondness for books, plays, and papers?"

"Yes." A leeriness filled her, like waiting for a trap to snap shut and cleave her dreams in two. "What about it?"

"I have nothing but the utmost admiration for anyone able to create such works. To fabricate worlds and invite others into them for a brief respite from the tedium of Polite Society's latest *on dit*, Parliament's pettiest arguments, or whatever other ridiculousness the world has spawned is an astounding talent."

The candor in his eyes threatened to bring her to tears. She swallowed hard and batted her lashes, thankful for her feathery mask. "You are most kind, Matthew. Thank you for not mocking me. Or laughing."

He smiled and took her hands in his. "We are friends, my lady, and I would do nothing to risk that."

Friends. A double-edged sword, that word. It stung even though she had always known they would never be anything more. She shook away the dismal feeling and squeezed his hands. "I consider myself fortunate on that count, my lord. Very fortunate, indeed."

"Then all is once again well between us?" His hopefulness shamed her for not being thankful for the gift of his friendship and trust.

She squeezed his hands again and smiled. "Yes, my lord. All is well between us."

"Good, because we must dance again. The pungent marquess is as persistent as the huntresses." He swept her back out onto the floor, turning and spinning them away from their pursuers.

"Oh dear. Mind your feet, my lord." Fortuity struggled to keep up with the oddly faster-paced waltz. "Should the tempo not be slower?"

"Ah, my observant little wren, did you not overhear Lady Atterley proclaiming to all and sundry that she would be the first to introduce this latest style of waltz to Mayfair?"

"I did not, and I take umbrage at being called a plump little brown bird with a loud song."

He laughed as he guided her through another twirl, not even wincing when she stumbled across his feet yet again. "Wrens are known for their cleverness. Have you never heard the tale of the little wren who hid in the eagle's feathers to win the title of the king of birds? Whoever soared the highest won, and when the eagle reached its limits, the little wren emerged and flew even higher."

"In Irish folklore, they symbolize betrayal," she countered. "One flapped its wings and showed St. Stephen's attackers where he was hiding."

Matthew laughingly shook his head. "I prefer my story over yours."

She couldn't resist a sheepish grin. "So do I." She glanced down at his poor feet as the music stopped, and she took a step back and curtsied. "Oh my. Your valet will be most displeased with me. Please offer him my apologies when he's fetching water to soak your poor bruised feet and then polishing your shoes."

He bowed, then held out his hand for her to take. "My feet are fine, my lady, and he polishes my shoes after each wearing, anyway. Come, let us join your sister so as not to rouse Serendipity's ire."

"Look," Fortuity whispered as she took his hand.

"What?" He turned to follow her line of sight.

"Lord Smellington has cornered your huntresses. Neither Lady Serafina nor Miss Genevia are pleased."

"And Lady Theodora may cast up her accounts," he whispered back. "She is as green as her gown."

Despite herself, Fortuity felt bad for the ladies. "Should you not be gallant and rescue them?"

Matthew huffed and walked her faster toward the other side of the room. "I am not the only gentleman present and am otherwise detained attending to your sister's wishes that we not allow Blessing to tire herself excessively."

As they reached Blessing, she eyed them with a sly expression that could only mean trouble. "Two waltzes? What will everyone surely think?"

"Stop, Essie," Fortuity said. "Chance and Serendipity are bad enough without your crossing over to their side in the war to marry off all the Broadmere sisters."

Blessing ignored her. Instead, she aimed a calculating smile at the viscount. "Then you would be my brother, Matthew."

"Where is your esteemed husband?" he asked, blatantly ignoring her remark.

Blessing puckered with a moue of bored displeasure. "Still speaking with Lord Atterley."

"No puckering," Fortuity told her sister in a teasing tone, feeling somewhat sorry for her being temporarily abandoned. "Remember what Mama said."

Blessing smoothed her expression, then hissed a dramatic sigh.

"I must ask," Matthew said. "What did your mother say about *puckering*?"

"Causes lines and gives one the appearance of a shriveled piece of fruit," Fortuity said.

"I am hungry again," Blessing said. "Will they never announce supper?"

Matthew bowed. "Allow me to fetch you a lemonade and some treats to tide you over, my lady. My future godchild must not go hungry."

Blessing brightened. "That would be lovely and shall be remembered when Thorne and I choose godparents for little Aloysius Starpeeper."

Matthew backed up a step, and Fortuity snorted with laughter. "Surely, you do not mean to name the child Aloysius Starpeeper Knightwood?" she asked.

Blessing shrugged and gave her an evil grin. "One never knows."

"I shall fetch the refreshments." Matthew hurried away, chuckling and shaking his head.

"He would make you a fine husband," Blessing said while watching the viscount weave his way through the crowd.

"We are friends," Fortuity said, wishing her sister would stop. "Nothing more. The only reason we danced together twice was to avoid Lord Smellington and those three he currently has cornered."

"Friendship is a fine foundation for marriage."

"Has your condition of pending motherhood rendered you deaf?" Fortuity scowled at her sister. "Viscount Matthew Ravenglass is a friend to all of us, I might add. That is all. Besides, did Thorne not tell us the man swore off marriage years ago? Something about the woman he loved tossing him aside to marry a duke?"

"You could heal him. You would never betray the man you loved."

"Who says I love him?"

Blessing took a step closer, and her demeanor shifted. She was no longer acting sly or teasing. "I know you, Tutie. I have seen the way you look at him."

"Then you also know how much it would hurt me to lose his friendship because you pressured him into something he would never wish." Fortuity bowed her head, fighting for composure. "Please, Essie. Leave it alone. For me?"

"But—"

"Please, Essie," Fortuity forced through gritted teeth. "Stop. I write romantic stories with happy endings. I do not experience them firsthand because I am…me."

Chapter Two

A s Matthew made his way to the refreshments, he caught sight of his younger cousin and came up short. Eleanor was standing entirely too close to the Earl of Fetterill, the *married* Lord Fetterill, a man known to be on the hunt for a new mistress.

He scanned the ballroom for Eleanor's mother, dreading what he knew he would have to do if she was still cowering in the ladies' retiring room. Her thankless daughter's removal from possible ruin would fall to him. A most undesirable situation, since Eleanor would just as happily trap him in a marriage of convenience as she would any other eligible male of the peerage.

"Anything I can do to help, old man?" His closest friend and Blessing's husband, Baron Thorne Knightwood stepped into his path. "Even with your mask on, you've a face like thunder." Knightwood followed his line of sight. "Ah… Never mind. I should have known it had something to do with *her*."

"No good deed goes unpunished. I should have rescued Agnus on the condition that Eleanor stay in India and marry the man her father's family chose for her."

"I very much doubt Mrs. Sykesbury would have agreed to that. She appears most devoted to her daughter and quite blind to her behavior." Knightwood shifted in place, scanning the large room with a sweeping gaze. "I do not see her, though. Shall I interrupt your cousin's conversation for you?" He tipped his head in her direction. "You have rescued me once or twice, as I recall.

Time to return the favor?"

While tempted, Matthew decided against it. "No. I would not do that to you and your wife—who, by the way, is famished and champing at the bit for them to announce supper. The last thing you need is the hungry woman carrying your child to be enraged with jealousy."

Knightwood's demeanor immediately shifted to one of concern. Even behind his purple satin mask, his expression shouted regret. "Old Atterley loves to hear himself talk. Our meeting lasted longer than I expected."

"I am sure if you take Blessing a plate of those Naples biscuits along with some lemonade, she will forgive you." Matthew kept his focus locked on his cousin, willing her to step back and put more distance between herself and the lecherous lord. The reckless, dark-haired wanton in her glittering mask that matched the silvery sheen of her satin gown glanced his way and smiled.

"You do realize she knows what she is doing?" Knightwood asked as he filled a plate with an enormous pile of biscuits, then accepted a goblet of lemonade from a servant.

"Making me look the fool?"

"No. She thinks she is stirring your jealousy."

"She should know better than that by now." Matthew lowered his voice even more. "I want her married and out of my home as soon as possible."

Knightwood brightened. "To make room for a wife, I hope? A particular Broadmere sister, even? One with whom you danced this evening not once, but twice, according to the whisperings I heard while plowing through the guests?"

"You are as insufferable as your wife."

Knightwood bowed. "Thank you." Dodging a rather portly fellow headed for the refreshments, he nodded in the direction from which Matthew had just come. "I best get these to Essie. And know this, old friend—she is very protective of Fortuity and thinks the two of you are a perfect match. I know how you feel about marriage after... Well, after. So, consider yourself warned.

If Essie has you in her sights for her sister, the issue will not go away easily."

Matthew stepped aside while extending an arm to open a path for his old friend. "Best get those to the lady. A hungry woman is not a happy woman." His past was a closed subject even though it had cemented his future. He would not discuss it, not even with Knightwood.

Before heading off to join his famished wife, Knightwood nodded his understanding of the unspoken request. As he disappeared into the crowd, Eleanor appeared at Matthew's side.

"Your glower frightened my prey before the trap could spring," she said.

"Your *prey* is married, cousin." He refused to mince words as he had done when the Sykesburys first arrived. "You need a husband, not a benefactor who will cast you aside once your beauty fades."

Rather than the crestfallen attitude he had hoped to trigger, Eleanor beamed at him. "So you think I am beautiful?"

"Where is your mother?"

A haughty sneer curled the girl's lovely mouth, revealing her true nature. "She promised we could stay until after supper, or have you already forgotten?"

"If you do not adjust your behavior and purport yourself in a manner befitting a virtuous lady seeking a socially acceptable match, we will leave immediately, no matter what your mother promised. Am I understood?"

She stared up at him, narrowing her dark eyes. "You have no right to speak to me in such a manner. Especially not publicly."

"I have maintained contact with your father's side of the family, and they have assured me their home remains open to you, since you are the last of their lineage, even though they consider you a foolish, stubborn girl. Need I clarify what that could mean for you?"

She backed up a step and caught a hand to her throat. "You would not dare. Think of what that would do to Mama."

He shrugged. "It could not cause her any more damage than her daughter becoming a courtesan."

"I was merely talking to Lord Fetterill," she said in a hissing whisper.

"If you had positioned yourself any closer to the man, you would have been inside his waistcoat."

"I hate you."

"Good." He rolled his shoulders, attempting to uncoil the weighty tension of his poor decision to bring his cousins under his roof. As he had learned long ago, but apparently failed to remember, no good deed went unpunished. "I suggest you disappear into the ladies' retiring room for a while and give Lord Fetterill a chance to forget about you and latch on to someone else."

Eleanor flounced away, but Matthew noted the direction she chose was the one he had suggested.

"Well done, my lord."

He cast a sideways glance at Fortuity and immediately relaxed. Strange how she always had that effect on him. He tried to assume a sternness and failed. "Someone once advised me that poking one's nose where it does not belong could be considered quite rude."

"No. I said it *was* quite rude, no consideration necessary."

At that, he couldn't help but smile. The teasing in her tone warmed his heart a great deal more than it should. "Forgive me for misquoting you, my lady." He angled a glance toward the last known sighting of Blessing in the crowded room. "Have you abandoned your sister after promising Serendipity to watch over her?"

"I was thirsty," she said, "and my charming brother-in-law only brought lemonade and treats for his wife. *He* is watching over her."

"Allow me to help." Cutting through the throng much easier than her, he shielded her from the crush and escorted her closer to the refreshment table that now appeared somewhat depleted.

He got her a glass of lemonade, but the Naples biscuits and other nibbles were gone, and the plates taken away. "Here you are, my lady, but I fear the lemonade will have to hold you until the supper gong."

"No worries." She stayed close to his side as they made their way to a less crowded area within full view of Blessing so as not to be accused of lying to Serendipity. "I followed Mama's advice. I am just fine until supper."

Intrigued yet again, he had to ask, "I must know. What advice was that?"

She pointed at him, and her stormy blue eyes flashed with the seriousness of the sternest tutor. "Your word that you will tell no one."

"You have it, my lady. I shall take your secrets to the grave." The tensed knot of frustration between his shoulders brought on by his cousin's antics disappeared completely. Fortuity was a balm to his soul.

"Well…" She glanced around, then eased a bit closer to shield their conversation from others. "Mama always had Cook serve us a healthy portion of mashed potato before we went out for the evening to attend such soirées as these. Mama knew the heartiness of the dish would not only shield us from the effects of an overly strong ratafia but also keep us quite hale should supper run late or the treats run short."

A warmth filled him, not from the crowded room but from thankfulness at having been accepted as a friend to such a close, loving family. "Your mother was very wise."

Fortuity ducked her head. "Yes. Very wise, indeed," she agreed quietly. "We all miss her very much."

Determined to shoo away her sadness, he nodded across the way at Blessing eating her biscuits with amazing speed. "I wonder if your sister forgot that sage advice?"

"I am sure she did not. Have you not been around her at tea or mealtimes recently? The rounder she becomes, the more voracious her appetite. She attacks her food with such gusto that her knife and fork send off sparks and clang like dueling swords." Fortuity clamped her mouth shut, and her eyes flared wider. "Pray do not tell her I said that!"

He strained to keep from roaring with laughter. "As I said, your secrets are safe with me."

The dinner gong sounded, causing every guest to turn toward the front of the room and slowly form a somewhat orderly line that jostled a bit as the various members of the peerage shifted to their appropriate places.

"Lining up in pecking order is ridiculous," Fortuity said as her brother the duke moved closer to the front of the line and offered his arm to a dowager duchess whose name Matthew couldn't recall. "We are all guests, for heaven's sake. Are we not?" She reached for her reticule and withdrew her folded bit of parchment and tiny stub of graphite. "I must make a note to avoid this silliness in any of my stories."

"Shall I assist you in removing your mask before you take your place in line with your partner?" As a viscount, Matthew regretted his place was farther down the way than whomever the daughter of a duke might pair with. In this instance, the age-old ritual disappointed him. He would much rather stand in line with Fortuity.

She looked up from her scribbling and eyed him with a mischievous smile. "Shall we be naughty?"

The sultriness of her tone belied her innocence and caused him an immediate awareness of the increasing tightness in the crotch of his pantaloons. He shifted in place, doing his best to shadow the bulge of his rather uncontrollable reaction to her question. "Naughty, Fortuity? You? Surely not." While he didn't wish to be fed to one of her sisters for ungentlemanly conduct, neither could he resist her. "What, pray tell, do you suggest?" He shifted again and loosely clasped his hands in front of the part of his person causing him issues.

"My goodness, you do fear Serendipity and Blessing, don't you?" Her lighthearted laugh softened the accusation. "It is nothing serious, my lord. A mere shuffling in the supper line to stir the guests properly before they sit down to enjoy their meal. It would be a most useful experiment to observe their reactions, and how the situation is handled with courtesy and decorum."

"A shuffling in the supper line? You do realize I cannot step in front of a higher-ranking peer?" In other words, he *would not.* He prayed she understood.

"Oh no, you couldn't possibly take such a risk as that, and I would never ask you to do so." But mischief danced in her eyes as she looped her arm through his. "Shall we see what happens when I partner with you, thereby causing an upward shift of rank among the ladies?"

"I should say the ladies would be quite pleased. But one must wonder how the gentlemen will look upon it."

"Exactly. And that is the usefulness of the experiment. How will they react?"

"Lady Atterley could very well pull you aside and direct you to your correct position," he warned. "Would that not be embarrassing for one who usually secludes herself in the draperies with her scribbling?"

"Lady Atterley was a dear friend of Mama's. She will more than likely send Chance or Serendipity after me." She patted his arm. "But we shall never know unless we try. Are you willing?"

"Are you, my lady?" He did not wish her shredded by the *ton*'s sharp tongues. Something about this rare woman made him determined to protect her, even if it meant protecting her from herself. "According to your brother-in-law, the gossips are already whispering about our two waltzes together. If you toss your head at standard decorum and plant yourself at my side, will it not stir them into a frenzy? Have them assume we are something we are not?"

The mischief in her eyes extinguished like a candle's snuffed flame, and something about her changed, became diminished. She quickly turned aside and gazed at the supper line. "You are quite right, my lord. What was I thinking?" She dipped a quick curtsy his way, then rushed off, moving to her appropriate place in the ridiculous pecking order waiting to be seated in the dining room.

Matthew groaned and damned himself for being a bacon-brained fool. While attempting to save her from public scrutiny and ridicule, he had bruised her feelings himself. While he hoped she cherished their warm friendship as much as he did, did any woman truly want it thrown in her face that their relationship would never be anything more?

But then, did Fortuity *want* more from him?

Something stirred deep within him, a dangerous wondering, the tiniest flickering of something he might once have called hope. With a roll of his shoulders, he tossed the implausibility aside. No. Fortuity did not want more than friendship. None of the Broadmere sisters portrayed themselves as eager to wed, and he most definitely did not wish to marry.

He kept his gaze locked on her as she waited in line up ahead but still within view, her head held high, occasionally huffing at the crimson feathers on her mask and rubbing her nose. His heart went out to her. Did she not realize she was the only guest still masked? Even with the silly red featheriness of the thing, she was beyond beautiful, a precious jewel. He had never understood how anyone could think her plain.

Tossing his own mask to a nearby table, he settled in his proper place and offered a detached nod to the viperous Lady Serafina Mellincotte, one of the three huntresses who had hounded him all evening.

"We meet again, my lord." She looked up at him through her dark lashes, then batted them with such fervor, he was tempted to inquire if she had something in her eye. "Are you enjoying your evening?"

"Lady Atterley never fails to host the perfect gathering." A vague answer was always best when dealing with the more dangerous members of the *ton*. Lady Serafina might not be the daughter of a duke as Fortuity was, but her viscountess mother had trained her well. Rumor had it that she had already reduced more than one of her fellow debutantes to tears, and several gentlemen feared she would eviscerate them next.

"Are you not going to inquire if I am enjoying *my* evening?" She quirked a brow, strangely making him think of a pine marten he had once come across in Scotland. Her brown hair and elaborate gown strengthened that impression with its creamy front inset in a dark cocoa satin. The mask dangling from her wrist even bore fur. And the tiny member of the weasel family fit her perfectly. While the animal could be quite pleasing to watch in its natural habitat, one must always remember not to touch it because of its fierce teeth, sharp claws, and appetite for smaller mammals.

"Well?" she repeated, a little more sharply.

"Forgive me, my lady." He didn't attempt to sound at all contrite because, frankly, he didn't care. "Have you enjoyed your evening?"

She moved closer until their shoulders subtly touched while they made their way to the dining room. "Indeed, I have—except for the waltzes." She tapped on the dance card dangling from her wrist beside her mask. "I saved both spots for you, but you chose another."

He simply smiled, then shifted his attention elsewhere, refusing to rise to her bait.

"Well?"

Not attempting to stanch a disgusted huff, he turned back to her. "Well what, my lady?"

She jutted her chin higher and narrowed her eyes. "I see."

He doubted that very much but was not rash enough to say so. Instead, he ambled into the room and, with great relief, broke off to the hostess's right of the long dining table, feeling sure Lady Serafina would go to the host's left. While she would inevitably seat herself across from him, at least the bloodthirsty woman would no longer be at his side, or so he had hoped. Unfortunately, since the places of honor had already been taken by higher-ranking peers, the remaining guests could seat themselves wherever they liked. Lady Serafina remained at his side.

The only saving grace was that Fortuity sat on the other side of the table, not close, but not so far down that he couldn't see her. In fact, he stared at her, willing her to look his way so he might apologize with a smile.

But she didn't.

A heavy sigh escaped him before he could stop it.

Lady Serafina leaned in entirely too close and whispered, "When can we expect the announcement, my lord?"

He frowned at her while bloody well wishing he had insisted on himself and his cousins ending this evening early. "Announcement?"

She turned her head and gave Fortuity the sort of smile that made one's blood run cold. "A courting announcement? Engagement? Pending nuptials?" With a coyness he found most revolting, she turned her chilling smile his way. "A Broadmere daughter, no less. Quite the catch. Although I hardly thought you would choose that particular one."

"Lady Fortuity is a friend whom I hold in the highest regard. A friend only," he repeated louder than intended, making several at the table look his way with raised eyebrows. He risked a glance at Fortuity and locked eyes with her, willing her to know he meant her no harm or insult.

She gave him a little nod and a smile that made her seem even sadder.

Damn and blast it all. He had hurt her even more.

"Forgive me, Lord Ravenglass," Lady Serafina said, "but your *friend* does not appear impressed with your high regard for her." She cast a disinterested glance up the table, then took a victorious sip of her wine.

The thing of it was, he was trapped, and the cruel Serafina knew it. If he bolted now, it would only fuel the gossips further. He clenched his teeth, knowing there was nothing for it but to sit supper out and speak to Fortuity at another time and preferably another place. After all, thanks to their two dances and Lady Serafina's actions, all eyes would be on Fortuity and himself for the remainder of the evening.

"Do forgive us. My wife suddenly finds herself feeling unwell," Knightwood told Lady Atterley in a voice loud enough for all in the room to hear. Before their hostess could comment, he looked Matthew's way. "Lord Ravenglass, would you be good enough to follow? I need a word. Urgently."

"Of course, Lord Knightwood." Matthew abruptly rose, concerned for Blessing as well as thankful for a brief respite from the room. He couldn't quit the party completely, not without his cousins in tow. But at least he would be free of Lady Serafina's company for as long as possible.

Every Broadmere sibling rose and curtsied to Lady Atterley, then hurried out behind Blessing, who clutched her husband as if she were so ill that she could barely walk. Matthew followed, praying that both the lady and her unborn child would be all right.

Once they all reached the large entryway and were well out of earshot of the other guests, and the footman had left them to summon the carriages, Blessing emitted a low growl and marched over to Fortuity. She caught hold of her sister's arm and towed her over to Matthew. "You will apologize for embarrassing my sister. I thought better of you, Matthew. How could you be so cruel?"

"Essie, stop!" Fortuity wrenched her arm free. "He merely told the truth."

"Fortuity," Matthew began, then went silent, uncertain what to say. All he knew was that he hated he had put such unhappiness in her eyes. "I…"

She held up a hand. "You do not owe me an apology. The gossips caused this treachery simply because we made the mistake of sharing two dances to escape less-than-desirable partners."

But neither her tone nor the teary sheen in her eyes matched the sentiment of her words. Unable to resist, he reached over and gently removed her mask. "Damn the gossips and everything else. Forgive me, Fortuity. I should not have chosen my words so poorly and reacted to Lady Serafina's goading."

She avoided his gaze by keeping hers lowered. "It is quite all right, my lord. Honestly. There is nothing to forgive."

"And forgive me for hurting your feelings when I balked at the experiment," he added softly.

"What experiment?" Fortuity's brother Chance pushed in closer.

"Nothing sordid." Fortuity glared at her siblings. "Must you all surround us as if we are a pair of prizefighters about to box?"

"Yes," Blessing said. "We must. I gave up my meal to provide you an escape from that room. Now, what experiment?"

"A mere shuffling in the supper line," Matthew said, hoping to draw their irritation to him rather than Fortuity. "We were curious about what might happen if Fortuity took a position beside me rather than farther to the front of the ladies' line where she belonged. But then we both had second thoughts about what the tongue waggers would say—what with our sharing two waltzes this evening."

"You mean *you* had second thoughts," Serendipity said with a withering glare. "Hence the apology for hurting her feelings. What did you say to her?"

"I was a coward," he said. "And I told her as such."

"And now you are lying." Fortuity rolled her eyes. "He warned me the gossips would stir into a frenzy and consider us courting, which would not be at all accurate, since we are only friends. He did not wish my marriageability harmed or any possible true loves dissuaded because they thought I was no longer available."

"But it hurt your feelings," Blessing said to her sister with a look at Matthew that made him feel lower than the soles of his shoes.

"It did not." Fortuity brushed her fingers across her forehead and looked everywhere but at anyone's eyes. "I was merely tired and growing hungry. They kept supper quite late."

Knightwood cleared his throat and tipped a nod at a footman coming their way. "I suggest we resolve this matter at another time and, most definitely, another place."

"There is nothing to resolve," Fortuity said, sounding much stronger. "All is well. We merely erred in allowing the gossips to take temporary control of the narrative. We shall not make that mistake again. Shall we, Matthew?"

"No, my lady. We shall not." But something about her made him feel ill at ease, quite unforgiven and as if he had done something much worse than naming her as his friend. And the more he thought about it, the more he wondered if he had been the worst sort of fool. She was not happy with him, and he hated himself for it.

A trio of maids appeared bearing the ladies' cloaks. A pair of footmen followed them with Thorne's and Chance's greatcoats and toppers. Another footman appeared and bowed to Matthew. "Do you require your things as well, my lord?"

"Yes. Along with my cousins. Have them fetched from the dining room and summon my carriage." Not even the hounds of hell could drag him back to that table and the poisonous Lady Serafina.

And he had much to think about. His heart ached for Fortuity, and he would be damned if he allowed her suffering and humiliation at the hands of the *ton* to continue.

You mean her suffering and humiliation at your hands, his conscience argued.

He bowed his head and accepted the damnation. Yes, the suffering, humiliation, and, worst of all, the sadness he had caused her.

Chapter Three

Fortuity crumpled the paper and tossed it aside, then propped her elbows on her writing table and dropped her head into her hands. Her characters' conversations had left her. Last night's painfully embarrassing debacle repeatedly squalled through her mind like a relentless storm, drowning out everything else.

"What was Blessing thinking?" she muttered. How could her sister not realize that if they had simply allowed the evening to play out however it would, the gossips would have soon grown bored and forgotten Matthew's rather loud proclamation that she was nothing more than his friend? After all, she was a wallflower no one ever noticed unless to comment that they thought her the plainest of the Broadmere sisters, which was fine.

Well, no, it wasn't fine. It hurt. But she refused to allow those mean-spirited sorts to dictate how she lived her life. Or, at least, she *tried* to refuse them most of the time. Sometimes that particular battle became wearisome and difficult to fight. A heavy sigh escaped her. Who was she attempting to trick? Those cruel, back-biting churls cast a shadow over everything.

Once the *ton* discovered her sympathetic sister had quickly recovered from her sudden ailment, the tongue waggers would realize what had actually happened: that a frailness of health was a mere ploy to remove the infamous Broadmere wallflower from an unpleasant situation. Everyone knew the siblings were close and would do anything to protect one another. It would take no stretch of the imagination for the tattle sheets to weave an intriguing tale everyone would easily believe. All of them were well and surely doomed.

"Dearest Blessing." Fortuity gave in to a despondent groan as she spoke aloud to the sister whom she no longer shared a home with. "I thought you better at this game than me. What in heaven's name were you thinking?"

A rapid tap on the door and the creak of its hinges made her lift her head.

"Chance has called for a gathering of the flock," her youngest sister Merry announced. "I tried to tell him you were unwell, but he didn't believe me." She offered a sympathetic shrug. "If it helps, he's angry with all of us, yet not so unhappy with you. At least you set your notes aside and danced. Or how did he put it?" She tapped her chin, staring upward as if the answer floated somewhere near the ceiling. "Ah, yes—you took part in the evening like a dutiful sister rather than the four selfish ones who did whatever they wished."

"I presume Serendipity possesses immunity, since she assists him in throwing us at potential husbands?" Fortuity leaned back in her chair and rubbed at her ink-stained fingers. "Somehow that seems less than fair, since she must also eventually find love and marry."

"When have you ever known Chance to be fair? He wants us starry-eyed, in love, and married off as quickly as possible, so he can be more than *a duke in name only*, as he puts it." With her hand still on the door latch, Merry waved for Fortuity to follow. "Come along. Serendipity might not fight on your side, but the rest of us will. We swore an oath last night."

Fortuity could just envision her four younger sisters joining hands and giving a hearty war cry, as they had often done as children when waging pretend wars against Chance and his chums at their country estate. Even though they were girls, Mama and Papa had indulged their every interest and imagination, never once limiting them to only subjects proper for young ladies.

"I might as well come down." She eyed the crumpled balls of paper scattered across the floor. "I am doing no good at all up here."

Merry looped her arm through hers and tugged her out into the hallway. "Blessing had a word with us last night."

Fortuity cut a leery glance at her youngest sister. "Your tone concerns me."

"She confirmed what the rest of us already knew. We are not young, oblivious things anymore, you know."

"Oh, I know," Fortuity said, trying not to smile. "Why, you yourself are the ripe old age of ten and seven now."

Merry lightly pinched her. "We know you love him."

Fortuity swallowed hard before assuming as bored an expression as possible. "Love whom?"

Merry arched a feathery brow and stared at her, waiting for the truth as Mama used to do when one of them had been caught in a lie.

"I love my writing," Fortuity said, but it came out weaker than she intended. She cleared her throat. "Matthew and I are friends, as he is friends with all of us."

"He didn't dance with *all of us* last night. Only you. Twice."

"We were escaping Lord Smellington and Lady Serafina."

"Hmm." Merry studied her as they descended the stairs to the main hall. "That excuse is hard to counter." She shuddered. "I do believe that man reeks worse than he did last Season."

"I am sure he hasn't bathed since last Season." Fortuity slowed their pace as they neared the parlor. "Matthew says the man believes that bathing causes illness."

"I thought only Scots felt that way?"

"I believe that was long ago. Remember Lord MacKenzie? Even when he was ancient, that man smelled so divine, all the ladies flocked around him."

Merry halted. "Surely you are not that naïve? While I agree

the man had an irresistible aroma that even I noticed as a child whenever he visited Mama and Papa, I overheard Serendipity whisper more than once that it was his *charm* that drew the ladies to him."

"His *charm?*" Fortuity couldn't decide if Merry meant the way the beguiling old Scot always treated the ladies, some magical gift, or a forbidden carnal talent.

"The man fathered twenty-seven children, Fortuity. The last one was born the year he died at the ripe old age of four and eighty." Merry leaned closer and lowered her voice. "And every woman he married was a great deal younger and always happy to become his wife and remain that way."

"How do you know all this?"

"I never divulge my sources."

Fortuity rolled her eyes. "You sound like Serendipity." She nodded at the closed parlor door. "You go first."

"Coward," her sister accused with affection, then charged forward and threw open the door. "All right, brother. We are here. Commence with the inquisition."

"Really, Merry?" Chance shot her a withering glare.

Fortuity took a seat between Serendipity and Grace. Old habits died hard. They always arranged themselves in birth order. Joy sat on the other side of Grace, Felicity next, and Merry took her seat at the end. "As Merry so eloquently put it, commence with the inquisition, brother," Fortuity said. She was in no mood for what would surely be as humiliatingly painful as last night.

"How are you today?" he asked, the tensed line of his jaw softening.

"I am well. You?"

He scrubbed his forehead and groaned. "I am not the one who appeared to be the subject of the masked ball last night. Nor was I selfishly used to escape debutantes, then cast aside like a useless bit of parchment. I intend to have a word with Ravenglass. Friend or not, I do not appreciate his casual treatment of you, especially when it brings ridicule down around your ears."

"I used him just the same to escape Lord Smellington. Matthew did nothing wrong. He simply stated the truth. We are friends, nothing more." *Nor will we ever be anything more,* she silently added. She rubbed her temple in a vain attempt at ridding herself of the subtle pounding that was getting stronger by the moment. That was just what she needed today, one of her terrible megrims. "Lady Serafina goaded him into raising his voice. You know he would do nothing to hurt us or cause us embarrassment."

"And yet he did." Serendipity reached over and gave her hand a sisterly squeeze. "Why do you not speak to him about this *friendship* of yours?"

"Am I the only one who remembers what Thorne told us?" Fortuity pulled her hand away, frustrated with this painful subject. "Have I not been humiliated enough? Why would I confront the man and force him to tell me he would never want me as his wife because he has sworn he will never marry? I daresay that would do wonders for our friendship."

"His *incident* was over five years ago," Chance said. "Perhaps he has reconsidered."

"I would rather have him as a friend than confront him and lose him completely." And that was the bloody awfulness of it all. She heard Mama's voice in her head, scolding her for using such unacceptable language even in her thoughts. She pulled in a deep breath and forced herself to maintain control. "Might we move on? I was not the only plump little Broadmere goose hanging in the butcher shop window at last night's ball."

"I did not go to the stables nor visit Lady Atterley's hounds," Grace said, lifting her hands in surrender.

"No, you hid most of the night," Serendipity accused. "I only found you when you emerged from the jungle of the conservatory to fetch yourself a lemonade."

"Poor planning on my part," Grace grumbled. She tipped her head down the line at Joy and Felicity. "These two were no better."

"I fattened my purse at a rollicking game of Commerce," Joy said, "and I am not ashamed to admit it."

Felicity twitched a shrug. "I simply had to discover how Lady Atterley's cook obtained such a lightness to her Naples biscuits."

Merry pointed at Grace. "I hurried after Gracie when I saw Lord Smellington on the prowl."

Chance groaned again. "Lord *Pellington*," he corrected her. "If all of you insist on calling the man names, at some point, one of you will surely err and do so in public. Need I remind you how inappropriate such behavior is for a Broadmere lady?"

"Your Grace?" drawled a deep, raspy voice from the doorway.

"What?" Chance barked, then clamped his mouth tightly shut and bowed his head. "I beg your pardon, Walters. It is not your fault I am saddled with impossible sisters who drive me to the limits of my patience."

The ancient butler stood in the doorway, blinking like a great horned owl waking for its nightly hunt. The duke's apology obviously made him uncomfortable.

Fortuity had to smile. Old Walters had been with the Broadmeres since before any of them were born. The devoted servant refused to take his pension. And, in truth, she couldn't imagine their household without him and their equally ancient housekeeper, Mrs. Flackney.

Chance lifted his head and squared his shoulders. "What is it, Walters?"

The butler extended a small silver salver bearing a single note. "A messenger awaits a response, else I would have placed it in the library with today's correspondence for your later perusal."

Frowning, Chance took it, eyed the wax seal, then arched a blond brow at Fortuity. "It is from Lord Ravenglass."

It took everything within her to maintain a nonchalant façade. Her family already possessed an opinion regarding her feelings toward the viscount, but there was no sense in fueling that opinion. "Open it."

He opened the single page and stared down at it, slowly shaking his head as he read. "I cannot possibly," he said under his breath. He looked up and motioned for Fortuity to come closer. "He wishes us to join him on an outing to Dulwich Picture Gallery of Southwark. Today."

"Us? There are a good many of *us* currently in this parlor, brother. How many carriage loads of Broadmeres does Matthew hope to entertain?"

Chance gave her a look that shouted he did not appreciate her levity. "You and I, dear sister. But I cannot possibly. Not when our infernal solicitor insists upon my meeting with our estate steward before spring is fully upon us."

"I am sure Mr. Sutherland, the elder, is only following Papa's wishes." Relief filled her. If Chance couldn't accept the invitation, then neither could she, and that would relieve her of the uncomfortable task of facing Matthew again so soon. "Besides, I do not think it wise, do you? If Matthew and I are nothing more than friends, how would it look for me to join him on an outing today after dancing with him twice last night?"

Her brother's eyes took on a dangerous twinkle. "As I said earlier, perhaps Ravenglass's feelings toward you have changed. He needs an heir, since his cousins are female, and I daresay he would rather one of his own blood inherit the fruits of his labors rather than some distant relative he has never known." He turned and eyed the other five sisters still seated in the lineup always formed for family meetings. "Serendipity?"

With a pained look, Serendipity shook her head. "I couldn't, possibly. I already committed to tea with Lady Burrastone."

"I'll go," Merry volunteered.

"I cannot," Joy announced. "Lady Edith's daughter is dying to learn how to win at whist, and I promised to teach her this afternoon."

"Ahem?" Merry waved both hands. "I can go."

"I am busy as well," Felicity said, "helping Cook with next week's menu."

"What about me?" Merry asked quite loudly.

"You are the youngest, Merry," Chance said with a shake of his head.

"I am ten and seven and quite able to tattle on my sister should she attempt to steal a kiss."

"No," Chance told her, then pointed at Grace. "Congratulations."

Grace slid lower in her chair. "I abhor the Picture Gallery, and besides, I was not invited." She wagged a finger at him and Fortuity. "The two of you were named. It would be most rude of me to step in. Politely decline."

"She makes a fair point," Fortuity said. She didn't wish to go either but knew if she fought Chance too vigorously, it would only make him dig in and strive harder to make her go. Her brother was the most stubborn of all of them. "Besides, I agree with Grace. I would much prefer a visit to the British Museum. Perhaps we can consider an outing there at some other time when the memory of yesterday evening's gossip fades. All you need do is tell the messenger to relay our thanks, but today's diaries—in fact, the remainder of this week's diaries—are full." She inwardly cringed at Chance's thoughtful expression. Instinct warned she may have pushed a mite too hard.

"No. You and Grace shall go, but we will inform the messenger of your preference to visit the British Museum rather than the Picture Gallery. Lord Ravenglass may call for you at three, thereby making your outing quite appropriate and before intimate calling hours." He moved closer, his smile growing broader with each step. "Discover his intentions, Tutie." He turned and arched a brow at Grace. "Help your sister in this effort, please?"

Grace rolled her eyes and deflated with a dismal huff.

"Chance—" Fortuity closed her mouth, giving up before she even started. There was no use fighting him on this. He had made up his mind. All she could do was go along with it, apologize to Matthew, and advise him to stay as far away from the as-yet-unattached Broadmere sisters as possible. That realization hurt her heart and made her eyes sting with tears she couldn't possibly let anyone see. She shooed him away as she turned to leave the room. "Do as you wish—as you always do. As Blessing once so accurately noted, you are a male. You always get your way."

"WE SHOULD HAVE offered to meet him at the British Museum and then gone elsewhere." Grace dropped onto the settee in the small parlor, still pouting about being forced to act as chaperone.

"That would not have been kind," Fortuity said. Although she had to admit the idea held merit. "And sit properly. You know how Mama felt about poor posture."

Adopting her usual defiant glare, Grace remained slouched against the cushions. "Do you truly wish to see Lord Ravenglass today?"

"I think you know the answer to that." Fortuity paced the width of the small room, keeping an ear tuned to the entryway just beyond the partially open door. A distinctive clatter outside made her hurry over to the front window and peep through the sheer lace panels hanging between the heavy draperies of the deepest blue. Her heart fluttered like a captured bird beating its wings against the cage. "They are here."

"Calm down. You've gone all red in the face. You'll have Mrs. Flackney running for that awful bottle of tonic she and Mama always poured down our throats at the first sign of frailty. Sometimes I think they gave it to us out of spite." Grace rose from the settee, shook out her skirts, and grudgingly joined Fortuity in the middle of the room to stare at the doorway. "Are we going out there to meet them, or standing here and pretending we don't know they have arrived?"

"Shh." Fortuity turned her head and strained to pick up on every word from the hallway. The voices she heard perplexed her. "Matthew is not alone," she whispered, then wrinkled her nose and stifled a groan. "He brought his cousin."

Grace pulled a face. "The back-biting cow?"

Fortuity nodded.

"Lovely. Today should be interesting, to say the least." Grace resettled her stance. "I make no promises regarding my behavior."

Fortuity eased closer to the door, picking up on another voice. "And Mrs. Sykesbury as well." She turned and grimaced at her sibling. "Why on earth did he bring the two of them?"

Her sister immediately brightened. "With such a wealth of chaperones, I shall not be needed after all."

Fortuity caught her arm and tugged her closer. "Oh yes, you are. Do not think to escape. *I* need you for moral support."

Grace rolled her eyes. "As you wish."

Walters pushed open the door to the small parlor and gave Fortuity what she interpreted as a befuddled scowl. Or, at least, the poor old butler appeared more confused than usual. "Lord Ravenglass, Mrs. Sykesbury, and Miss Sykesbury," he announced in a deep, raspy drawl Fortuity always heard in her mind whenever writing ghostly graveyard scenes. "Will refreshments be required before the outing?"

"No thank you, Walters. Only our cloaks, please." She invited the trio into the room with a wave of her hand, noting their expressions appeared somewhat strained. "Is something wrong?" she asked Matthew.

After angling a disgruntled glare at his cousin Eleanor, he tipped a formal nod that suggested he was tensed tighter than an overly wound watch. "I do hope the emergency that called His Grace away is not dire."

"Sorry?" Fortuity sidled a glance at Grace, who responded with a shrug that said she was just as confused.

Matthew smiled, but it was a tight, miserable smile that held no joy. "I simply found it strange that he would invite us on an outing if his diary was full, so I assumed today's meeting must have been urgent and unavoidable."

Fortuity noticed how Eleanor backed up a step and drew closer to her mother. There was ill afoot, and that little chit had something to do with it. "*You* invited us—Chance and I—on this outing, but we replied it would be Gracie and myself, since Chance had prior obligations. Shall I have Walters fetch the note to clear away any confusion?"

"No. That will not be necessary." He shifted and offered her another polite nod. "I understand everything now and will address it with the responsible party at another time."

"Are you not the lucky gentleman, cousin?" Eleanor said in an overly bright tone. "Escorting four ladies to the British Museum?"

"Return to the carriage, Eleanor. Immediately."

Eleanor's mother gasped. "My lord, please do not be harsh with her."

"You may go with her," Matthew said in a somewhat gentler tone. "I wish to speak to Lady Fortuity and her sister privately before we are on our way."

"But cousin—" Eleanor stepped forward, then halted at the viscount's icy glare. "Come, Mama. Let us wait in the carriage."

After the women departed, Matthew closed the parlor door behind them, then turned back and faced Fortuity and Grace. "I must apologize for my cousin. It would appear she took it upon herself to create today's outing. I presume she did so to draw closer to your brother. After all, he is an eligible duke and quite coveted by the Marriage Mart—or so I am told."

"But she had to know he wouldn't be joining us," Fortuity said. "We sent a reply explaining his full schedule."

"Why would she continue the game if she failed at drawing in all her players?" Grace asked.

"She overplayed her advantage." Matthew's jaw flexed as if he struggled to restrain himself from baring his teeth in a snarl. "She probably told me about the invitation and arranged our part of the outing before she knew her prey had escaped her snare."

"I see." The painful realization that Matthew had not instigated the meeting knotted in the pit of Fortuity's stomach like a poorly digested meal. He hadn't wanted to see her. In fact, had probably not planned on seeing her again until another function accidentally brought them together. And apparently, she was the silliest of ninnies for dwelling on last night's events. She could now do the only thing she knew to do: dismiss the poor man and give him his means of escape.

"Do not feel obligated to continue this farce," she said. "I am sure you have much more important things to do."

"Nothing is more important to me than you."

Grace bumped into her hard enough to bounce her to one side. "I am going to go see where Walters has gotten to with those cloaks. Leave the door wide open and maintain an appropriate distance between each other until my return, or I shall set my hounds on you."

Before Fortuity could stop her, her sister rushed from the room. She threw up her hands and shook her head. "Today's madness appears to be contagious. I am so very sorry." When he didn't smile or answer, she caught her bottom lip between her teeth and wondered how one of her characters might handle this situation. How would she write her way out of this scene? "All really is well between us, Matthew, if that is your worry."

"But it is not," he said softly while moving closer. "I hurt you last night. Do not deny it, Fortuity. Your eyes reveal everything you feel."

She forced a smile, inwardly cringing when she felt it slipping. "You protected me from Lord Smellington, twice. You helped me fight the crush to get a glass of lemonade, and you told me I am your friend. How is any of that hurtful?" She swallowed hard, wishing he would just go away and take his cousins with him. Could they not just pretend as if his overly loud conversation with Lady Serafina hadn't happened?

He stared at her, the somber gray of his eyes darker than she had ever seen them before. "When I say that you are my dear friend whom I hold in the highest regard, I beg you to know that there are very few in my life whom I trust as I trust you." Closing the distance between them, he took her hands in his.

"Your sister's hounds can just be damned," he said with a sad grin, then fixed her with a woeful gaze. "I no longer trust easily, Fortuity, and I am sure your brother-in-law has told you why. The man gossips worse than the tattle sheets." He squeezed her hands, sending such a series of warm tingles through her that she struggled to breathe.

"I know of your history, my lord." She cut herself off and clenched her teeth. No, she could not *nudge* him as Chance and Serendipity wished her to.

"You know of my history—but what?"

She tried to pull her hands away, but he held them tighter. So she bowed her head, finding herself too great of a coward to look him in the eyes. "How is it you read me so easily?"

"Because I have watched you closely at every opportunity. You fascinate me," he whispered.

With a hard yank, she pulled her hands free and turned away from him. "Why do you say such things?"

"Because it is the truth. Should I not always speak the truth with you?"

"You should not speak the truth and make it sound as if it is so much more." There. She'd said it.

"So much more?"

At the risk of her already aching heart, she faced him. "Chance and Serendipity wished for me to use this outing to discover if you had perhaps changed your mind about marrying. They feel your behavior shows more than simple friendship."

"And how do *you* feel, Fortuity?"

"Very confused." She allowed herself a heavy sigh.

He nodded and bowed his head. "I am sorry."

"As am I," she quietly agreed.

He scrubbed a hand across his face, looked aside, then faced her once more, clearly uncomfortable with the conversation, just as she had known he would be. All was ruined between them now. Now she would not even have him in her life as a friend.

"Perhaps you should go," she gently suggested. "I promise Gracie will not be disappointed. She was my chaperone under duress."

He frowned at her, not an angry or unhappy frown, but an apologetic one. "Perhaps I should, but I would like to make amends and heal our friendship. I cherish you, Fortuity, and wish for things to be well—truly well—between us."

She shook her head to deny him, but he held up a hand to silence her.

"I can help you publish your stories if you will let me."

Those words would have been magical to her at one time, but now they were hollow, no longer holding a bright, shining hope for the future. She felt as if she had just unwrapped a much-longed-for gift only to discover it wasn't what she wanted after all.

"Publish my stories?" she repeated, forcing the question through the dismal fog clouding her mind. She had to say something but didn't have the heart to disappoint him by declining an offer that would invariably cause her more pain by bringing her into his presence more often.

"I am well connected with several reputable publishers who will listen to my recommendations."

His surge of confidence made her want to weep and shout that she didn't want that from him. He had made her want so much more, made her want that which she could never have. She swallowed hard, afraid to speak, afraid her composure would slip. The best she could manage was a smile and a nod.

"Of course, I would need to read your stories to speak intelligently about them, but I am sure they are wonderful. How could they not be, after all the care you took to study human nature?"

"My studious scribbling from the shadows," she said more to herself than him.

He laughed, oblivious to her struggle. "Yes, indeed. I have no doubt your studies have been quite fruitful. Will I recognize any of your characters? Have you changed the names to protect their true identities?"

No longer able to face him, she crossed over to the front window and swept the panels of lace aside. "All the names are different, my lord. Never fear." After all, it would seem strange indeed if every dashing hero in her love stories was called Matthew. "Your cousins must be quite cold by now. Should you not get them home?"

"They have throws. I am sure they are fine." He joined her at the window. "What say you, Fortuity? If you gave your stories to me today, I could read them tonight and start speaking with publishers tomorrow."

The idea of allowing her stories out of her possession made her bristle. Her precious tales were the last of her privacy, the last of her soul, the deepest imaginings of her heart. How could he expect her to hand them over like yesterday's tattle sheets? "I am not comfortable with that, my lord, but I thank you." She kept her gaze locked on the street outside the window, willing him to go away and leave her to the task of licking her wounds.

"Not comfortable with what? I must read them to more intelligently convince the publishers of their worth."

Fisting her hands, she forced herself to look at him. "Why are you doing this?"

"Doing what?"

"This," she said, hissing the word through her clenched teeth. "Go home, Matthew, and busy yourself with whatever viscounts do."

His dark brows drew down, and he dragged in a deep intake of air. "I cannot give you marriage, my dear little wren, but I can give you my friendship and help you achieve your life's dream. I beg you—please—let that be enough."

"I think it best we part ways and be done with it."

"With my help, your stories will be published. The title pages will read: *written by Lady Fortuity Abarough*. Alone, you have no option other than your brother using his power to coerce someone into accepting them. Is that what you wish? For your tales to be published because of coercion?"

"Is that not what you offer?" she snapped. "Using your connections to force your business acquaintances into doing what you wish?"

"No." He scowled at her. "I intend to read your stories and sing their virtues until every publisher I know begs for permission to be the one to put your books out into the world. I shall start a bidding war for your tales."

"For one who has never read them, you think highly of my writings."

"That is why you should give them to me today."

"No. My stories do not leave my possession. If you are to read them, you may do so in my presence, then give your opinion." She jutted her chin higher, determined to hold strong. "They are all I have, Matthew, and I daresay I do not trust allowing them into your household without myself to guard them."

"I would guard them," he said in a hurt tone.

"The way you guarded the details of today's outing?"

He flinched and bowed his head. "I understand, my lady."

"Good day, Matthew. Take your cousins home. Get them in out of the cold."

He fixed her with a stare that sent a shiver through her. "Only if you promise to bring your stories to me tomorrow. Bring your sister or however many sisters you deem appropriate to protect your reputation, although I will take great pains to ensure that Agnus is also there as a proper chaperone. In fact, as far as anyone is concerned, you are coming to visit her. I daresay it would be too great a stretch of the imagination for anyone to believe you are coming for tea with Eleanor."

"Why?"

"Because I want to do this for you," he said. "I *need* to do this for you."

"Why?" she asked again, softer this time.

"Because this is the only thing I can offer you, Fortuity. Please, allow me to do this."

Chapter Four

"I THINK YOU should tell the fool to make up his mind," Grace said. "From what I overheard yesterday, the man loves you but is too great a coward to admit it to himself."

Fortuity clasped her gloved hands tighter inside her fur muff and shivered as the Broadmere carriage drew ever closer to Ravenglass Townhouse on Chesterfield Street. It was a damp, bone-chilling day, and the task at hand only made her colder. "I think you should remember that eavesdropping is most rude."

"Do not be a hypocrite, sister. I have seen you lean in close to take in conversations you were not a part of."

"We should turn around and go back home."

"We should not." Grace wagged a finger at her. "The more he is around you, the more he will realize his life is incomplete without you at his side."

"Since when do you know so much about love? I thought your only interest was your puppies."

Her sister pursed her mouth into a tight pucker and looked aside.

Fortuity smiled, thrilled that she'd discovered a secret about Grace, the sister no one ever got one over on. "You are in love. Who is he?"

"I am not in love." Grace huffed and glared upward, as if sending up a prayer for divine guidance. "If you must know, I have read your stories, and your current difficulties leave me to wonder how you could ever write such romantic tales when you can't seem to get it right in real life."

"My characters do as I bid them. Unfortunately, no *real* persons seem inclined to grant me such courtesies."

Grace eyed her. "I can see how that would be true. Even so, I do not think today a mistake. Make the most of it." She nodded at the bundle on the seat beside Fortuity. "Did you bring them all?"

"Almost all. I left the unfinished works in my hideaway—which I apparently must relocate, since you know where it is." Fortuity pulled aside the window covering and peeked outside. "Oh my. We are here. I thought the carriage was slowing."

"Calm down." Grace scooted forward as the vehicle rolled to a stop. "Make the man realize he wishes to marry you, so I will not be forced to shake him."

If only it were that easy, Fortuity thought, but didn't dare voice her insecurities. Grace was by far the strongest willed of them all. Nothing shook her. At times, she even outwitted Serendipity. "Thank you for coming with me today. Seri can be unbearable at times since she decided to help Chance find us husbands."

"You are welcome," Grace said with surprising gentleness. "After yesterday, I feel somewhat invested in your future and mean to see it through to a successful outcome."

The carriage door swung open, and their footman, George, stuck his head inside before folding down the steps and helping them out. "Mind the walkway, Lady Fortuity and Lady Grace. Not yet icy, but soon will be."

"Thank you, George." Fortuity scooped her bundle of stories into the crook of her arm and tried not to lose her muff in the process.

"Might I carry your package for you, my lady?" The trusted young man eyed her with worry as she teetered in the doorway, attempting to balance the bundle, her fluffy handwarmer, and her reticule while disembarking without snagging her cloak or gown somewhere in the process.

She handed it over, then accepted his help in stepping down.

"My goodness, George, you were quite right about the slippery way of things." She cast a glance back. "Mind your steps, Gracie. The stonework is quite treacherous." A glance upward at the heaviness of the dreary gray clouds made her wonder if the weather was an ill omen. The chilling drizzle came down harder. "Perhaps we should go home."

"We are staying," Grace said. "However, does Ravenglass have shelter for our people and horses? I refuse to make them sit out in this weather while we are warm beside a fire."

"If there is no shelter for our team, nor a good, hot drink for our servants, we shan't be staying." At least they agreed on that count. Fortuity carefully picked her way to the front door and banged the heavy metal knocker shaped like a raven.

The same butler she had met during last year's visit opened the door. "Good day, Lady Fortuity. Lord Ravenglass is expecting you."

"Thebson, isn't it?" At least, she thought that was the man's name, recalling it because it was so unusual.

The man bowed. "Yes, my lady."

"Before my sister and I may enter and visit in good conscience, we must know that our servants and team shan't be left out in this horrid weather. Is there room in Lord Ravenglass's stables for our animals and a bracing cup of tea for our people?"

"Tell her *yes*, Thebson," came a familiar voice from deeper within the house. "Have Thomas and Mr. Turnmaster see to the lady's request."

"Yes, my lord." The butler disappeared before ushering Fortuity and Grace inside.

"Bloody fool." Matthew hurried to help them enter and accepted the bundle containing Fortuity's stories from her footman. "Thebson has never been able to manage more than one task at a time, and, as you can well see, his prioritizing of duties leaves much to be desired." He turned back to the open doorway and addressed the Broadmere servants. "To the back of the townhouse is the mews. Mr. Turnmaster is my head groom and will see to the team. Thomas will bring you both into the kitchen for tea and food."

George bowed. "Thank you kindly, my lord."

The coachman tipped his hat. "Thank you kindly, indeed, my lord."

After shutting the door to the gusty, wet weather, Matthew bellowed, "Mrs. Greer?"

Fortuity jumped and squeaked, "What on earth, Matthew?"

"Forgive me for startling you, my lady." He gave her a curt bow, then glared down the hallway. "Brace yourselves," he warned, then roared even louder. "Mrs. Greer!"

"Aye, my lord! I be a-comin'!" An ancient matron of considerable girth careened into view from around the corner. Her round face plumped with her ever-widening smile. "Be that yourself, Lady Fortuity? And you as well, Lady Grace? 'Pon my soul, 'tis good to see you both again."

A comforting rush of happiness washed across Fortuity. She and the housekeeper had formed a bittersweet friendship during the time the dear old woman had helped the Broadmeres care for their dying mother. Fortuity rushed forward and hugged the grandmotherly angel who had concocted numerous poultices and tonics that had brought Mama the only relief to be found during her final days. "It is so good to see you, Mrs. Greer. I hope I didn't lead you into a poor place of employment when I recommended you to Lord Ravenglass?" She turned and fixed him with a hard glare. "How dare you bellow for Mrs. Greer? Have you never heard of a bell?"

"Mrs. Greer told me to shout for her because Mary Louise dismantled the bell system for a good greasing." Matthew glared right back at her. "You know very well that I treat my servants like people and not property."

Fortuity arched a brow and turned back to the housekeeper. "What say you, Mrs. Greer?"

The matron chortled and clapped her beefy hands together. "I am quite happy here, Lady Fortuity, and I thank you for making it come about." She chortled again, much like a contented hen settling into the nest. "Although this house could use a fine mistress to see to the running of it."

"Thank you, Mrs. Greer," Matthew said. "Tea in the parlor, please. And also, please let Mrs. Sykesbury know our guests have arrived."

Her eyes bright and twinkling, Mrs. Greer nodded, then gave Fortuity a wink. "Aye, my lord. Right away."

"Since Thebson has yet to reappear and tend to his duties, allow me to help you with your cloaks, ladies." Matthew gave Grace a strained smile as he accepted her outerwear and hat. "My word, how long did he keep the two of you standing on the step? This cloak is quite wet."

"It's not entirely Thebson's fault," Grace said. "Tutie kept trying to turn tail and run." She aimed a smug look at Fortuity. "I had to convince her to stay."

With Grace's damp things draped over his arm, Matthew slowly turned to Fortuity with a look she could only describe as hurt. "Is that true?"

Fortuity squared her shoulders. "I was merely concerned about leaving our people and horses exposed to the dreadful weather." She shot Grace a warning glare. They would discuss her traitorous behavior later.

Matthew piled Grace's things on the entryway bench and moved to help Fortuity with hers. "Are you being truthful?" he asked so quietly she almost didn't hear him.

She flipped her cloak off so quickly that he almost dropped it. "I do hope my stories haven't drawn damp. Where are they, so I might check them?"

Before he answered, a thunderous pounding rumbled down the stairs. A snorting, barking fury of tawniness sped past her, slowing long enough to latch on to her fur muff, snatch it from her hand, and charge down the hallway with it.

"Come back here, you!" Fortuity gave chase while Grace shrieked with laughter.

"Ignatius!" Matthew roared. "Halt. Sit."

The thieving pug skidded to a stop and plopped down on his plump behind, black face wrinkling with pride as he woofed around the mouthful of Fortuity's furry handwarmer.

"Oh dear. Ignatius," Mrs. Sykesbury called out from the base of the stairwell. "Bad, bad puppy. Shame on you."

Fortuity moved to recover her stolen goods, and the teasing little dog skittered back, staying just out of reach. His bulging brown eyes lent such a comical look to his joyful expression that she couldn't help but laugh. "Give it back, you little terror, or I shall be forced to set Gracie on you. She knows how to handle naughty puppies."

"Ignatius." Matthew pointed at the floor. "Drop it. Now."

The dog shook with another muffled woof, revealing his reluctance to obey.

"Drop it," commanded Matthew in a sterner tone. "Now."

The muff hit the floor, and Fortuity almost swore she heard the little animal give a disgruntled snort. She hurried to recover the even damper hand warmer. "Thank you, Ignatius."

The playful scamp wiggled his curly little tail and smiled.

Gracie rushed forward, dropped to her knees, and patted her hands together. "Come see me, you handsome boy. Thanks to you, this visit might just be bearable."

"Thank you, Lady Grace," Matthew said, his tone dripping with sarcasm.

"You are quite welcome." Grace scooped the dog up into her arms and glanced up the hallway. "Which way to the parlor?"

Matthew nodded at the second set of double doors, then narrowed his eyes at the butler hurrying toward them. "The ladies' outer garments are wet with rain, Thebson. See that Mary Louise tends to them, and moving forward, you will clarify which task I wish you to attend to first, since you appear unable to sort that out for yourself."

The butler tucked his chin, seeming to wilt before them. "Yes, my lord. I do beg your pardon for mishandling my duties."

"Don't be cross with him," Fortuity whispered. "He's older and probably cannot help it. Like our Walters at Broadmere."

With his jaw clenched, Matthew stared down at her a moment longer than necessary.

Please? she mouthed.

He bowed his head, then turned back to the butler and spoke in a kinder tone. "Thank you, Thebson. That will be all for now. As I said, please see that the ladies' garments are properly dried and brushed."

"Yes, my lord."

"Thank you," Fortuity said quietly to Matthew. "Perhaps one of your footmen could help Thebson keep things sorted. Make the footman a butler in training to save Thebson's pride."

"The man left you standing in the cold rain, and you wish to help him?"

"He didn't do it maliciously."

"No. He did not." He frowned at her, as if unable to define what sort of creature she was. "But most ladies do not appreciate a good soaking with icy rain."

"Well, I don't either. However, what's done is done, and there is no reason to be petty about it. As I said, he did not do it maliciously." She angled her way past him and smiled at Mrs. Sykesbury. "We didn't get to speak the night of the masquerade ball. Your dress was so lovely."

Mrs. Sykesbury gave a graceful curtsy. "Thank you, Lady Fortuity. You are too kind." She moved closer, wringing her hands. "And please forgive Ignatius for his rudeness. He has not been with me long, and we are still working on his manners."

Fortuity waved away the apology. "Do not apologize. I am quite used to rambunctious puppies. Gracie has several who have the run of the townhouse."

The older woman tucked her chin and tipped her head, appearing as shy and retiring as a wallflower nearing spinsterhood. "Again, you are most kind. Excuse me while I ensure Mrs. Greer has a proper tea in the making."

Fortuity watched her go, her heart aching for the poor woman whose world had fallen apart when her husband died. "I wish I could help her," she said more to herself than Matthew.

"Agnus is better than she was, which I suppose is something."

Unable to resist, Fortuity eyed the staircase. "And will Eleanor be joining us?"

"Eleanor will not be joining us. She is spending the day in her rooms." Matthew went to the side table beside the entryway bench and picked up the bundle wrapped in a dark cloth and secured with a matching ribbon. Staring down at the package as if it were as rare and precious as smuggled jewels, he gently rested his hand on top of it. "Thank you for entrusting me with your stories."

"I am not leaving them here." He needed to understand that. "Gracie and I shall stay while you read, and when we leave, my stories leave with me."

He frowned at her—but not really a frown, more of a pained expression, a realization that perhaps they were no longer the close friends they once were. "You do not trust me."

"I trust no one with my stories."

"Then how do you hope to ever get them published? Publishers will need time to review them before deciding whether they wish to print them."

She hadn't thought of that, but it didn't matter. That still didn't mean she would leave them unguarded with Matthew.

Maybe he was right. She no longer trusted him. Not since the masquerade ball and then his cousin's manipulation of the outing that never happened. "I brought them here for you to read and provide an opinion. I will decide on my course of action once I hear your recommendations. Until that time, they shall remain in my possession."

"Will things ever be right again between us, Fortuity?" he asked softly.

"Of course," she lied with her best fake smile. "After all, we are friends. Are we not?"

EVEN THOUGH THE prose of Fortuity's story was compelling and entertaining, try as he might, Matthew could not concentrate on it. Instead, he repeatedly found himself watching her as she and Grace played with the impertinent Ignatius by tossing the dog's favorite bit of knotted rope.

It wasn't just her beauty or the way she laughed that drew his focus back to her again and again. It was something he couldn't define, an impossible-to-ignore magnetism, as if she were a rare vintage wine and he was dying of thirst. How was it that every eligible male of the *ton* wasn't beating down her door, begging for her hand in marriage?

"Well?" she asked as she rose, returned to the center table laden with the offerings of a proper tea, and poured them all another cup. "How far have you gotten?"

He stared down at her flowery script and couldn't recall a single detail of anything he had read. A skimming of the last few sentences revealed it was some sort of garden scene where the hero was attempting to charm his lady love. "Uhm… How could she be in the garden without a chaperone? Does he ruin her?"

Fortuity stared at him as if he'd sprouted a unicorn horn in the middle of his forehead. "Her maid is right there cutting flowers. How did you miss that?"

He blinked and lifted the page higher, hiding behind it like a schoolboy caught short in his studies. What the devil was wrong with him? He had promised to do this to repair their friendship, hadn't he? He cleared his throat and resettled himself in his chair. "Ah… Yes. Right here. How could I have missed that? Forgive me."

She perched on the edge of the chair next to him, still frowning. "The garden scene is the opening of the first chapter. Do you mean to tell me you haven't gotten past the first page?"

"I need quiet in which to read and reflect properly. How am I supposed to concentrate with all the noise?" He tipped a jerking nod at the pug where it sat in Grace's lap, crunching on a biscuit.

"He eats no louder than you do," Grace said. "Do not blame the dog for your own shortcomings."

"My shortcomings?" He opened his mouth to say more, then thought better of it. It would not be wise to give Fortuity's younger sister a curt answer. One never knew how Lady Grace might respond, and he didn't wish to upset Fortuity more than he already had.

"Gracie." Fortuity gave her sister a stern frown, then turned back to him and narrowed her eyes. "Please forgive her. Gracie is protective when animals are unjustly blamed."

"Unjustly blamed?"

"Yes. Unjustly blamed." She rose and snatched the papers out of his hands. "If you find my stories boring and impossible to immerse yourself in, simply say so. Do not blame the dog for being noisy."

"If you must know, you were the distraction." *Damn and blast.* He had not meant to say that.

"I was the distraction?" She arched a brow, clearly not believing him. "Do go on, my lord. Explain how I distract you."

He held out his hand. "Give them back so I may finish reading."

"From the sound of it, you haven't even started."

"Then give them back so I may start."

"No."

"No?"

"Yes, my lord. The answer is *no*, which means you do not get your way." She straightened the pages and returned them to the bundle on the table. The alarming rosiness of her cheeks warned she was furious or about to burst into tears—or both.

"Fortuity."

"Do not say my name like that."

"Like what?"

"Like you have the right to say my name like that, because

you do not."

"Come, Ignatius," Grace said as she hefted the wriggling dog up into her arms. "Let us stroll the halls and find the perfect place for you to lift your leg."

"Gracie!" Fortuity stared at her sister in open-mouthed dismay as Grace marched out of the parlor but left the double doors open behind her. After a barely audible groan, Fortuity slowly shook her head. "I do beg your pardon, Matthew. Gracie can sometimes be—"

"Shocking?"

She nodded. "Yes. I fear we have used that word more than once when describing her. Again, I apologize." She pressed her hands to her still-rosy cheeks. "We should not have come here today. It is too much to ask of anyone, of a friend."

His heart ached for her. Why was it that the harder he tried to repair the fracture between them, the worse it became? "I offered to read your stories, my lady. Forgive me for not forcing myself to concentrate."

"You see?" She jabbed a finger at him. "That is just it, isn't it? You should not have to *force* yourself to concentrate. A good story pulls you in and refuses to let you go until the last page."

The way the fullness of her bottom lip quivered made him yearn to pull her into his arms and kiss her until they both became senseless.

He blinked away the thought. *No.* They were friends. Friends did not kiss unless it was on the cheek in greeting or farewell. He raked a hand through his hair and looked away. "Forgive me, Fortuity. I do not know what has gotten into me. I have a great deal on my mind."

She immediately calmed, and sympathy shone in the stormy blue depths of her eyes. "Eleanor?"

"Yes. Eleanor." It wasn't a complete lie, but he damn well couldn't tell her she had become a distraction he was powerless to ignore. "I fear the ungrateful chit is headed for certain ruin and determined to take me with her."

"You don't believe she would trap you in a marriage of convenience, do you?"

"I believe she would if I were her only remaining option." He sipped his tea and wished it were something much stronger. "Your brother is her current target. Warn him to take the greatest care."

"I shall warn him." She returned to her chair and thoughtfully stirred her tea. "What will happen to Mrs. Sykesbury when Eleanor successfully snares a husband? While she seems to love her daughter very much, Eleanor sometimes seems as though she forgets she even has a mother."

"Agnus is welcome to stay here as long as she wishes." A happy woof from the hallway made him roll his eyes. "Her and that infernal dog, who in a moment of weakness I bought for her, thinking it might help her overcome her extended grief."

Fortuity gave him a wistful smile that hit him as so sad it squeezed his heart. "You are a kind man, Matthew, even though you do not wish anyone else to realize it."

There was so much he wanted to say to her but couldn't. Admittedly, he was a coward, but he feared losing a cherished friendship by making the mistake of trying to turn it into something more. In his experience, love never lasted. His parents had gone to their graves hating one another, and when he'd risked opening his heart, it had won him the humiliation of standing at the altar, waiting for a bride who had run off to Gretna Green with a duke.

He snorted and waved away her compliment. "Do not tell anyone I am nice, I beg you. My reputation would be ruined."

Mrs. Sykesbury swept into the room, wringing her hands as she always did. "Forgive me. I didn't realize Lady Grace had taken Ignatius for a walk and left you unaccompanied."

"There is nothing to forgive," Fortuity said. "The doors remained wide open, and as you can see, I am in my chair enjoying my tea and Matthew is in his."

The perpetually nervous woman flittered over to the settee

and perched on the edge of the cushion, looking on with the misery of one waiting to march to the gallows.

Matthew stifled a groan and turned back to Fortuity. "May I please read your story now? I promise to do better." With poor Agnus souring the room, he should be able to concentrate. "Please?"

Fortuity stared at him with a critical glare, then rose and picked up the pages she had tucked back into the bundle. "I shall grant you one more hour. No more." She handed them over. "Gracie and I do not wish to overstay our welcome."

He gratefully accepted the pages and settled deeper into his chair. "I daresay Ignatius shall be distraught once you leave."

"He is enjoying himself with Lady Grace," Mrs. Sykesbury said as she picked up her needlework and held it for Fortuity to inspect. "Do you enjoy embroidery, Lady Fortuity?"

"I am afraid I have no talent for it," Fortuity said. "Yours is quite lovely, though. I particularly like that shade of green you selected for the sprigs."

Matthew easily immersed himself in Fortuity's story this time. With such riveting conversation in the room, he was grateful for the escape. It never ceased to amaze him how Agnus could chat for hours about absolutely nothing. He noted Fortuity displayed the patience of Job as his cousin droned on and on about her needlework. Heaven help them all.

He forced himself to concentrate, finding the flowery script and turn of phrase pleasing and easy to read. Fortuity's personality shone in the prose. Whenever her heroine laughed or spoke, it was Fortuity's voice and mannerisms. It was Fortuity he pictured in every scene. He found himself smiling and perfectly content to stay inside the romantic tale for however long as he was allowed. The more he read, the more the hero infuriated him. One did not treat a lady with such casual disregard. Did the fool not see that the lady loved him?

When he reached the final page, the interruption in the tale jarred him. "I need the rest, Fortuity."

She shook her head and took the papers from him. "I am sorry, my lord, but it is time for Gracie and me to go. What did you think of the portion I gave you?"

He stared at her, frustrated beyond belief that she was actually going to leave and take the rest of the book with her. "Quite compelling. But some of your scenes are inaccurate."

"Inaccurate?" She arched a brow, daring him to continue.

Her scenes weren't inaccurate, but instinctively, he felt if he didn't stir her ire, they might not enjoy another visit like today's. "Yes. Inaccurate. For instance, the way the hero treats his lady love. I find it hard to believe she would remain in love with him when he behaves like such a churl."

"It is known as *growth*, my lord. No character is perfect, and neither are relationships. They must get to know one another, work through each other's faults, and *grow*."

He delighted at the irritation in her tone. If he nurtured it just enough, she might agree to another visit, so they could work through her stories. This afternoon had been most enjoyable even with its few bumps along the way. She brought a brightness to his home that wasn't there before. He hungered for more. "I agree that some growth is expected, but do you not believe a proper kiss should have happened between them by now? They dance around each other somewhat, but he is barely pursuing her."

"Maybe he is extraordinarily dull-witted and wouldn't know a fine opportunity if it bit him on the end of his nose. And they are not even engaged yet, so there should not be a kiss." She tucked the pages into the bundle, refolded the cloth around them, and secured the ribbons with a hard jerk. "Besides, they experience a stolen kiss in chapter three."

"Let me read it."

"No. I told you it was time for Gracie and me to go."

"Let me read the kiss first."

"Why? So you can tell me I wrote that wrong as well?"

"Have you ever been kissed, my lady?"

Agnus gasped from her perch on the settee. "My lord, that is not an appropriate question to ask a young lady."

"Purely professional, Agnus. If Lady Fortuity has never been kissed, how can she properly describe a passionate embrace?"

"I have observed such behavior at parties when couples sneak off to the gardens," Fortuity said with a low growl. "I assure you, my description is quite detailed. One does not have to experience everything one writes about. In chapter seven, the hero is shot, and I have never experienced that. All I needed to draw upon was my brother-in-law's experience to achieve the vividness required."

He feigned a disinterested shrug. "Well... There are other inaccuracies as well, but since you feel you must leave, we shan't discuss them now. But the story is well written and shows promise. I feel sure publishers would love it—once we revise and edit a few things."

"Edit a few things?" she said through gritted teeth.

With a smile that he knew would irritate her even more, he pushed himself up from his chair. "Only minor things, my lady. But since you feel you must leave, we've no time to discuss them now."

"Gracie!" she called out while narrowing her eyes at him. "Make haste. It is time for us to go."

Grace appeared in the doorway with Ignatius at her side. She eyed Fortuity, then shifted her gaze to him. "What did you say to her?"

"I merely advised her that her stories bear a few inaccuracies that some slight revisions would easily remedy."

She rolled her eyes. "Then I advise you to have your man fetch our things, because I can assure you my sister is most definitely ready to remove herself from your presence."

He turned to Fortuity, praying he hadn't foiled his plan for another pleasant afternoon in the lady's company. But then again, should he distance himself from her? No, he couldn't—or wouldn't. Gads, what the devil was wrong with him? What had the woman done to him? "You wished for an opinion, my lady. You know I mean no ill will, and I do feel the publishers will love your story."

"Our things, my lord, so that we might go." She hugged her bundle of stories as if it were a babe. "Posthaste, if you please. This visit is over."

"But there will be another visit, so I might review the rest of the tale?" She had to agree. He couldn't bear it if she refused.

She glared at him and hugged the bundle tighter.

"Please, Fortuity?" he whispered. "I shall do better and not be such an arse. I promise."

"I shall think on it," she said, her voice cracking just enough to give him hope. "Good day, Lord Ravenglass." She charged past Grace into the hallway.

Grace pointed at him as if sighting a pistol. "Stop hurting my sister."

"I do not mean to," he said, the confession catching in his throat.

With a loud snort of disbelief, she shook her head and left the room.

◆ ◆ ◆

Chapter Five

"FIRST, HE COULDN'T possibly immerse himself in my story, and then he dared to proclaim he was an expert and bemoan supposed inaccuracies after reading the first two chapters." Fortuity blew into the private sitting room shared by the remaining six sisters living at home, still unable to believe how the day had progressed. Why had she ever agreed to show Matthew her writing?

Maids emerged from the bedchambers on either side of the small parlor, hurrying forward to help with cloaks and things that had once again become damp with the dreary weather.

"Did he ever really say what he felt was inaccurate?" Grace asked as she tugged off her gloves and handed them to one of the maids. "Sorry about the dog hair, Nellie," she said. "They had the most delightful pug named Ignatius. You would love him."

Nellie smiled and gave an amused shake of her head as she gathered Grace's things.

"Well?" Grace said to Fortuity. "You never gave details. Are you being vague, or was he?"

"He complained about the hero's behavior and the lack of a kiss in the first few pages. They are just getting to know one another. How could he think my heroine was such a lightskirt?" Fortuity yanked off her gloves with her teeth, biting the fingertips as though she were one of her sister's hounds. They never should have gone today. She never should've shared her stories.

"May I be helping you, Lady Fortuity?" asked Anne, the second of the four maids assigned to help the six sisters with personal duties. The girl cringed, eyeing the delicate gloves as though she feared them about to be chewed to bits.

"Never mind me, Anne. I have had a most frustrating afternoon." Fortuity handed over her cloak, then perched on a low cushioned footstool to untie her boots. "I fear I plowed through several puddles. A pair of dry stockings would be most appreciated."

"Right away, my lady." Anne scooped everything up and went to the bedchamber on the right. She paused in the doorway and looked back. "Will you be wishing to change in here, my lady, or the dressing room? Shall I draw you a nice, warm bath to help you recover from your afternoon?"

"Just some dry clothes for now, and I can change in here, since the fire is already nice and toasty."

The maid nodded and disappeared to gather the necessary items.

"I think he simply wants to see you again," Grace said as she backed up to the hearth and lifted her skirts, basking in the heat. "Seemed to me he was teasing you to get you to growl." She wrinkled her nose. "Thorne does that with Essie too, I've noticed. What is it about men? It's as if they wish to poke a bear with a sharp stick in a rousing game of survival."

"Attacking my stories will most definitely make me growl." Fortuity joined her at the hearth. "Shove over. I'm cold too."

"How did it go?" Serendipity asked as she entered the room. After a few steps in, she halted and arched a brow. "Oh dear. Fortuity, you've a face like thunder. What happened?"

"He suggested my scenes were inaccurate."

"I see."

"What do you mean by *I see*?" Fortuity was in no mood for Serendipity to side with the enemy.

"I mean that I feared this might happen. Any time one asks someone for an opinion or recommendation about something, there is always a risk they might say something one won't appreciate." She tucked a snowy blonde curl behind her ear and idly paced back and forth in front of them. "What exactly did he say?"

"That my hero was a churl, and my heroine a lightskirt."

Serendipity stopped pacing and frowned at her. "What sort of stories are you writing?"

"Tales of romance where my characters are imperfect and must learn to love one another." Fortuity stepped away from the hearth, lifted her nose, and sniffed. "Gracie, you might wish to check your chemise. I smell a crispiness in the air that might not bode well."

"Drat!" Grace moved away from the fire while trying to turn and check the condition of her hemline.

"Grace Elena Daisy Abarough!" Serendipity scolded. "What would Mama say about such language?"

"Mama used that word on more than one occasion," Grace said as she headed for the bedroom on the left. "I am going to get Nellie to see if I've ruined this one too, and then I'm having a good cuddle with my hounds. I hereby pass off chaperone duties to you, Seri. May God have mercy on your soul."

"I do not need to be chaperoned in my own home," Fortuity shouted after her before turning to Serendipity. "And she played with the dog the entire time she was there, so do not believe her act of being so sorely put upon."

"When did Ravenglass get a dog?" Serendipity asked. "I don't recall one there last year when we took Blessing to see him."

"Ignatius the pug is a newer member of the household. Procured to help Mrs. Sykesbury with her grief."

Serendipity gave Fortuity a syrupy smile that almost made her gag. "How precious. Lord Ravenglass is such a caring man."

"Matthew Ravenglass is a selfish, pompous arse."

Serendipity's eyes flared open wide. "Fortuity Marion Ivy Abarough! What has gotten into you and Gracie today? Perhaps an afternoon with that gentleman was ill-advised. The two of you are using language from the gutter."

"It thrills me to no end that you remember our full Christian names, sister." Fortuity rolled her eyes at the scolding. She much preferred railing about the imperious Lord Ravenglass than jousting with Serendipity. "We had been there over an hour, and he hadn't even gotten through the first few pages of the story. First, he blamed the dog for making too much noise, and then he blamed me for distracting him."

"Did he now?" Her sister's tone suggested that once again Fortuity had overshared. "And how did he say you distracted him?"

"He didn't."

"Didn't what?"

"Didn't say."

Serendipity frowned. "I may be confused. Did he say you distracted him or not?"

"First, he blamed the dog, then me, and then Eleanor—and from what I observed of her behavior at the ball, I believe she was the actual distraction. He said we should warn Chance that he is her goal."

Serendipity huffed. "Many in the Marriage Mart are after Chance, but he is far from ready to be *caught*." She slowly shook her head, as though confused. "If he was so distracted that he only made it through the first few pages of your story, how did he conclude that there were inaccuracies in the first two *chapters* in need of repair?"

"I foolishly gave him another hour to redeem himself for only reading the first pages. In that last hour of our visit, he completed the first two chapters."

"And then gave his recommendations."

"Which I intend to ignore."

"Tutie," Serendipity said, "publishers often change manuscripts. Remember how they did Papa's journal when they published his novel about his travels? The changes are to make the books more pleasing to the general public, and therefore, more saleable and successful. Lord Ravenglass is considered an expert in the publishing industry. Perhaps all he was trying to do was save you from experiencing that with a publisher. If you submit a perfect manuscript to them, they shall have nothing to pick apart."

"Whose side are you on?"

"Always your side, sister. Always." Serendipity wrapped an arm around her and gave her a gentle shake. "Never doubt that. If you never wish to see the man ever again, then do not do so. We shall find you another." She pulled a note out from behind the neckline of her gown and held it out. "I came up not only to hear about your day but also to bring you this. It arrived while you were gone."

"Must you carry my mail tucked against your bosoms?" Fortuity plucked the stationery away from her sister.

"I didn't wish the younger ones to see that you are the only one of us to receive an invitation to dinner at Thorne and Blessing's." Serendipity grinned. "Even I was not invited."

"I smell a poorly hidden snare." Fortuity tapped on the broken seal. "And why was this opened if it was addressed to me?"

"Forgive me. I saw it was from Blessing and assumed it was to all of us. I was wrong."

While Serendipity did sound contrite, Fortuity still wondered what sort of plot was afoot. Just because Blessing's lying-in would soon start in no way meant she would remove herself from the matchmaking game. She herself had admitted that she enjoyed it almost as much as studying her stars. "What is she up to?"

"Up to?"

"Do not play innocent, Seri. It does not suit you."

"It is dinner with her and Thorne. Saturday next. How could that possibly be sinister? You wouldn't even require a chaperone to enjoy a private meal at your sister's home." Serendipity brightened even more and tapped on the note. "Why don't you take her one or two of your stories? Her days of being able to leave the house are numbered, you know, and the observatory

Thorne is having built for her is far from finished."

Fortuity almost felt sorry for Blessing's husband, doing his best to keep his expectant wife happy. "I hope he realizes that nothing he builds will ever compare with her observatory from Papa."

"I am sure he realizes that, but I also feel certain Essie will make sure he knows his efforts are appreciated. She knows he dotes on her." Serendipity nodded at the invitation. "So you will go, then? Surely you would never wish to disappoint Essie."

"I will go." Fortuity dropped to the settee and rested her head in her hands. The tensions of the day had wearied her beyond comprehension. "Matthew plainly said he could give me nothing more than friendship and help to publish my stories," she said without looking up. She couldn't bear to see the pity she knew would be in her sister's eyes.

"I see." Serendipity settled down beside her. "And will you be all right with that?"

A sad laugh snorted free of Fortuity. "What choice do I have?"

Her sister folded her hands in her lap and waggled her head back and forth. "You could pursue him and attempt to change his mind."

"If the man has his mind set, I refuse to demean myself and beg for his affections," Fortuity said. She might be the plainest of the Broadmere sisters and a confirmed wallflower, but she had her pride. "Besides, once I am established with a publisher, I will need to write more stories for them to print." She swallowed hard against the knot of emotions choking her. Heaven help her, she sounded pathetic even to herself.

"Tutie…" Serendipity's tone dripped with pity, making every nerve Fortuity possessed bristle.

"Do not do that." She rose and returned to the fire to warm her hands. "If that is all, I would like to enjoy some time alone, Seri. I found today very tiring. I am sure you have somewhere else to be or something else to do."

"It is not true, you know?" her sister said while remaining firmly ensconced on the settee.

Fortuity stared down at the yellow flames dancing throughout the coals. "If I inquire *what is not true*, will you go away?" Shuffling behind her gave her hope that Serendipity was heading for the door. When the hinges squeaked, she allowed herself a relieved sigh.

"You are not the plainest of us," her sister said from the doorway. "You are simply different, as you should be. Mama and Papa always told you that. I heard them many times."

"*Different* is a questionable compliment in the best of times, and the kindest insult in the worst, dear sister." Fortuity shifted and managed a wry smile for Serendipity's benefit. "I will be fine, Seri. Go along now and grant me some time to myself."

Serendipity stared at her, clearly not pleased and fretting.

"Remember what Mama said about worry lines," Fortuity reminded her softly as she rubbed her forehead.

With a sad smile, Serendipity mimicked the gesture. "I love you, Tutie, and I promise, all will be well."

Fortuity huffed a mirthless laugh. "I love you too." She didn't add that Serendipity shouldn't promise that which she could not control.

MATTHEW WAS IN no mood for a dinner party, no matter how relaxed and intimate Knightwood promised it would be. He prayed that meant that neither Fortuity nor any of the other Broadmeres would be there. Ever since the masquerade ball, he'd struggled to control his thoughts about her. And the afternoon he'd read her stories had fouled his mind even more. Truth be told, he had always liked her best of all the Broadmere sisters, always finding comfort and joy in her presence, a genuine affinity, a friendship. Why the devil did he have to ruin it now by thinking of her as so much more, *feeling* her as so much more? As the months had passed, the impossible-to-ignore feeling became stronger, but he'd managed it. But then came the masquerade ball, and heaven help him, his ability to *manage it* was weakening.

"I do not wish to do this," he grumbled as he climbed the front steps. He should have asked if Fortuity would be there, but good manners had held his tongue. If not for Knightwood swearing his wife would be reduced to tears if Matthew didn't accept, he would have spent the evening at the club rather than the Knightwoods' dining room. And since when did Lady Blessing crave his company so badly? Yes, they had grown quite close over the past year since she had married his best friend, but, to be honest, Fortuity's currently low opinion of him could very well endanger his friendship with several from his inner circle—namely all the Broadmeres and possibly even Knightwood himself.

Gritting his teeth over what could prove to be a most uncomfortable evening, Matthew knocked on the door and hoped no one answered, so he might escape to the club and disappear into a dark corner with a strong drink. But, alas, the steady thump of someone approaching dashed all his hopes.

"Good evening, Lord Ravenglass." Cadwick, the Knightwood butler for many years, swung the door open wider and bowed as he entered, then held out a white-gloved hand. "May I take your things, sir?"

Matthew shed his greatcoat, hat, and gloves and handed them over, but before the butler gave his things to a waiting footman, he stopped him. "This is a *small* dinner gathering, correct? So small it could in no way be defined as a dinner *party?*"

"There is but one other guest yet to arrive, my lord," the emotionless man said in a monotone that would send the liveliest of souls into a deep sleep.

Still unsatisfied, Matthew blocked the butler's way again. "And how many guests have already arrived?"

As expressionless as always, Cadwick slowly blinked several

times as though emerging from a trance. "Lord and Lady Knightwood await you in the parlor, my lord, along with the dowager baroness and two others." The barrel-chested man swelled with a deep intake of air. "And a multitude of cats, as I am sure your lordship expected." He handed Matthew's things to the footman and headed down the hallway. "This way, my lord. Mind where you step. The most recent litter of kittens delight in tripping the unwary."

Matthew tried not to laugh. The butler hated the felines that Knightwood's mother adored. Matthew wasn't all that fond of cats either, but the dowager baroness was a dear, sweet lady struggling with the plight of losing her hearing, and if cats made her happy, then so be it. As he entered the parlor, the cat-loving matron rushed to greet him before he was fully through the double doors.

"Lord Ravenglass, we feared you might not make it."

He bowed to the lady and kissed both her hands. "Lady Roslynn, how could I possibly miss a dinner with you?"

Her eyes danced with happiness as she tugged him over to the rest of the group. "Just one more to arrive, my dears. Excuse me while I ensure Cadwick has properly fed my babies."

Matthew didn't recognize the couple standing with Blessing and Knightwood. He bowed to his hosts. "Knightwood. Lady Blessing."

"Allow me to introduce Viscount Simon Carronbridge and his sister, Lady Sarah," Knightwood said, then turned to the pair and tipped his head toward Matthew. "Carronbridge, Lady Sarah, this is Viscount Matthew Ravenglass, one of my oldest and most trusted friends."

The pretty but somewhat shy lady curtsied, and Carronbridge bowed. "A pleasure to meet ye, Lord Ravenglass," he said with a faint Scottish brogue.

Members of the Scottish peerage. No wonder Matthew had failed to recognize the two. He bowed. "The pleasure is mine, Lord Carronbridge, Lady Sarah."

"Lady Fortuity Abarough," Cadwick announced from the doorway.

Matthew turned to look at her and found it impossible to breathe. Her eyes were even stormier than usual, lending a thrilling fury to the loveliness of her delicate features. Her hair was carelessly swept up into a lively mass of dark golden curls that reflected the candlelight like a dragon's coveted hoard of coins. Moving forward with her chin up, she fisted her hands, and the soft line of her jaw hardened as if she clenched her teeth. She was angry, but she still floated her enchanting beauty across the floor in a gown of the deepest blue, a contrasting portrait of serenity. She flashed her displeasure at him and her sister, glaring at them both and narrowing her eyes as though sighting a target on their foreheads.

Damn and blast it all. It was impossible to deny that he wanted her like he had wanted no other. What the devil was he to do? They were *friends,* or they had been until he had goaded her into hating him. *Friends.* He suddenly discovered he hated that word.

Blessing hurried over to Fortuity, linked her arm through hers, and escorted her to their little group. "Dearest sister, you must meet Thorne's friends from Scotland. They are a delight." With a graceful sweep of her hand, she motioned to the pair. "Lord Carronbridge, this is my sister, Lady Fortuity. Fortuity, this is Viscount Simon Carronbridge and his sister, Lady Sarah."

Impressive and powerful in his kilt, even in Matthew's grudging opinion, the ruddy-haired Scot made a leg. "'Tis an honor and a pleasure to meet ye, Lady Fortuity."

Fortuity dropped a modest curtsy. "The pleasure is mine, my lord." She offered his sister a polite nod. "It is lovely to meet you as well, Lady Sarah."

"And yourself, my lady," the reserved Lady Sarah said with the shyest of smiles.

"Lady Fortuity," Matthew said with his best bow. "It is good to see you again."

She glared at him until Blessing nudged her. "Good evening,

Lord Ravenglass."

Lord Ravenglass? He had indeed assumed the role of his own worst enemy, potentially ruining any possibility of friendship or anything else with the exquisite lady. *Anything else?* Was he brave enough to attempt *anything else?* If it took the hatred for him out of her eyes, indeed he was foolish and courageous enough to rush in where angels feared to tread, as Alexander Pope had once so wisely written.

He rolled his shoulders and opened his mouth to speak to her, only to find himself cut off by the determined Scot.

"Lady Fortuity," Carronbridge said, gallantly offering his arm, "would ye think it forward of me if I escorted ye to the dining room? Your fine sister here mentioned we would go in as soon as ye arrived."

She stared at him for a long moment, as if confused by his ardent attention. "Why no, my lord. I would not think you forward at all." She took his arm and fell in step beside him.

Matthew clenched his teeth so tightly his jaws ached, but he still found the presence of mind to offer his arm to Lady Sarah. "My lady? Might I escort you?"

She gracefully nodded even though she never lifted her gaze as she lightly rested her hand on his forearm. "Thank ye, my lord," she said so quietly, he almost didn't hear her.

Blessing and Knightwood brought up the rear even though they were the hosts. Matthew silently cursed them both for whatever purpose this cruel game of theirs was supposed to serve.

Once seated, Matthew found himself across from Fortuity and Lord Carronbridge, with Lady Sarah to his right. Blessing sat at one end of the table, and Knightwood the other. Lady Roslynn's place remained empty to Matthew's left. He arched a brow at Knightwood. "Surely Cadwick would not be so unwise as to fail to feed the herd?"

"Feed the herd?" Carronbridge repeated before Knightwood could answer. "Have ye livestock, man? Here in town?"

Knightwood laughed. "A herd of felines. Mother's cats are her pride and joy. I sometimes wonder if she loves them more than she loves Blessing and me." He nodded at Matthew. "And if Cadwick values his life, Mother will find all the dishes and bowls full of kippers and cream."

"Do ye like wee moggies?" Carronbridge asked Fortuity, leaning toward her with obvious admiration and an intent to charm her.

She eyed him with uncertainty. "I am not sure, my lord. What are *moggies*?"

"Ah, forgive me," he said with a chuckle. "Cats, my lady. We Scots call them moggies."

"I do like them," she said, with a smile that Matthew wished she would turn on him. "I particularly enjoy their antics."

"And their purring is most soothing," Blessing said, before turning to the Scot's sister. "Dogs or kitties, Lady Sarah. Which do you prefer?"

"I love them all," Lady Sarah said with an almost cowering twitch of her shoulder. "Animals are the best sort of friends."

Lady Roslynn blew into the dining room and took her place. "Do forgive me. I discovered the outside bowls were quite empty and had to correct that immediately. Zeus was beside himself waiting for his dinner."

"Is Cadwick still alive?" Matthew couldn't resist asking.

"Temporarily," she said with a curt dip of her chin, then she smiled at Blessing. "Forgive me, my dear. I did not mean to keep your guests waiting."

"There is nothing to forgive, Mother Roslynn." Blessing rang the bell beside her plate and a pair of footmen appeared, one bearing a tureen of soup and the other prepared to ladle it. "Cook prepared our favorite artichoke soup. I do hope you'll enjoy it."

Matthew noticed Carronbridge had scooted closer to Fortuity than he considered appropriate. Had Blessing gone blind? Was she not supposed to see that her sister behaved properly? Although, in Fortuity's defense, it was Carronbridge who had arranged his chair closer to hers. But everyone smiled and chatted as if nothing was amiss.

"We will be in London another fortnight, Lady Fortuity," Carronbridge said. "I would consider it an honor to call upon ye during that time. Would ye find that acceptable, my lady?"

Fortuity paused with a spoonful of soup partway to her lips. After stealing a glance around the table, she lowered it back to the bowl, drew her napkin up from her lap, and dabbed at the corners of her mouth. "That would be very nice, my lord. I look forward to seeing you again."

"Is the soup not to your liking, Lord Ravenglass?" Blessing asked with pure wickedness gleaming in her eyes.

He was too bloody well angry to eat it, but couldn't very well say that. "It is fine, my lady," he forced through clenched teeth with a pointed glare at Fortuity and Carronbridge that Blessing needed to heed and do something about.

The infuriating woman simply smiled at him, then turned her attention to Lady Sarah. "Is there no way you can convince your brother to stay in London longer? The two of you are most welcome, and as spring approaches, there will be so many delightful gatherings."

"But your confinement approaches as well, my lady," Matthew told Lady Blessing with the slightest narrowing of his eyes. What was she trying to do? Marry Fortuity off to a bloody Scot?

"I would be most happy to provide introductions should you decide to stay longer," Fortuity told Lady Sarah. "And the first would be to my sister, Grace. She loves animals too. In fact, her hounds have the run of our townhouse."

Lady Sarah blushed and smiled broadly, seeming to relax for the first time the entire evening. "Thank ye for such warm hospitality, but I fear I am at the mercy of my brother and whatever he decides."

Carronbridge laughed and lifted his glass. "If my wee sister wishes to stay longer, then we shall stay longer." He touched the crystal to Fortuity's goblet, sending the clearest *ting* through the room. "I look forward to an extended visit."

"As do I," Fortuity said, then sipped her wine.

Bloody hell, Matthew thought. What the devil was he to do now?

Chapter Six

"Do my eyes deceive me?" Grace whispered in Fortuity's ear. "You are not in the shadows, furiously writing on your scraps of paper?"

"Lord Carronbridge keeps flushing me out. It's as though I am a plump little pheasant just begging to be shot." Fortuity forced a smile at the attentive Scot headed their way with yet another glass of lemonade. "Please stay close, Gracie. If I drink much more, I shall surely flood every chamber pot and bourdaloue in the ladies' retiring room."

"Then decline when he asks if you wish for more."

"It is the only way I can be rid of him for longer than a matter of minutes." Fortuity kept her fake smile fixed on the Scottish viscount as he drew ever nearer. "I have introduced him to every debutante whose name I can recall, yet he follows me like one of your devoted hounds."

"I thought you liked him?"

"He seems to be a very nice man," Fortuity hurried to say, then stepped forward and accepted the glass of lemonade from Carronbridge. "Thank you, my lord. You spoil me with such attentiveness."

"Ye are quite welcome, my lady," he said with a gallant bow. "And one such as yourself deserves every attentiveness." He nodded at Grace. "And how are ye this fine evening, Lady Grace?"

"Quite well, thank you." Grace stretched up on tiptoe and peered around the crowded ballroom. "Is your sister here, Lord Carronbridge? I thought she might like to know that Lucy finally had her puppies. A healthy litter of seven."

"Seven pups? Well done, indeed." He turned and joined her in scanning the crowd. "Last I saw her, she was dancing with a gentleman whose name I canna recall, but she seemed happy enough with him. The ladies ye introduced her to have been quite kind. Sarah has always struggled with being overly shy and retiring. I am glad she has been so well received."

"Lady Sarah is kindness itself," Fortuity said, wishing the young woman would come and fetch her brother for at least a little while. As she'd told her sister, Carronbridge seemed nice enough, but something about him made her as uneasy as walking through the parlor in her stocking feet before Grace's hounds went outside for their morning run. Invariably, the gorgeous pattern of the parlor's Turkish rug always hid a warm, disgusting puddle the pups left behind.

Fortuity wondered what undesirable things the handsome Scottish lord's charming attentiveness hid. It was nothing he had said or done, but *something* was there just beneath the surface, and it wasn't good. She would wager her favorite quill on it. She choked down another sip of lemonade and tried to control her runaway suspicions. Perhaps she was just being silly or maybe just missing Matthew, a man known for his brutal honesty. A melancholy sigh escaped her.

"Miss Eleanor Sykesbury is here," Grace said, then wrinkled her nose.

Carronbridge chuckled. "I take it ye dinna care for Miss Sykesbury?"

"Miss Sykesbury and her mother are cousins to Lord Ravenglass," Fortuity hurried to explain before Grace launched into a scathing diatribe about Eleanor's cutthroat tactics on either finding a husband or preventing others from doing so. "Would you like an introduction?"

The wily Scot waggled a ruddy brow at her, but his rich brown eyes hardened ever so slightly and somehow seemed colder. "Are ye trying to be rid of me, my lady?"

"Never, my lord," Fortuity lied, then curtsied and handed him her empty glass. "Do forgive me, but I must excuse myself to the retiring room for a moment."

"I shall anxiously await your return, my lady," Carronbridge said, then handed off her empty glass to a passing servant.

"He does get up one's nose a bit," Grace said as they wove their way through the crowd. "If you do not wish to encourage him, you may have to speak plainly. Or do you wish to encourage him long enough to shake some sense into a rather slow-witted viscount for whom we all know you possess a certain fondness?"

"Gracie, hush!" Fortuity rushed into the ladies' retiring room and hurried behind the screen in the back corner. Thankfully, the chamber pot and bourdaloue appeared to have just been emptied, cleaned, and returned to the cabinet. Lady Burrastone thought of every comfort for her guests when trying to outdo Lady Atterley in giving the Season's most enjoyable parties.

Fortuity selected the bourdaloue, since it was much easier to hold up under her skirts rather than attempt to squat over a chamber pot and not wet her chemise or gown.

"I am merely stating what everyone knows," Grace told her from the other side of the screen. "Or, at least, our family knows. And we appear to be the only two in here at the moment, so calm down and finish with your necessities."

After making the bourdaloue a great deal heavier, Fortuity carefully set the full vessel on the cabinet. Then stepped out from behind the screen and immediately halted at the sight of one of Lady Burrastone's maids waiting with a pitcher of water, a bar of soap, and a linen towel.

"For refreshing yourself, my lady?" the young girl offered with a proper curtsy.

"Thank you." Fortuity glared at her sister for the lie about their being alone. Everyone knew servants were the lifeblood of the *ton*'s gossip. They found out everything and reported the information to their mistresses. She washed her hands and dried them, then seated herself in a chair beside the door.

"Are you unwell?" Grace asked as she perched on a chair beside her.

"I simply need to sit a moment and gather my thoughts." Fortuity aimed a pointed look at the two maids flitting around the room, attending to the ladies who had just entered.

Grace leaned over and bumped shoulders with her. "He is here, by the way. Sulking in your usual corner."

"I do not have a *usual* corner," Fortuity said, staring straight ahead.

"Yes, you do. No matter the party, you always hover in the back corner of the room on the same side as the refreshments table." Grace bumped shoulders with her again. "Perhaps he is waiting for you."

"Stop doing that." Fortuity scooted her chair to the side, increasing the distance between them. "And why would he possibly wait for me? He has made himself quite clear."

"Are you going to allow him to help you with your stories?"

"I am not."

"Tutie."

"Do not use that tone with me. It does no good, and you know it."

Grace huffed and plucked at the embroidered flowers dotting the skirt of her gown. "May we go back out now? Serendipity charged me with keeping Joy away from the gaming rooms, so I really should at least *appear* to be putting forth some effort in that regard."

"You go." Fortuity pulled in a deep breath and released it with a soul-cleansing sigh. "I need more time. I am not used to being the subject of such ardent attention, and I find it not only annoying but most tiresome."

"You don't trust him." Grace poked her in the shoulder. "What did he do?"

"Keep your hands to yourself, Gracie." Fortuity rubbed her shoulder even though the poke hadn't hurt. "And he's done nothing. It's just…"

"Just what?"

"A feeling."

Grace rose to her feet, stepped in front of Fortuity, then bent and looked her in the eyes. "Animals survive by their instincts," she said quietly. "Listen to your feelings when they're attempting to warn you about something."

Fortuity tipped her head toward the door. "Go find Joy, or Serendipity and Chance will sputter at you."

Grace grinned. "I enjoy making them sputter." She wagged a finger. "Do not stay in here too long. If you don't wish to return to *Scotland*, seek the land you know."

Fortuity nodded, then massaged her temples as Grace exited the room. The beginnings of a headache throbbed behind her eyes, making her wonder if an overindulgence of lemonade caused the same aftereffects as an overindulgence of wine. Not that she would know. Mama had taught them all that a lady must always remain in control, and too many spirited drinks stole one's control away. She closed her eyes and continued rubbing the sides of her head. If this continued, she would go home early and seek refuge in her bed.

"There you are."

Biting her tongue to keep from groaning aloud, Fortuity opened her eyes. "Eleanor." She hoped her disgusted tone would make the chit go away.

Eleanor widened her eyes as though Fortuity had raised a hand to strike her. But then she took hold of Fortuity's arm and tried to tug her to her feet. "Lady Blessing begged me to fetch you. She is in the garden and not feeling well at all."

"What on earth is she doing out there in the cold night air? Where is Thorne? Surely he didn't allow her to go outside alone?" Fortuity rose and hurried along behind Eleanor, cursing the crowded room that made getting to the veranda's doors even more difficult. But the more she fought the crowd, the more she found the entire situation strange. She pulled Eleanor to a stop. "How did you happen to come across her? Outside in the chilly March air? And alone?" She narrowed her eyes. "Is this another of your tricks, Eleanor? Because I assure you, we all know how you are by now. We are not as dull-witted as you like to believe."

The usually defiant Eleanor bowed her head. "I deserve that for my past behavior, of which all I can do is continue to apologize and beg forgiveness." She lifted her dark-eyed gaze to Fortuity's and appeared on the verge of tears. "I asked Lady Blessing to step outside so I might apologize to her personally for the way I behaved when she and Lord Knightwood were courting."

"After all this time? Why now?" Fortuity eyed the woman, who was either telling the truth or was a remarkably talented liar. She couldn't decide which. "Why this evening? You could have just as easily sent her a written apology at any time over the past year."

"I felt it would be more sincere if I spoke to her directly. Notes can be so cold and impersonal." Eleanor waved for Fortuity to follow. "And as we stand here arguing, your sister needs you. She sent me to fetch you and her husband both."

"I would hope you took him to her first and then came to find me?" Fortuity still didn't believe this wild tale, but a glance around the ballroom revealed that not only was Blessing nowhere to be seen, but neither was Thorne among the crowd, nor any of the other Broadmere siblings. Was Eleanor actually telling the truth for once?

"Of course. He has gone to her as we speak."

Still doubtful but worried about Blessing, Fortuity waved Eleanor forward and hurried after her. As they charged outside, the bracing chilliness of the clear night made Fortuity catch her breath. "Essie should not be out here. Why could you not have spoken to her in an unused room?"

Eleanor halted and stared out across the moonlit gardens. "I don't see them. Lord Knightwood must have carried her inside."

"I sincerely hope so. This coldness could not possibly be good for her."

"But I promised to bring you to her," Eleanor said. "I am trying my best to show her I have changed and regret my past behavior."

Fortuity turned to go back inside. "I will assure her you kept your word to fetch me. Come. All we are accomplishing out here are numb fingers and toes."

"But I must keep my word. Let us check Lady Burrastone's library. Perhaps he carried her there so she might rest in the quiet until their carriage is brought 'round." Eleanor caught her by the wrist and hurried her along. "I am so concerned about her."

"Should we find Lady Burrastone? I have no idea where her library is." Fortuity pulled her arm free. "I prefer not to be dragged."

"Of course, forgive me." Eleanor didn't slow her pace. "The library is down this hall and off to the right. Lady Burrastone was kind enough to give Mama and me a tour when we had tea with her recently."

Fortuity hadn't realized that the Sykesburys had ingratiated themselves with Lady Burrastone, but it made sense. The dear old woman hungered for those who blindly followed wherever she led. Mama had often said the lady longed to be placed on a pedestal and worshipped as if she were the patron saint of the *ton*.

"Here it is," Eleanor said as she opened a door on the right. She stepped back to let Fortuity enter first. "I remember a pair of fainting couches at the far end of the room in front of the hearth. Surely he took her there."

Entering the shadowy room, Fortuity turned in the direction of the candles glowing on the mantel. "Essie, are you there? Thorne?"

"Fortuity?"

She halted, and every hair on the back of her neck stood on end. "What is this? A trick?"

Matthew stepped out of the shadows with a scowl as dark as the devil's waistcoat. "You should not be in here alone with me. Leave at once."

"Do not order me around, Lord Ravenglass. I am not one of your servants." But she hurried back to the door. She indeed needed to leave before anyone saw her in such a compromising situation. The latch clicked, but the door refused to open. "Matthew," she said, struggling to force out the words, "your cousin has locked the door. Why would she do that?" Panic rising, she tried again. All it did was rattle and remain shut. Perhaps the mechanism was just a bit tricky, or it stuck in damp weather. She closed her eyes, clenched her teeth, and tried again—and again. The door was indeed locked.

She leaned forward and rested her forehead on the door. "How did she lure you here, or was this your idea?"

"Fortuity." His injured tone cut through her. "I would never do such a thing to you, and you should know that."

"All I know," she said without turning to face him, "is that I am locked in a room, alone, with a man the *ton* paired me with only weeks ago." She turned, tempted to throw something at him. This had to be his fault, his and his dratted cousin's. "I will be ruined. My sisters will be ruined."

"Only if we are found." He took a step forward but halted when she jabbed a finger at him.

"Has your unbelievable arrogance done away with any good sense you ever possessed? If Eleanor took the time to lure us both here and lock us in, do you not think, at this very moment, she is gathering every tongue wagger she can find to drag here and reveal our contrived debauchery?"

He jutted his chin higher as he moved closer. "Then we will marry."

"WE MOST CERTAINLY will not marry," Fortuity squeaked in a high-pitched whisper.

The entirety of her person trembled, making Matthew draw closer still so he might catch her if she swooned. Even in the dimly lit room, her pallor was unmistakable. Her disgust for him wrapped cruel, icy fingers around his heart and twisted, nearly ripping it out of his chest. Gads, she hated him more than he'd ever imagined possible.

"If we are found, it is the only way," he said quietly, hoping the certainty in his tone would calm her. "You know that as well as I. Your reputation would be compromised."

She pointed a trembling hand at the window. "I will climb out that window. All I need to do is escape this room. Don't think I won't do it."

"Has your hatred for me truly grown that strong?"

She stared at him, blinking rapidly, then swiping at tears that appeared to make her angrier. "I do not hate you," she said with another shudder. "But I refuse to marry a man who does not want or love me. I am not a duty or a lesson in chivalry." She went to the window and grunted with the effort of trying to raise the sash.

He couldn't hold back any longer. He strode forward and pulled her into his arms. "Fortuity—stop."

"Leave me alone," she said, growling with her teeth bared. She twisted back to the window and tried in vain to open it. "Why will this dratted thing not give way?"

He caught her by the wrists and yanked her back into his arms. "I said *stop*, and I meant it. You will be my wife. Either by announcing the bloody banns three Sundays in a row, special license, or Gretna Green. I do not care. But I will not have you and your family ruined by Eleanor. I will deal with that conniving chit later."

She glared up at him, the hurt in her eyes stinging him worse than a slap in the face. He ached to tell her that everything happened for a reason, that perhaps this was fate's way of shoving him in the direction he had needed to take all along. But he couldn't. Something inside held him back, kept him from making himself even more vulnerable to her than he already was. Gads, he was still such a coward when it came to love.

"And to answer your earlier question," he said, trying to shift his thoughts from his own failings, "Eleanor informed me that your brother wished to speak with me regarding a matter of the utmost importance and asked that I meet him here in the library. *That* is how I came to be in this room."

"And that does not anger you?"

"Of course it angers me."

"Then why are you so bloody calm?" She tried to twist away. "Let me go and help me open this infernal window."

"The drop from that window would injure you." He stepped between her and her faulty means of escape. "How would that help your reputation, my little wren? Having the servants find you crumpled in a heap on the carriage road?"

She stared up at him, her chest heaving and becoming quite the distraction. "Break down the door while I hide behind the desk. After an appropriate amount of time has passed, I shall sneak out and rejoin the party."

He would laugh if her determination to escape him didn't cut him to the quick. "I daresay that breaking down the door might draw the attention of anyone close enough to hear."

"Then we both need to hide. Or...or discover if there is a secret passage out of here." Her eyes lit up, and she tore away from him, running her hands along the walls and shoving on the bookcases. She cast a glance back. "Well, come on. I would think a man who does not wish to marry would be more helpful."

"What if I said I changed my mind and now wish to marry?"

She shot him a glare that could have incinerated him on the spot. "I would call you a liar."

"I never lie."

Her fisted hands trembling, she backed up against the wall. "Can you honestly tell me you intended to ask me to be your wife? That you have recovered from your painful past and are ready to marry?"

"I—" He couldn't lie. She would know.

"I thought not," she said as she returned to the window and thumped the facing, determined to unstick the stubborn thing. "Come help me open this bloody window. Now!"

He held out his hand, regretting every time he had ever told her they were nothing more than friends. "Fortuity—come. The evil herd approaches. The clatter of their cloven hooves in the hall is unmistakable."

She stared at the door and shuddered. "This cannot be happening. Not to me. Matthew, this cannot be happening to us."

He went to her, took her hand, and gently led her to the center of the room, closer to the door. "I will protect you, my little wren. Always. I swear it."

Staring up at him with tears in her eyes, she opened her mouth to speak but then snapped it shut again as the latch on the door rattled, then the thing swung open, revealing a smirking Eleanor leading several of the most vicious and gossiping members of the *ton*.

"Cousin! Lady Fortuity!" The chit adopted a convincing expression of shock, then turned to the back-biting pack surrounding her. She weakly attempted to shoo them away, as if trying to keep them from seeing that which she had already revealed to them. "Why don't we all return to the ballroom, ladies?"

"Wait," Matthew ordered her, ensuring his powerful voice echoed well into the hallway. "I have an announcement."

Eleanor narrowed her eyes, and her victorious smile faded the slightest bit. "An announcement?"

"Yes." Turning to Fortuity, willing her to trust and forgive him, he pressed a tender kiss to the back of her gloved hand. "Lady Fortuity has honored me with a *yes*. She has agreed to be my wife."

"Nothing more than friends?" Lady Serafina Mellincotte

snapped with a bitter snarl. "I thought you abhorred lies, my lord?"

"And what of her Scottish admirer?" taunted Lady Theodora Worsten. "This evening, his lordship has served her better than any lackey I have ever seen."

"I refuse to tolerate such insulting behavior toward my future wife." Matthew slammed the door in their faces, then turned to find Fortuity had lowered herself into a chair and rocked forward with her face in her hands. "Fortuity?"

"Go away," she said, her voice trembling.

He went to her and knelt. "I will not leave you here in tears for them to discover and pick the meat off your bones." With the lightest touch, he rubbed a finger across her gloved hand. "Look at me," he implored softly.

She shook her head while keeping her face buried in her hands.

"Fortuity."

"Do not say my name like that," came her muffled scolding from between her fingers.

"Like what?" Perhaps if he teased her, it might give her the courage she needed to face the prying eyes of the *ton*.

"Like you have the right to."

"I do have the right to. You are going to be my wife."

"Not if I can think of a way out of this." She dropped her hands to her lap and stared at him with such desperation that his heart clenched. "You made it quite plain that you never wished to marry," she said, "that we would never be anything more than friends. I will not be party to an agreement where my husband was leg-shackled to me against his will out of some ridiculous sense of honor and duty."

"You are too overwrought to plot anything at the moment. We will sort this out. Together." Still kneeling beside her, he eased both her hands into his and gently squeezed. "Come," he said with a grin. "Let us find your brother and sisters. Eleanor may have locked them in the pantry."

The library door burst open with such force that it bounced off the wall. In the doorway stood Viscount Simon Carronbridge, red-faced and his chest heaving. "Get away from her, ye filthy cur! Stand and face me, I say!"

Rage like he'd never felt before surged through Matthew, pushing him to his feet. "This is none of your affair, Carronbridge. Calm yourself and leave."

The Scottish lord tipped a hard nod at Fortuity. "That fine lady is mine, and I find your behavior loathsome. Luring her in here. Attempting to ruin her in my eyes."

"Lady Fortuity is to be my wife." Matthew squared off in front of the man, shielding Fortuity.

"Ye lie," the man said with a rumbling throatiness. "I have courted this lady for the past fortnight. If what ye say is true, where the devil have ye been while another man pursued your woman?" He shifted to one side and glared at Fortuity. "And what sort of woman willingly receives another man's attention when she belongs to someone else?"

"I did not encourage you, Lord Carronbridge." Fortuity set her chin to a defiant angle. "I spent time with you and your sister to help you ease into London Society more easily. It was not *courting*. It was kindness and extending friendship." She shifted in the chair as if uncomfortable, then pushed herself to her feet. "And I belong to no one because I am neither chattel nor an animal purchased for breeding. I belong to no one but myself."

He narrowed his eyes and shook his head. "Ye dinna ken your place, woman. Such an attitude is most unbecoming. While I regret speaking ill of the dead, did your parents not have the sense to raise ye properly?"

"Do not dare to insult my parents, you arrogant churl." She fisted her hands and started toward him. "They were far better people than you could ever hope to be."

Matthew caught her and pulled her back, tucking her close to his side. "Leave, Carronbridge, or I shall personally escort you out."

"I wouldha taught her how to behave, but now that I see she's nothing but a brazen whore, ye can have her." Carronbridge spat on the floor. "Good riddance to her, and I pray ye know for certain ye are the father of anything that comes out of her."

Matthew lunged and landed a solid blow to the Scot's jaw, knocking the man out into the hallway. Driven by uncontrollable rage, he charged forward, grabbed the rude lord up from the floor, and struck him again. "Insult her again and die!"

"A common lightskirt," Carronbridge sneered through the blood streaming from his nose.

Clutching the devil by the waistcoat, Matthew drove the man back into the wall and pummeled him. "You are the only thing common here, you bastard." He hit him again, a red haze of fury roaring through him, deafening and blinding him to all else.

"Ravenglass, stop! You are going to kill him!" Lord Knightwood caught hold of Matthew, attempting to pull him away.

Matthew twisted free, determined to finish the man. "He insulted my Fortuity. He deserves to die!"

"We will see him ousted from London," the Duke of Broadmere said as he grabbed Matthew's other arm. "No one hurts any of my sisters and gets away with it." He and Lord Knightwood forced Matthew back from the Scot, who sank to the floor and went still.

Lady Sarah pushed through the gathered onlookers and hurried to her unconscious brother. "Oh, Simon. Not again." She turned and looked up at Matthew, Knightwood, and the duke. "I am so sorry. If someone could please place him in our carriage, we shall be gone from here and never return. Please forgive him. He canna help himself."

Tears streaming down her face, she went to Fortuity, curtsied low, and bowed her head. "Forgive us, Lady Fortuity, I beg ye. He is a good man most of the time. At least, he is until his demons break free. Please find it in your heart to forgive him, and remember us in your prayers."

"Stay here with us. We will protect you." Fortuity sent a pleading look to her brother.

Chance nodded. "You are most welcome to shelter at Broadmere House, Lady Sarah, while your brother returns to Scotland."

The lady gave them both a sad smile, then turned her gaze to her brother. "I canna leave him. He is my twin, and I fear what he might do, what harm he might bring down upon himself, were I to desert him." She curtsied again. "But I thank ye for the offer."

"Remove him to his carriage," Lord Burrastone ordered his footmen. He turned to Matthew and narrowed his eyes. "Do you require a room and the assistance of my valet, my lord?"

"Thank you, but no, Lord Burrastone." Still struggling to compose himself, Matthew offered the portly gentleman a bow. "However, for the sake of your wife's delightful party, I feel it best that my cousins and I depart." He turned to Fortuity's brother. "Your Grace, I shall call upon you tomorrow. Lady Fortuity has agreed to be my wife."

"Has she?" Chance eyed Matthew, shifted his gaze to Fortuity, and then offered them both a knowing smile. "Until tomorrow, then, Lord Ravenglass. I look forward to our meeting."

Matthew moved to Fortuity, took her hand, and kissed it. "All will be well. I promise."

Her eyes glistened with tears, but she offered him a curt nod. "We will speak more tomorrow, Lord Ravenglass."

His heart fell. *Lord Ravenglass.* He bowed, kissed her hand again, then exited the library, striding down the maze of hallways toward the front of the Burrastone home. Eleanor and Agnus were already there, donning their cloaks. Agnus appeared confused. Eleanor looked frightened.

"Cousin," she started, but he silenced her with a look.

"What have you done now, Eleanor?" her mother whispered.

"Not a word until we get in the carriage," Matthew said as a footman held the door, and they descended the steps to their vehicle.

"But cousin," Eleanor began, "I—"

"You will shut your mouth and do as you are told," he informed her as he held her hand as she climbed inside.

"My lord, please," Agnus began.

"You will not speak either, Agnus. You and your daughter have abused my hospitality and familial responsibilities for as long as I shall allow." He settled into the seat opposite them. "But since I am not an entirely heartless bastard, I shall give the two of you a choice. Return to India to live with the departed Mr. Sykesbury's family and all that entails, or move to the smallest of my properties in the country, never to return to London or any other Ravenglass holding ever again."

They gasped in unison and stared at him, aghast.

"But it is the *Season*," Eleanor said, her high-pitched whine angering him even more.

"You ended your London Season when you attacked the Broadmeres, a finer family never to be found." He calmly folded his hands in his lap. "What shall it be, cousins? India or the country?" He focused on Eleanor. "Or perhaps one of each? Eleanor to India to proceed with her arranged marriage and Agnus to the country? I rather like the sound of that."

Agnus fisted her lacy handkerchief, clutching it to her chest. "Please do not separate us, my lord. I beg you."

"Then both to India?" He arched a brow, knowing they would choose the small cottage on the edge of the Lake District near the village whose name he couldn't recall.

Agnus reached over and clutched Eleanor's hand so tightly that her knuckles turned white. "We shall move to the country and be grateful for your tolerance."

Chapter Seven

"**D**ID YOU NOT think it strange that Essie would send *Eleanor* to fetch you?" Grace gently asked. "I mean—of all people."

"I do not need reminding of my naïveté or my stupidity, but thank you, dear sister, for being kind enough to do so anyway." Fortuity paced the breadth and width of the siblings' shared sitting room that connected their bedrooms. How in the world had she allowed Eleanor to trap her so easily? And after she'd informed the conniving little chit that they were all smarter than that and knew better than to trust her? Eleanor must surely be laughing so heartily right now that she spewed tea out her nose.

"Other than joining a nunnery, I can think of no way out of this that will not drag us all into ruin." Fortuity stopped pacing and threw up her hands. "I could tolerate being ruined. Who knows? Such a scandal might even make my books more enticing to publishers and readers alike. But it would also taint the rest of you. It is simply not fair, and there is nothing I can do about it. I am truly doomed."

Grace hefted one of her overly plump hounds up onto the settee beside her. "But you do love him, so it will be all right in the end. Will it not?"

"Would you want the man you loved forced to marry you out of a sense of duty? He never wanted to marry, Gracie. Never!" Fortuity hugged herself tighter as she made another circuit around the room. The hot chocolate she had forced down hours ago raged in her stomach like a stormy sea. It would surely be a miracle if it didn't come sloshing back out. "And Chance is less than delighted with what happened. Did you see his face at breakfast?"

"That is only because your marriage of convenience does not satisfy the requirements of Mama and Papa's will. He knows if Mr. Sutherland gets wind of your marrying for the sole reason of saving the rest of us from ruin, things will get messy, and he might never come into the full of his inheritance. You know how Chance hates the restrictions of his monthly stipend. He considers himself a duke in name only until all of us are happily married, and Mr. Sutherland presents him with the key to all the coffers."

Fortuity gave up on pacing and plopped down onto the lounge in front of the hearth. "I cannot marry him, Gracie. Not like this. It isn't right. Not when I love him, but he does not love me." Her stomach churned harder, making her curl her toes and tense to keep from casting up her accounts. "I would only end up loving him more, and when he eventually took a mistress, it would break my heart."

"Why would you think he would take a mistress?" Grace scratched behind her dog's floppy ears until the beast started kicking its back leg in delight. "Did you sleep any last night? Your arguments are weak this morning, and that is so unlike you."

Serendipity and Merry entered the room, their cautious expressions tensing Fortuity even more.

"He is here to speak with Chance, isn't he?" She clapped a hand over her mouth and concentrated on slow, deep breaths to keep from being ill.

"Oh dear. She has gone quite green." Merry rushed to the bellpull and rang for the maid.

Serendipity sat beside Fortuity on the lounge, grabbed her by the back of the neck, and forced her to bend forward and put her head between her knees. "Breathe in and hold it to a count of five, then breathe out, and do it all over again."

Fortuity twisted away and straightened. "I am not about to swoon, Seri. I am about to eject my breakfast chocolate into the chamber pot."

Her sister gently wrapped an arm around her shoulders. "But I thought you were quite fond of Lord Ravenglass?"

"I shall ask you"—Fortuity turned and glared at Merry—"and you as well, the same thing I asked Gracie. Would either of you wish for the man you loved to be *forced* to marry you?"

Merry shrugged. "It would simplify things, actually."

"What?" Fortuity stared at her, unable to understand her youngest sister's reasoning.

"Once married, he would be trapped, and I would have more time to make him love me back." Merry bobbed a satisfied nod. "Much easier than trying to win him when he still had options."

Serendipity gave young Merry an impressed look. "I agree completely."

Fortuity sagged forward and held her head in her hands. "The two of you defy logic."

"Why?" Merry asked. "Because we know how to make the best of a situation?"

"She thinks he will take a mistress," Grace told them in an overly loud whisper.

Fortuity lifted her head. "I can still hear you."

"Good. Then listen to me when I say that Lord Ravenglass would not take a mistress. Essie's husband was the rake—not your Ravenglass. I've not heard a single disparaging word about your man until last night." Grace clamped her mouth tightly shut, then covered it with her hand.

"Indeed, you *should* clap a hand over your mouth, sister!" Serendipity glared at Grace. "That is not at all helpful." She returned her attention to Fortuity, rubbing and patting her back as if she suffered from colic and needed to break wind. "I did overhear some news you are sure to find encouraging."

Fortuity allowed herself a despondent sigh. "What news?"

"The Sykesburys have moved to a small village in the Lake

District. Permanently. Or, at least, they leave for their new home today, so you won't have the displeasure of sharing a household with Eleanor."

"That *is* a bit of a bright point." Although, to be honest, Fortuity hadn't even gotten that far in her worries. She felt sure she would have eventually dreaded living under the same roof as Eleanor but simply hadn't thought of it yet. "How long does he intend to stay?" she asked Serendipity.

Her sister frowned. "How long does who intend to stay where? Lord Ravenglass? Here, today?"

"Who else, Seri?" Fortuity groaned and rocked forward, hugging her middle. How had life become such a mess so quickly?

"Sorry. I was still reveling in Eleanor's departure before she wreaked any more havoc." Serendipity rose from the lounge. "I am unsure how long Lord Ravenglass intends to stay, but he inquired about you, and left me with the impression that he would not be averse to seeing you." She offered a compassionate tip of her head. "The question is: do you feel well enough to go downstairs and see him? You have gone a bit pale again."

"But she's not as green." Merry came forward with a cup and offered it to Fortuity. "I had Jenny bring it up. It's one of her best tonics for settling ill humors." When Fortuity didn't move to take it, Merry pushed it into her hands. "It's minty and not foul at all. Nothing like the tonics from Mrs. Flackney and Mama we used to have to take."

Fortuity sniffed the pale concoction that resembled weak tea. It did indeed smell of mint. She hazarded a sip, hoping it would calm her breakfast beverage that was churning to escape her stomach.

"See? Not terrible at all."

Merry's usual cheeriness grated on Fortuity's nerves, but she kept herself from snapping at her well-meaning sister by taking another sip. "No. Not terrible at all," she said, wishing the remedy would ease her tumultuous feelings as effectively as it calmed her stomach. "I suppose I shall go down now and discover what

Matthew and Chance have decided about my future." Tears that begged to be cried stung her eyes, making her blink faster. Why should she even call it *her* future when it was quite clear that nothing about it was within her control?

She mentally shook herself. Wallowing in self-pity did nothing but make her weaker. She might not have control over *what* happened to her, but she controlled how she reacted to it. After all, she was a writer and created such dramatic plots all the time. How would she write her heroine's way out of this? Deuced if she knew.

She rose from the lounge and set the cup on the table. "Is everyone ready, then? I am sure you all wish to overhear what is discussed between my future husband and myself."

Serendipity and Merry gave her astonished looks while Grace glared at her and said, "Shall I fetch Felicity and Joy so you can bathe them in this lovely mood of yours?"

A twinge of guilt nipped at Fortuity. This situation was not her sisters' fault. "Forgive me. You three are not the enemy."

"You know we will help you in any way we can," Serendipity said.

"And if he does choose to take a mistress, we will make him sorry," Grace promised.

"We swear," Merry added.

"A sister cannot ask for more than that." Fortuity led the way downstairs and turned into the hall leading to the parlor.

"Library," Serendipity called out from behind her. "Chance had loads of paperwork to sort through, so they are in the library."

Of course they were in the library, what with the marriage agreement details to settle. Fortuity shifted directions, accessing the different hallway by using the servants' corridor. The closer she drew to the room, the harder her heart pounded. She knew what she wanted and prayed she could convince Chance and Matthew to add it to the contract. After a hard swallow, she pushed onward, quickening her pace and feeling like a lamb headed for slaughter. At the closed library door, she halted and knocked.

"Yes?" Chance's response came quickly and wasn't as surly as she'd expected.

"It is Fortuity, Chance," she said, "along with three members of the flock to uphold my confidence, I suppose you could say."

The door opened, and she immediately found herself floundering in the concern filling Matthew's flinty gray eyes. "Matthew," she whispered, then corrected herself and said louder, "Lord Ravenglass."

Disappointment furrowed his brow. "I prefer Matthew."

She curtsied, then stepped around him, entering the room with her sisters in tow. Heart still pounding, she braced herself for the men's reactions as she put forth the only condition over which she hoped to have any control. The condition that would not only save her pride but also her heart in this untenable situation. "I have a request," she told her brother as she halted in front of his desk.

Standing beside his leather wingback chair as he waited for his sisters to be seated, Chance fixed her with a warning look. "Fortuity, you understand the ramifications should you refuse Lord Ravenglass's offer of marriage?"

"I do not intend to refuse it."

Her infuriating brother had the audacity to smile. "Good, then I believe he and I have come up with a most agreeable marriage contract."

"I wish to add something," she said, squaring her shoulders. She didn't dare look at Matthew, fearing she would lose her nerve.

"Add something?" Chance motioned for her to sit, then seated himself as well.

"Whatever it is, give it to her." Matthew lowered himself into the chair next to her.

Chance glanced to the right at Serendipity and ratcheted both brows higher.

She shook her head and shrugged.

"Seri has no idea, Chance. This request came to me on the way down here." Fortuity folded her hands in her lap. "I wish for this union, this marriage of convenience, to be in name only. We may reside under the same roof to keep up appearances, but that is all."

"In name only?" Matthew repeated, appearing dumbfounded.

"Yes, as in *unconsummated*, my lord. A business agreement between two like-minded parties. And you will also see that my stories are published, as you previously promised." She angled her chin higher. "After all, you stand to benefit from my generous dowry and personal holdings. It is only fair that I benefit as well from this wicked trap set by your cousin Eleanor."

Thankfully, her voice hadn't quivered, even though her throat ached with the need to sob. She didn't want a marriage like this. She wanted love, happiness, and babies, and wanted all of it with Matthew. But she refused to *force* him, knowing he would eventually resent and grow to hate her. That would be more than she could bear.

She cleared her throat. "You may satisfy your"—she fluttered a hand, struggling for the genteel wording—"*manly* requirements elsewhere. I merely ask that you be discreet so the gossips do not shred me any more than they already have."

He stared at her, the hurt in his eyes threatening to make her crumble. "Why, Fortuity?" he asked softly as if they were the only two in the room. "Why are you doing this?"

She tightened her hands into fists, forcing herself to remain calm. She could shatter to bits later. "You made it quite clear you never wished to marry and could never offer me anything more than friendship. My addition to the agreement ensures your wishes are met while protecting my interests as well. We shall live together as friends, nothing more. Just as you wanted."

He reached over and cupped her jaw, gently stroking her cheek with his thumb. His touch threatened to break her. "What if I want more?" he asked.

"As I said…" She closed her eyes, cursing herself for the weak quiver in her voice. "You may satisfy your *wants* elsewhere. All I ask is discretion, my lord." She risked opening her eyes and meeting his gaze. "I have been hurt enough by your family," she whispered. "Please bring no further harm or humiliation upon me."

"I wish you to be my wife. Utterly. Completely." His stare hardened to a piercing glare. "I have sworn to protect you because I care about you and your family."

"You prove my point, my lord. This offer of marriage is out of duty, not love. I am merely defining your duty and making it less odious to you so we might remain friends."

Matthew scrubbed his jaw. With a low, throaty growl, he bared his teeth. "Everyone out. I wish to speak to my future wife alone."

"I am not comfortable with that, Ravenglass. Not in your current frame of mind." Chance glanced at the trio of sisters lined up on the settee against the wall, then curtly nodded at the door. "I shall remain. Sisters, you may leave."

Serendipity, Grace, and Merry quickly filed out and softly closed the door behind them.

Fortuity forced herself to stare straight ahead, focusing on the cluttered bookcase behind Chance's desk. It needed dusting. Did he never let the maids in here? Maybe if she concentrated on such ridiculous things, the pounding of her heart would calm and the sickening weight in her stomach would lighten.

"Are you afraid to speak to me alone, Fortuity?" Matthew asked.

She refused to look at him. Instead, she pulled in a deep breath and held it to a count of five before releasing it and answering. "I am not afraid to speak to him, Chance. Lord Ravenglass would never physically harm me." He would break her heart and shatter her dreams, but she knew he would never lift a hand to strike her. "You may wait in the hall with the others while he says whatever he has to say to me."

"You are dismissing me from my own library?" Her brother snorted in disbelief.

"According to our esteemed solicitor, Mr. Sutherland the elder, until you marry us all off for love and come into the entirety of your inheritance, this library belongs to the estate, not to you or any one of us."

"God help you," Chance told Matthew before he pushed up from his desk, charged out of the room, and thumped the door shut behind him.

"Why are you doing this?" Matthew asked with such heartfelt quietness that she flinched.

"I already answered that question once, my lord," she said without looking at him, reminding herself that she had to be strong. "I daresay my answer has not changed since a few moments ago."

"What if I told you I wished to marry you because…"

His voice trailed off, making her huff a mirthless laugh. She shifted in her seat and faced him. "You cannot finish that thought, can you?" Her poor Matthew was honest to a fault. She doubted the man could lie if his life depended on it. "Finish your sentence, Lord Ravenglass."

"Fortuity, I wish to marry you because I *need* to marry you."

"Need?" She shook her head and huffed again. "Why? Because of duty? Your friendship with my brother, the *duke*? Or your friendship with Thorne and my sister?" She forced herself to stiffen her spine and sit taller. "You loved a woman once. Loved her enough to ask her to be your wife. Do you feel for me what you once felt for her?"

"It is not the same."

"Exactly." She sagged into the depths of the chair with the conclusion that attempting to remain strong was extraordinarily wearying and not entirely worth the effort. "You do not love me. You are marrying me for every reason *except* love. That is why I wish our union to be in name only. I will not be used any more than I already have been."

"I have never used you."

"Perhaps not you personally, but you see, dear Matthew, women are pawns in this ridiculous Society in which we live. Our families barter us to align bloodlines, bring forth heirs, and increase fortunes. One would think we are no better than pedigreed hounds or purebred horses. And sometimes, in this unjust game for females, we are taken or given out of pity or duty because a player moved incorrectly across the board and must be penalized for breaking Society's rules." She gulped in a breath of air, realizing too late that she had forgotten to breathe during her heartfelt speech. She braced herself for his response.

Once again, he stared at her in open-mouthed amazement.

"Well?" She gripped the arms of the chair, digging her fingernails into the padded upholstery. "Does that clarify things for you, my lord?"

He slowly smiled and shook his head. "You are by far the most exquisite woman I have ever had the pleasure of knowing. Thank God Almighty you are to be my wife."

She studied him with increasing leeriness. He had never been known to behave as though his mind had left him, but perhaps he had sustained a blow to the head of which she was unaware. "What?"

"You are exquisite." Admiration shone in his eyes and echoed in his tone. "I shall obtain the special license this afternoon so we may marry before week's end."

"Before week's end?"

"Yes."

"So you accept the terms I wish to be added to the marriage agreement?" She wasn't budging on what she had requested and couldn't imagine his denying her. After all, the Lord Ravenglass she knew and oh so woefully loved would never force himself upon a woman, even if she was his wife.

"I will not lie to you and say that I like your terms, but if you insist on a marriage in name only or no marriage at all, it does not appear I have a choice, since I refuse to bring shame upon you and your family." But his expression gave her pause, making her wonder what he was plotting. "I already promised to do everything in my power to help you realize your dream of seeing your stories in print, so that point is irrelevant."

"I see." She cleared her throat. "Well, then." Now what the devil would she do? Marry him, of course, as she had no other choice. "I assume we shall remain in London until summer?"

He offered her a sultry grin that threatened to make her squirm. "Is that what you wish, my lady?"

She attempted a nonchalant shrug. "My wishes are not relevant in this matter. Your presence in the House of Lords during the session is."

"I have completed what is required of me during this session. Would a change of scenery, some time in the country, stir your muse and enable you to write more stories?"

He was up to something. She could smell it as plainly as the disgusting dish of onions, kidneys, and livers that she'd once told Mama would serve better as rat poison than dinner. That statement had required her to apologize to Cook and be sent to bed without her supper, which had achieved her goal of avoiding the meal entirely. But she couldn't read his expression or the emotions in his eyes, so she erred on the side of caution. "If it pleases you and your schedule, I prefer to stay in London until Blessing is safely delivered of my new little niece or nephew." She couldn't help but smile. "I am eager to meet him or her."

Matthew smiled back, and the rigid set of his broad shoulders appeared to relax. "Of course. I had forgotten about little Aloysius Starpeeper Knightwood's upcoming arrival."

Fortuity laughed with a very unladylike snort. "Oh my word, I fear I shall remember that name every time I cradle that precious child in my arms."

"I wonder what they shall call little *Starpeeper* if he is a she?"

"Perhaps Arabella Starpeeper Knightwood?" Fortuity snorted again, then covered her mouth. "Oh dear, forgive me. I am making the rudest of sounds."

He seemed suddenly sad. "I love your sounds when you laugh and want our future to be a happy one, Fortuity. Truly, I do."

She caught her bottom lip between her teeth and nervously chewed on it. "I cannot fathom what our future holds," she whispered. "I fear it, Matthew."

"Our future holds whatever we choose to place within it."

His words made her shake her head. "Platitudes, my lord. The future is not a sturdy bucket to be trusted. One never knows when the bottom will fall out and all your hopes and dreams will wash away—lost, never to be regained."

"What are your hopes and dreams, my little wren? Truthfully. Tell me so I might help you not only fulfill them, but protect them."

She hitched in a quick breath at the depth of his sincerity. "I no longer know, Matthew." With an apologetic shrug, she offered him a sad smile. "And that is the truth of it. I no longer know."

He dropped his head and shifted with a heavy sigh. "I understand."

Biting her lip to keep from saying that she truly doubted that he did, she bowed her head with a humble nod. She would adapt to this new life that fate, Society, and Eleanor had seen fit to give her. One way or another, she would adapt.

"I WANT SOMETHING original because the lady I am about to marry is beyond compare." Matthew slid the velvet display box back toward the jeweler. "And I need it today."

"Today, my lord?" The short, thin man with the longest fingers Matthew had ever seen puckered his mouth as if he had just tasted something extraordinarily tart. He repositioned his wire-rimmed spectacles higher on the bridge of his nose, then drummed his long, spidery fingers on the countertop. "Today is quite short notice for a ring like no other."

"What a pity, Mr. Eibertson." Matthew knew exactly how to compel the master jeweler to reveal the items he always held back for the most discriminating of customers. "In my travels, your creations are renowned not only for their beauty but how you seem to pluck them out of thin air upon the whim of your clients." He offered the artisan a polite nod and stepped back from the counter. "Thank you for your time, sir. I shall see if Mr. Lewisry can create what I require."

The reedy little man gasped, and his eyes flared wide with fiery indignance. "I assure you a Lewisry creation does not compare with that of an Eibertson." He rounded the counter, hurried to the door, and locked it. With a fluttering of his long fingers, he implored Matthew to follow him through a curtained-off archway at the back of the shop. "I just remembered a piece that might meet your requirements, Lord Ravenglass."

Matthew smiled to himself as he joined the man in his private workroom, which resembled what Matthew imagined a garden of gemstone blooms with gold and silver greenery might look like. "Impressive."

Mr. Eibertson accepted the compliment with a pleased nod as he unlocked a cabinet and withdrew a black velvet box from its depths. "I assume you are familiar with the *regard* rings that have become quite common?"

"Regard rings?"

"Yes. Some call them *dearest* rings." The craftsman lit another oil lamp and motioned Matthew closer. "Acrostic rings where the first letters of the gemstone's names spell *regard*: ruby, emerald, garnet, amethyst, ruby, and diamond." He lifted the lid of the small ring box and proudly turned it to face Matthew. "In my opinion, the word *regard* feels aloof. Informal. If one is your *dearest*, then why should you water down the sentiment to *regard*? I give you the Eibertson *dearest* ring. The only one of its kind."

The arrangement of gemstones, faceted and polished to create the utmost sparkle, was exactly what Matthew wanted.

"Diamond, emerald, amethyst, ruby, emerald, sapphire, and topaz. Set in a gold band. Exquisite, Mr. Eibertson, except for one thing." He pulled the ring from its velvet pillow and handed it to the jeweler. "I would like the word *trust* engraved inside the band."

With an avaricious smile, the artisan took the ring and the lamp and moved to a workbench beside the counter. He donned a pair of glasses with thicker lenses and selected a burin, a hardened steel spire with a handle, from his rack of tools. After what appeared to be an entirely inadequate amount of time, he returned to Matthew and handed him the ring to inspect. "Will that do, my lord?"

The word *Trust* now lived on the inside of the widest portion of the band, inscribed in a delicate script. "Mr. Eibertson, this ring shall become a Ravenglass family heirloom passed down through many generations."

The jeweler bowed. "I am honored, my lord."

Matthew took out his wallet and placed banknotes on the counter until the jeweler nodded for him to stop. Well pleased with his purchase, he secured the beribboned velvet box deep inside his pocket. "Thank you, Mr. Eibertson. You have been most helpful."

"Congratulations, my lord, on your upcoming nuptials. May you be blessed with years of prosperity and happiness."

Prosperity and happiness, Matthew repeated to himself as he exited the shop and returned to his carriage. He was not so much concerned about prosperity as he was happiness. Fortuity's request for a marriage in name only had stunned him, but the more he thought about it, the more he understood her motive. She feared he would resent her for forcing him into something he had sworn he would never do. But she had not forced his hand. Eleanor had. And that was hardly the point now, because this twist of fate had given him the shove he needed to admit that he had feelings for Fortuity, feelings that went far beyond friendship.

But she wouldn't believe him now. Not when he'd sworn to

all and sundry that they would never be anything more than friends, and had so poorly tied his own tongue when attempting to explain how he truly felt when they had met again that day in the library.

"I am such a bloody fool." He scrubbed a hand across his mouth, then rested his hand on the pocket bulging with the ring box. This was a start in reparations—the first onslaught in his war to win Fortuity's trust, earn her forgiveness, and convince her he would cherish her heart for all time, if only she could find the courage to entrust him with it.

Chapter Eight

MATTHEW STARED OUT the window at the blustery spring afternoon but kept his senses locked on the hallway behind him. He strained to hear approaching footsteps. The Broadmere butler had gone to fetch Fortuity and probably one of her sisters, although the need for a chaperone seemed silly at this point, since they would marry within days. With the special license already in hand, Fortuity had but to tell him which particular day she preferred. After all, a lady needed a little time to prepare not only for her wedding but moving her things to her new home.

He had come straight from the jeweler's, too eager to see what Fortuity thought of the ring to wait another day. He prayed she would love it, but more importantly, he hoped it would create the first of many cracks in the protective wall she had built around her heart.

The brisk and light tapping of approaching footsteps down the hallway made him smile. It was but one set of delicate feet. Fortuity came to him alone. Good. He turned toward the doorway just as she swept into the room.

"Lord Ravenglass." She dipped a formal curtsy, then, with a strained politeness that was most disconcerting, directed him to the settee and chairs in front of the hearth.

He sidled his way over to the seating area but remained standing. An aching sense of something akin to homesickness filled him, a longing for things to be as they once were when he was too great of a fool to appreciate them. He missed her infectious smile, her lighthearted laugh, and the easiness that always ran between them like the quiet waters of a peaceful stream. Her hopeless melancholy weighed heavy on his conscience. "What have I done now?"

"Done?" She cocked her head, reminding him of Ignatius the pug's reaction whenever someone spoke to him.

"I can always tell whenever I have displeased you because you address me as Lord Ravenglass rather than Matthew."

She lowered her gaze and rubbed her forehead as if her head ached. "You have not displeased me, my lord. Life has."

He crossed over to her, took her gently by the hand, and led her to the settee. "I know, my little wren, and I am truly sorry." With a nod at the seat, then a glance at the open parlor doors, he asked, "Would you sit with me? I have something for you."

Rather than appear pleased at the thought of receiving a gift, she looked even more pained—in fact, almost horrified—as they took a seat. "That is very kind, but I...I have no need of anything." She barely shook her head. "Truly, I don't."

He pulled the delicate velvet box from his pocket and placed it in her hand. "A gift is a *need* for the giver—not the recipient."

"Oh my. I see." She caught her bottom lip between her teeth and lifted the box higher, eyeing it as though it held something dangerous. "You really didn't have to, you know. It is not as if our marriage is..."

"Is what?"

"Uhm... *Usual*, I suppose would be a way of putting it."

"I know," he said quietly. "But I wish to make you happy again." He would not tell her of his hope that their marriage would one day be *usual* in the best way possible. She would never believe him. He nudged her hand that held the box. "Open it. It is my sincerest hope you will like it."

After another reluctant glance at him, she removed the ribbon and carefully opened the hinged lid. "A *regard* ring." Her tone revealed she was less than impressed but determined to be polite. "How lovely." But then something came over her, something that gave him hope. She cradled the box in both hands and studied the gemstones closer. "No, this one is different. The gems do not spell *regard*, do they?"

"No. They do not." He waited, holding his breath for her to discover the uniqueness of this ring that was intended for her alone.

"Diamond, emerald, amethyst, ruby, emerald, sapphire, topaz." Her voice had dropped to a whisper as she named the stones. She stole another glance at him, this time lingering long enough to meet his gaze. "*Dearest?*"

"Yes. Because that is who you are to me, my little wren. You are and always will be my *dearest.*" He took the ring out of the box and showed her the inscription inside the band. "And this is what our marriage shall be built upon. *Trust.*"

Tears welled in her lovely eyes. "It is wonderful, Matthew," she whispered. "So very wonderful."

"Shall I place it on your finger?"

"Yes, please." She breathed the words so softly he barely heard her.

As he slid it to the base of her ring finger on her left hand, he smiled. "A perfect fit. A good omen, wouldn't you say?"

She nodded while gazing down at her hand and slowly tilting it so the stones caught the light. "It is very lovely." Her smile finally shone in her eyes once again. "Thank you." She hugged her hand to her heart and twitched a little shrug. "I thought you might be here to inquire about the date we shall wed."

"Have you settled on one?" He wouldn't remind her that the sooner they married, the sooner the gossips would get bored with them and move on to torment some other poor soul.

"Felicity and Cook already have our wedding breakfast well in hand, and the maids have my trunks sorted. They assure me it will take no time at all to finish packing that which remains." She paused and swallowed hard, as if she had just forced down an overly large bite of biscuit. "Would the day after tomorrow be suitable for your schedule?"

"It would indeed, thank you." He hated this new, meek demeanor of hers. Where was his feisty little wren that warbled and darted through any situation with wit and fury? "I shall notify Mrs. Greer that the lady of the house will arrive the day after tomorrow. Shall I send for some of your trunks, or do you prefer to wait until your maid can accompany them to get your things properly situated in your rooms?"

She stared at him for a long moment, appearing bewildered. It was as if he had spoken in a language she didn't understand. "My maid?" she said under her breath, more to herself than him. "I suppose I shall need a maid, shan't I?"

"I fear Mrs. Greer cannot spare Mary Louise, and neither would she suit the task. While she is efficiency itself when it comes to many things, the duties of a lady's maid are not her strengths. Her shortcomings caused poor Agnus to lose her temper more than once."

Both of Fortuity's fair eyebrows rose nearly to her hairline. "Agnus Sykesbury lost her temper? More than once? With Mary Louise? I cannot imagine that."

Matthew chuckled. "It was quite remarkable. Even Eleanor was rendered speechless both times, and you can imagine my astonishment and joy at her mouth being shut for her."

"Oh my. I am sorry I missed that." Fortuity's gaze settled once more on her ring and her smile widened, thrilling him immensely.

"You truly like it?" he asked.

"I do indeed." With a sheepish dip of her head, she ran her thumb back and forth across the gemstones, barely spinning the ring on her finger. "I shall cherish it always." She went quiet and her brow slightly puckered. Shadows of worry blotted the light of happiness from her eyes.

"What are you thinking, Fortuity?"

"How we have always been such good friends, even from the

very start, and I do not wish us to lose that. I fear the loss of your freedom will cause you to resent me."

It took every ounce of restraint he possessed to keep from dropping to his knees and telling her he was glad they were marrying. He didn't dare, though, not yet. Because she would never believe him. Instead, he took her hands in his. "I do not now, nor will I ever, resent you."

"How do you know?"

He took her hand and pressed it to his chest, flattening her palm over his heart. "My heart knows. That is all that matters, because I have learned that my heart gets things right far more often than my head does."

She didn't speak, nor did she lift her gaze from where she had it locked on her hand on his chest. Then she eased her hand free and hugged it to her middle. "I am glad you do not resent me," she said quietly.

He longed to catch her up in his arms and beg forgiveness for being such a fool. But she looked ready to bolt, like a frightened fawn in the woods. "We will work out our life together and find happiness. I am sure of it."

Her forced smile brought him no comfort, but it couldn't be helped. The battle to win her heart and trust was a delicate and strategic balancing act of patience, timing, and the careful nurturing of her forgiveness for his stupidity and pride. And he would win this battle. For Fortuity. For himself. But most of all for their future children.

"YOU ARE LOVELINESS itself, my lady." Anne secured Fortuity's curls into a becoming bundle of ringlets high on her head, then tugged some free to cascade in an alluring temptation down over one shoulder.

"Thank you." Fortuity stared at her reflection in the dressing table mirror, already missing the chaos of her many sisters fluttering about while they all attempted to get ready at the same time. "Is everything packed and ready to be moved to Ravenglass Townhouse?"

"Yes, my lady. I've but to add the last of your items while you and his lordship attend your ceremony. Soon as I sort those things out, I'll have George load the wagon and take me over. He said he'd stay and help unload too, so's I can have everything ready for you when you arrive."

Fortuity swallowed hard and concentrated on breathing deeply—in, then out. She'd forgone eating or drinking anything as a precaution to keep from casting up her accounts all over the vicar. "And you packed my quills and ink? My foolscap and stationery? Everything?"

"Yes, my lady. Your writing desk too, because His Grace said you most certainly had to have it when he told me I was going along to be your lady's maid."

"I am glad you are coming with me, Anne. It will be strange to be one of so few females in a house." The unnerving quiet of the dressing room made her clench her fists. "Where is Gracie, by the way? And Merry and Joy? I know Felicity and Serendipity are busy seeing to the preparations of the wedding breakfast, but I cannot imagine why Gracie, Merry, and Joy are not up here lending me moral support."

Anne pulled a face as she held out a selection of necklaces for Fortuity to choose from. "Far be it from me to gossip, but Mrs. Flackney overheard His Grace instructing the ladies that if they dared help you escape your vows, he'd give away all of Lady Grace's hounds, ban Lady Joy from the gaming tables at every party, and condemn Lady Merry to dance with Lord Pellington at every ball." She tapped on the necklace in the middle. "This ruby was a favorite of your mother's and matches the embroidery on your gown."

Fortuity nodded, not really caring which necklace she wore. "What about Lady Knightwood?" She hated the whining in her tone, but she needed her sisters, and Chance making them afraid to gather around her was not fair in the slightest. Even if the others were too leery of his temperament to come to the dressing room, Blessing could come and keep her company. She was married and mistress of her own home. "Do you know if she has arrived yet?"

Anne fastened the ruby necklace around her throat. "She has. But it's my understanding that her ladyship is quite uncomfortable. She is in the parlor with her feet propped on a stool." She lowered her voice. "You should see them, my lady. Her ankles and feet have swollen so that her slippers look ready to pop right off."

Fortuity tried to suppress a heavy sigh and failed. She supposed she was being selfish, wishing for her sisters' support. After all, in their minds, she was marrying the man she loved. But what they didn't understand was that Matthew was being forced to do something he had sworn he would never do. Admittedly, his kindness and thoughtfulness only made her love him more, but he still thought of her as a *friend*—not a wife. She could see it in his eyes. Surely such a thing would doom their marriage to failure.

She squirmed atop the cushioned bench, remembering his unmistakable pity for her the moment they both realized they had walked into Eleanor's trap in Lady Burrastone's library. He was marrying her because he not only felt honor bound to do so, but because he felt sorry for her. He knew she had no other options, other than that temperamental Scottish lord whom she had intended to send back to the Highlands at her next opportunity.

Anne brought forward the ruby earrings that matched the necklace, then halted and frowned at Fortuity's reflection in the mirror. "Your sisters' ears are pierced, but yours…"

"Are not." Fortuity rubbed her earlobes, remembering the battle to keep them safe from Serendipity's needle. "The necklace is enough. Serendipity or one of the others can have the earrings."

She touched the simple necklace of a single ruby dangling from a delicate chain. "I prefer a quieter look."

"As you wish." The maid returned the earrings to the velvet trays of jewelry she had spread out across the top of the low dresser.

A persistent and ever-louder noise at the closed sitting room door made Fortuity turn that way. "What is that? It sounds like scratching."

Anne hurried over and opened it. "Oh my goodness. Shoo, Gastric. You are not supposed to be in here."

"Let him in," Fortuity said while reaching for Grace's favorite hound, named Gastric not only for his gluttony but his regular habit of filling a room with eye-burning flatulence. "Come here, old friend. At least you've come to see me."

With a happy woof, he ambled over and nudged his tawny head up into her hand for the pats he knew he deserved.

As Fortuity smiled down into his adoring brown eyes, she noticed a rolled parchment secured with a ribbon around his neck. "What is this, Gastric? Are you a spy for the Crown now?"

He merely wagged his tail in a faster circle.

She untied the ribbon, unrolled the parchment, and read to herself: *Even though we are not with you, we are with you. Never doubt it. Chance is an arse. But you knew that. Love, G.* Before rising from the bench, she scratched the sweet dog under the chin. "Thank you, Gastric. You have been a much appreciated messenger."

With a glance at Anne, who was pawing through a trunk in search of who knew what, she crossed to the hearth and tossed the note from her beloved sister into the flames so Chance wouldn't discover it and become even more annoying. Then she kissed the top of the dog's head and rubbed his floppy ears. "Tell Gracie I said thank you," she whispered against his velvety muzzle.

He responded with another happy woof, then trotted out of the room.

"Thank goodness," Anne said as she watched him go. "We

mustn't have a bride that smells of dog."

"Gracie bathes Gastric weekly. He does not smell."

Anne wrinkled her nose and shook her head as she closed the trunk in front of her. "He is a sweet dog, my lady, but his *fragrance* is unmistakable at times."

"With that, I cannot argue."

The small clock on the dressing table chimed the nine o'clock hour, and Fortuity's heart jumped. "Oh dear. It is time for me to go down." She was about to marry the man she loved, and yet the moment was filled with dread rather than excitement, brightness, or joy.

"It is a lovely morning for a wedding, my lady." Anne gave her an encouraging nod. "Warm and sunny enough to speak the vows in the garden. 'Tis a prosperous sign, I am thinking."

"Yes." Fortuity smoothed her hands down the delicate folds of her favorite gown, a creamy satin embellished with embroidered roses scattered across the skirt and trimming the empire waist and neckline. "I suppose when next I see you, I shall be Lady Ravenglass, and we shall be in our home." She almost choked on the words. If her knees didn't give way and send her crashing to the floor, it would surely be a miracle.

Anne clutched an armload of wraps to her chest and gave her a wistful look. "Yes. Go, my lady, and God be with you."

"Yes," Fortuity agreed under her breath. "God be with me." She forced herself out the door and down the staircase before she gave in to her fears and climbed down the trellis on the back wall and ran away to who knew where. She loved Matthew so much. Had even entertained daydreams of becoming his wife. Yet now that it was about to happen, she dreaded it, knowing he would come to resent her because honor had forced him to marry her. He would eventually hate her, even though he denied it.

Her *dearest* ring caught her attention as it sparkled in the light, whispering that all would be well. All she had to do was *trust*. She snorted at the thought. Trust. That word was as fickle as *friendship*.

"There you are," Chance said as he met her at the base of the stairs. He offered his arm. "Would you grant me the honor of escorting you to your betrothed?"

"You are trying too hard, brother," she said, but took his arm. It was taking all her energy to get through this. She had none to spare for a tussle with Chance.

"I want you happy, Fortuity." Genuine concern shone in his dark blue eyes that tended to flash to a hearty amethyst whenever his temper was stirred. "Please know that."

"I do, Chance. This is just not how I thought I would come to be married."

He patted her hand. "I believe he fosters a genuine fondness for you, sister. Do not give up hope."

"Let us just do this, shall we?"

He escorted her through the formal dining room and out the double doors to the garden their mother had loved so. Her sisters rose from their seats in front of Matthew and the vicar and beamed at her, silently encouraging her with their love and support.

Her steps faltered as she risked a look at her husband-to-be, standing in front of the ivy-covered arbor. He was resplendent and entirely too handsome for her ability to remain calm with his black dress coat, matching black waistcoat, creamy white cravat, and buff trousers. But it was his wide, gleaming white smile and the joy dancing in his eyes that made her stumble. He seemed, dare she hope, actually happy to be marrying her.

Chance squeezed her hand and whispered, "Steady on, Tutie. All will be well. I promise."

Since she couldn't very well argue with her brother as she walked forward to say her vows, she simply held her head higher and forced a smile that came easier when she noticed that doddering old Vicar Darbley gently swayed back and forth as though about to fall asleep and topple off his perch. Heaven help the poor man who refused to step aside and hand over his flock to his much younger curate.

Chance must have noticed the man's demeanor as well, because he trembled against her arm with silent laughter.

When they reached the *chopping block*, as she had come to think of the place where she would recite her vows, her brother kissed her cheek and whispered, "I love you, Tutie, and wish you every happiness."

She thanked him with a smile, then swallowed hard as Matthew took her hand and gently tugged her forward to stand beside him.

He grinned down at her, then cast a sideways glance at the vicar. "Shall we wake him?"

"Since we cannot marry without him, I assume we must."

Matthew cleared his throat. "Vicar? We are ready."

A soft snore came from the balding man with his chin tucked to his chest.

"How does he not fall over?" Fortuity whispered to Matthew.

"Horses sleep standing up."

"Yes, but they have four legs with which to balance better. A much sturdier base, I would think."

Chance stepped around them and touched the elderly man's arm, then gently shook him when he still didn't awaken. "Mr. Darbley," he said quite loudly. "We are ready to proceed with the vows."

"By the power vested in me by God Almighty and the Church of England, I now pronounce you man and wife," the vicar said, then blinked and glanced around the garden. "Will the wedding breakfast be here or elsewhere?"

"Here," Matthew said in a tone that indicated his patience was wearing thin. "After we have said our vows. You got the last bit right. Might we now go back and do the first part?"

Unfazed, the vicar chuckled and fumbled with the pages of his prayer book. "Ah, yes. Do forgive me. I tend to wander off a bit now and again."

"Indeed," Matthew said.

Fortuity held her breath to keep from snorting with laughter.

Mr. Darbley squinted at her over the tops of his smudged spectacles. "Do you…" He paused and licked his thin, pale lips. "What is your name, child? It escapes me at the moment."

The vicar had christened each and every one of the Broadmere children, but that had been quite some time ago, so Fortuity granted him some grace. "Fortuity Marion Ivy Abarough."

The man leaned forward and cupped a hand to his ear. "Say again, please?"

"Fortuity Marion Ivy Abarough," she shouted.

"No need to bellow, young woman." He rumbled with a long clearing of his throat, adjusted his spectacles, and squinted at his prayer book. "Do you, Fortuity Marion Ivy Abarough, take… Oh dear." He gave Matthew a pained frown.

"Matthew Dorian Ravenglass," Matthew said with an unmistakable growl.

The vicar's brows rose to where his hairline had once been many years ago, then he looked to Fortuity once again. "Do you, Fortuity Marion Ivy Abarough, take Matthew Dorian Ravenglass to be your lawfully wedded husband? To obey him in sickness and in health, through prosperous times and times of woe, setting aside all others and keeping yourself to him alone?"

"I do." She flinched at the nervous squeak in her voice. "I do," she repeated louder to ensure the vicar heard her.

"I heard you, young lady. Eagerness is most unbecoming."

Ratty old goat, Fortuity thought, then sent up a quick prayer asking for forgiveness.

Mr. Darbley shifted his attention to Matthew. "Do you, Matthew Dorian Ravenglass, take Fortuity Marion Ivy Abarough to be your lawfully wedded wife? To honor her and forsake all others, to protect her and comfort her, keep her at your side in sickness and in health, through prosperous times and times of woe?"

"I do," Matthew said so loudly that the vicar backed up a step as though startled.

"Then, as I said earlier, by the power vested in me by God Almighty and the Church of England, I now pronounce you man and wife." Mr. Darbley wet his lips again and nodded. "Now I believe my question regarding the wedding breakfast was never answered. Is it here, or shall we be traveling to another venue?"

"It is here, Mr. Darbley." Serendipity jumped up from her seat, went to the old man, and firmly led him away while casting a *you are welcome* smile at Fortuity.

"Help me rise," Blessing called out as the rest of the Broadmere sisters surrounded Fortuity and Matthew, patting and hugging them.

"Oh, dear sister." Fortuity pulled on one of Blessing's arms while Gracie pulled on the other.

"*Oh, dear sister* is correct." Blessing groaned as she teetered to her feet. "In the past few weeks, I have become as enormous as a Clydesdale about to deliver twin foals."

"Where is Thorne?" Fortuity asked her, suddenly realizing she had yet to see her dashing brother-in-law who was also Matthew's best friend.

"He is abed with a terrible cold and has confined himself to another part of the Knightwood townhouse to avoid sharing his malady with all and sundry." Blessing patted the pronounced rounding of her middle while holding her lower back. "In fact, he wishes me to remain here until he is recovered, since Aloysius Starpeeper's arrival will be upon us before we know it."

"Already a wise father," Matthew said. He moved to stand beside Fortuity and rested his hand on the small of her back as if unwilling to go without touching her. "It would not do for you to fall ill, my lady."

"No," Blessing said with a sly look at Matthew positioning himself as a devoted husband.

Fortuity tried to ignore her. Instead, she widened her smile so much that her face ached.

"Essie," Grace said while waving Merry and Joy forward. "Come, let us get you settled in the dining room at a place where we can place a cushion for your poor feet."

"Brilliant idea." Blessing kissed Fortuity on the cheek, grinned at Matthew, then waddled away with her sisters fluttering around her.

"Could they possibly have been more obvious?" Fortuity said under her breath as she watched them go.

"They are trying to be nice and give us our first moment alone as a married couple." Matthew gave her a thoughtful yet concerned look. "How are you? You appeared quite pale when you first entered the garden."

She pulled in a deep breath, held it for a few moments, then let it ease back out. "I am better and will be all right. Change has always been difficult for me." The threat of tears suddenly stung her eyes. "And I realized just this morning how much I shall miss my sisters and all their chaos." She gave a defeated shrug. "I guess you could say I fear the deafening quiet of your home."

"*Our* home," he gently corrected her. "And we will have a small amount of hopefully controllable chaos."

"Oh?" His mysterious tone intrigued her.

"Ignatius is still there."

The thought of the comical little pug lightened the weight of worry on her heart. "But I thought he belonged to Mrs. Sykesbury?"

"He did, but she feared she would be unable to control him in the country, since she had little or no control over him here in town." Matthew resettled his footing and appeared to be uncomfortable about *something*.

"What else are you not telling me?" Fortuity eyed him, bracing herself for the worst possible news, such as Eleanor returning to live with them.

He frowned and shuffled in place again. "I had thought about how quiet the townhouse would be for you, what with your sisters and Grace's hounds here. I spoke with Thorne about it, and he and his mother recommended that I take in four of their liveliest kittens—which I did before I found out that infernal dog would be staying put."

"Four kittens and Ignatius?" Fortuity tried not to laugh, but she couldn't help it. "And how do the five get along?"

"They stampede the halls at all hours of the night and sleep during the day." He swiped a hand across his eyes, then pinched the bridge of his nose as if weary beyond all comprehension. "I have not had a proper night's sleep in ages."

She couldn't resist giving him a sympathetic pat on the chest. "Never fear, my lord. I shall get them sorted, and if I am forced to call reinforcements, Gracie would be delighted to help. You know how she loves Ignatius."

He caught her hand and pressed a kiss to her fingers before she realized what he was about to do. "I know you will get them sorted, my little wren. The townhouse already seems a brighter and better place because you will soon be there with me."

She caught her breath, and a little gasp escaped her before she could stop it. "Uhm, perhaps we should go inside? They cannot start the breakfast without us."

His smile dimmed the slightest bit, but he nodded and offered his arm. "To our wedding breakfast, my bride."

"Yes," she said, finding herself still somewhat breathless. "To our wedding breakfast."

Chapter Nine

FORTUITY HAD SPOKEN very little during the carriage ride and seemed apprehensive as he helped her step down. Matthew kept hold of her hand as she eyed Ravenglass Townhouse before ascending the steps to the front door. A slight breeze tugged at her curls, making them dance and shimmer like liquid gold in the sunshine of the unseasonably warm spring day.

"You are beautiful, Fortuity," he said on impulse. "Absolutely stunning."

Her gaze dropped, and her cheeks flushed with color. "Matthew," she said in a softly scolding tone.

"What?"

"You don't have to say such things." She gently eased her hand free, caught hold of her skirts, and started to climb the front stairs.

He blocked her way and cupped her chin in his palm, tilting her face upward. "I say such things not only because they are true, but because I feel them in my heart."

She watched him, visibly weighing his sincerity. He felt her judgment of him sway between *is he good?* and *is he evil?*

"Then thank you for the compliment," she replied with a slight caginess before quirking a brow. "Might we enter our home now?"

"Indeed." He offered his arm, relaxing at her tone's slight shift to a teasing lilt. "Brace yourself for the menagerie."

As they reached the door, it opened, revealing the servants lining the front hall and standing at attention to greet the new lady of the house. The beaming Mrs. Greer stood at the head of the line, bouncing in place in her excitement at welcoming Fortuity to her new home.

"There she be," the jolly housekeeper crowed while clapping her hands. "Welcome home, Lady Fortuity."

Fortuity rushed to hug her. "Thank you, Mrs. Greer. How thoughtful of all of you to greet me. Thank you all."

The servants smiled and bowed, then a thunderous pounding resounded from the stairway.

"Here they come," Matthew said with a groan.

Two half-grown kittens, both of them solid black with white bibs and paws, were in the lead, followed by Ignatius and two more half-grown kittens, one of them a ginger tabby and the other a solid white feline with a long, fluffy tail. While the dog happily barked and yipped at them, the cats playfully flattened their ears, bowed their backs, and alternately danced sideways and swatted at him while scampering around and over him with amazing speed and agility as they all descended the steps.

"Ignatius! Heel!" Matthew pointed at the floor to his left.

The pug barrel-rolled down the remaining three steps, recovered awkwardly to all fours, then scurried to obey. His claws clickity-clicked across the polished marble floor. Once he skidded to a stop, he plopped his rump against Matthew's left foot and gazed up at him in adoration.

The cats scattered and sought the safety of high ground, perching on tables and cabinets—one scrambled to the top of the floor clock at the end of the hall.

"Oh my," Fortuity said with a poorly stifled giggle. "They are rather exuberant, aren't they? Have you named them yet?" She bent and scratched Ignatius behind the ears. "Are the wicked kitties getting you in trouble, little man?"

Panting heavily, tongue lolling out the side of his mouth, the pug seemed to grin in agreement as he wiggled his curly tail.

"The cats came with names," Matthew said, trying to remember which one was which. He pointed at the black kittens with the white bibs. "One of them is Horatio, and one is Jervis. I have no idea which is which, nor can I tell them apart. Only your sister possesses that ability." He nodded at the ginger cat. "That one is Abercrombie. Where the devil did the white one go? Wherever he is, the large, fluffy white one is Wellington."

"British war heroes. How appropriate." Fortuity snorted with laughter, then covered her mouth. "Oh dear. I am sorry."

"Do not be sorry, my little wren, because this chaos is yours as well now." Although her merriment made it all worthwhile. He would fill their home with cats and pugs if it kept her happy. Her laughter washed the house in joy and light. Gads, he loved this woman—if only he could make her forget his stupidity in denying it for so long.

Mrs. Greer cleared her throat, then scattered the servants and cats with a sharp clap of her hounds. "There's chores to be done, my lovelies. We mustn't have the mistress thinking we would ever fail her." She bobbed her head at Fortuity. "I am sure your Miss Anne has your rooms ready. Such a good worker, that girl. I remember her from before. Shall I fetch a fine tea for yourselves and bring it to the parlor, my lord and lady? Your first together in your new home?"

Fortuity looked to Matthew as if uncertain about what to say.

He moved in as if to press a kiss to her temple and whispered in her ear, "This is your house now, my dearest. You are mistress of it. Do as you wish. I merely want you happy." And then he took advantage of the opportunity and brushed a kiss to her warm, sweet skin before drawing back. He couldn't help himself.

She drew in a quick breath and glanced at him as though startled. "Uhm… A proper tea would be lovely, Mrs. Greer."

The housekeeper chortled with glee, then hurried away, bellowing for Thebson the butler to stop dawdling with the animals and take care of the master and mistress.

"Poor Thebson," Fortuity said as they made their way into

the parlor. "He may never forgive me for recommending Mrs. Greer to you."

A slight sense of disappointment came over him when she settled in a chair rather than on the settee, where he might sit next to her. Determined to think of a way to coax her into joining him, he sat on the end of it closest to her. "When our tea arrives, I think it most appropriate to sweeten it with a bit of brandy in celebration of the day. What say you?"

She didn't answer. Instead, she continued with what appeared to be a disapproving look around the parlor. "You don't have books stacked everywhere as you did before." She turned to him with concern. "I loved the way books were piled about as if they were pieces of fine art. You didn't get rid of them because of me, did you? I adore books and thought having them at your fingertips was just perfect."

"The day the cats arrived convinced me to rethink the care and storage of our precious books." He shuddered at the memory of the avalanches caused by the felines when they used the stacks of books to launch themselves to even greater heights.

"Blessing says they settle down once they get older. Many of hers rarely find the energy to rise from their favorite sunny spots on the window ledges."

"One can only hope." He reached for her while patting the cushion next to him. "We are married now. You may sit beside me without the risk of anyone accusing you of being a lightskirt."

A grim somberness settled over her, making him wish he had kept his mouth shut. Then she forced a smile with the slightest incline of her head. "I am quite comfortable right where I am, my lord, but thank you for the reminder."

Unwilling to surrender in his war to convince her that their marriage could be *very* real, Matthew adopted a nonchalant demeanor. "As you wish, my lady. But your behavior surprises me. I never thought of you as one with tendencies of cowardice."

"Cowardice?" Her brow shot up and her eyes narrowed.

He nodded. "There is no shame in admitting your fear of

sitting next to me."

"I do not fear sitting next to you."

He gave her his best patronizing smile. "Of course you don't."

With a snorting huff, she rose from her chair, flounced her way to the other end of the settee, and plopped down in a very unladylike manner. "There."

"You are still not next to me."

Her mouth fell open in either shock or outrage. He wasn't sure which.

"There is but one seat cushion between us," she said. "Do you wish me to sit in your waistcoat pocket?"

He tried not to chuckle and failed, heightening the color of her rosy cheeks to an even lovelier shade of red. "I daresay that would be interesting."

And then she laughed, thrilling him immensely.

"That is so much better, my little wren."

"What is?" She angled herself more comfortably into the corner of the cushions, leaning back and filling his imagination with visions of his stretching over her and possibly siring the first of their many children right here in the parlor.

She cleared her throat. "My lord?"

He reminded himself to stay focused on winning this battle so he might soon enjoy the spoils of this war. "This day has you tensed tauter than a bowstring. When you laugh, you relax."

Her gaze dropped, and she plucked at the folds of her skirt. "This new life will take some adjustment."

"Yes, it will." Perhaps if he showed her the second surprise he'd planned for her arrival? He rose from the settee and held out his hand. "Come. There is something else you must see."

"What?" She remained seated, appearing not to trust him, but mischievously so.

"Come, little wren. I honestly believe you will be pleased."

"What about our tea?"

"I assure you that Mrs. Greer will find us when our tea is

ready. Nothing in this household escapes that woman." He wiggled the fingers of his outstretched hand. "Give over now. You know you wish to see what it is."

With a roll of her eyes, she took his hand and rose from her seat. "I think *you* wish me to see what it is."

"Well, of course I do," he said as he tugged her into the curve of his arm. "Surprising you with presents gives me great joy. Although…"

"Although?"

"The cats are regrettable."

"They are not. I think they are delightful."

What was delightful was the way she fit so perfectly against his side with his arm wrapped around her, but he was wise enough to remain quiet about that. Instead, he basked in her warmth and breathed in the sweetness of her lilac scent. "This way, dearest. The front room beside the library."

"In Broadmere House, that is our smaller parlor for when unannounced guests come calling."

"It was once the same here, but no longer." He pushed the door open with a flourish and stepped back. "Your personal office, my lady. After all, a writer needs space in which to disappear into her worlds and put them to the page."

She stood at the threshold, her lips barely parted as her gaze darted all around the room. "Oh, Matthew," she said with a satisfying breathlessness. "This is… This is…"

"Yes?"

"So wonderfully thoughtful of you." She slowly entered the room, as if afraid it would disappear.

"I know this is not the writing desk you brought with you. I instructed George and Anne to place that one in your dressing room. But I hope you find this one suitable." He stepped around her and went to the decidedly feminine desk that was just as large as his desk in the library, but this one had curved lines and rounded edges. It was softer, like a woman's form compared to the hard, muscular lines of a man. He pulled out the leather wingback chair that was also smaller and would fit her much better than the usual desk chairs.

"Oh, Matthew," she repeated with the same breathlessness as before. "It is absolutely perfect." She sat in the chair and smoothed her hands along the rich, reddish-hued wood of the desktop. "This is not mahogany. Is this rosewood?"

"It is," he said. "Rosewood symbolizes romance and love. I thought it perfect for the desk of a romance author."

She surprised him by leaning forward and resting her cheek on the satiny surface while continuing to run her hand across it. "The desk is gorgeous, but your speaking about my life's dream as if you believe in it too is the greatest gift you could ever give me."

"I do believe in you, Fortuity." He wanted so badly to touch her, stroke her cheek, or kiss her hand, but he remained strong. If he attempted to convince her of his feelings too quickly, she would never believe him. "Your stories are as lovely as you are."

"Thank you so very much, Matthew. This means the world to me."

"I am glad."

A knock at the door interrupted the moment and made him grit his teeth in irritation. "Yes?"

"The proper tea ordered by Mrs. Greer is set up in the parlor, my lord," Thebson told him. "And a messenger just arrived with a letter he says the sender informed him was quite urgent."

"Place the letter on my desk in the library, Thebson. Today is my wedding day, and nothing is more urgent than my bride." No matter what it was, Matthew would address it later. He would not cast Fortuity aside when she had only just arrived. She was his priority.

Thebson nodded, then disappeared to do as requested.

"But if the messenger said it was urgent," Fortuity said, "you should see to it. It could be something regarding your cousins in the country."

His cousins could go to the devil, but he refrained from saying that aloud. Not that he no longer cared about them, but they had created nothing but problems ever since he had rescued them from India. He shook his head. "You are my priority, and we have only just arrived home." He meandered around the room, motioning to the shelves filled with several of his favorite books. "I thought you might enjoy these. They might even provide helpful resources for your stories. Is the color right? I read somewhere that color can sometimes influence thoughts."

"The color?"

"Of the room. Draperies. Walls. The earthy tones of the rug?"

"I adore the pale greens and browns." She hugged herself as she looked all around. "I feel as though I have stepped into an enchanted forest. It is perfect, Matthew. Absolutely perfect."

"As you are, my little wren."

She ducked her head as she rose from the chair and went to the window. He noticed her fingers trembled slightly as she idly ran them across the folds of the damask draperies in the soft shade of green the window dresser had recommended. "You do not have to try so hard, Matthew. I know you never wanted this, but I shall do my very best to make it as painless as possible."

His heart fell. *Damn and blast it all.* He had overplayed his hand and failed. At a loss for how to make it right, he went to her and held out his hand. "Our tea is ready in the parlor, my lady," he said quietly.

With a wan smile, she took his hand. "Yes. Tea will be nice."

They moved down the hall in strained silence. When they reached the parlor door, she paused and laid a hand on his arm. "Why don't you see to your urgent message? Then we can enjoy our tea at our leisure. I shall wait for you in the parlor."

Something about the way she said it felt both like a dismissal and a request for some time to herself. He gave her a polite nod. "As you wish, my lady. I shall return to you shortly."

"Take your time, my lord."

He almost flinched, but stopped himself just in time and offered her another nod instead. Winning his wife's heart and her trust would be more difficult than he thought.

WHATEVER THIS GAME was, Matthew needed to just stop. Fortuity paced the length of the large parlor that had formerly always reminded her of a delightfully cluttered reading room, a room she had fallen in love with as deeply as she loved Matthew. But the scattered stacks of books were gone, removed from every table, chair, and shelf. He had blamed the cats, and from what she had observed upon meeting the fearsome four, that excuse seemed plausible enough.

She rubbed her hands together as she paced, wishing their nervous dampness would cease. She hated this tense situation, and it was obvious Matthew hated it as well. Why else would he try so hard to make her feel as if he wanted her here? The *dearest* ring, the cats, and now that breathtaking office of her very own? Did he not realize how much his kindnesses tortured her? She already loved him, would go so far as to say she adored him, even though he only thought of her as a friend. Why could he not just leave her be and give her the time she needed to get her feelings under control, so they might manage this uncomfortable arrangement? Surely, he didn't wish to break her heart more than he already had? He had never been cruel.

Approaching footsteps down the hallway alerted her that her much-needed time alone had ended all too soon. She forced a smile and turned toward the doorway, then alarm shot through her. "Matthew, what is it?"

He had gone quite pale, a feat in and of itself, since the man had always looked like he spent a great deal of time out of doors even in the dead of winter. Part of it was his natural coloring; the rest was his passion for riding. These things kept his skin from being considered fair in any sense of the word. He had never possessed what she and her sisters had dubbed as the usual pasty peerage pallor. His weathered handsomeness lent a wildness to him, drawing her in and daring her to love him. But his current lack of color concerned her.

She went over and led him to the settee in front of the table set with their tea. "Matthew? Tell me. You look as though someone you know has died."

"I did not know them. Only *of* them." He stared straight ahead at nothing, scowling at whatever he was seeing in his mind.

"Tell me where the brandy is and I shall pour you some. I do not believe tea will be sufficient for whatever is troubling you."

He didn't answer, just kept opening and closing his fists where they rested on his knees.

Fine. She would find the brandy herself. Turning, she spotted a likely cabinet and went to it. Upon opening the double doors at its front, she discovered several crystal decanters and the sort of glasses best used for port or brandy. She chose the honey-colored liquid, unstoppered it, and gingerly sniffed the contents. The heady smell of fermented peaches heated her nostrils and made her nose twitch. Rather than pour it into a glass, she carried the decanter back to the table and poured him a generous cupful.

"Would you like some tea with your brandy?" she asked, realizing too late that she had left little room in the cup for anything other than the strong drink. "If you do, I need you to drink some of this first so I can fit it in there."

Still staring off into nothingness, he held out his hand. "No. Neat is perfect."

She wasn't certain what *neat* meant, but he took the cup, drank from it, and didn't complain, so she must've gotten it right. After pouring herself a cup of nothing but tea, she sat beside him and waited, remembering how Mama had always treated Papa whenever he was upset. Her mother had silently supported her father until he was ready to share whatever problem had him worried.

Matthew downed the contents of his cup, then stared down into it as if surprised it was empty.

"Shall I pour you another?" she asked.

"No, Fortuity," he said quietly, as if suddenly remembering she was there. He frowned at the teapot surrounded by multiple platters of biscuits and cakes. After what felt like an eternity, he turned his head and looked at her. His troubled gaze pierced her heart and soul. "You know I would never lie to you, do you not?"

Rather than placate him with platitudes, she braced herself and chose brutal honesty. "I have witnessed your telling the truth even when it was uncomfortable for you to do so."

"I would never lie to you." He huffed a mirthless laugh, then shook his head. "Even when I said I *wanted* to marry you, I was not lying, even though I know you think otherwise."

She forced herself not to react. Now was not the time. Not when he was so overset. "Is there any way I might help you with whatever is wrong? What has it to do with lying? Is there another unsavory rumor out there of which we were unaware?"

He pulled a folded paper out from his waistcoat and held it out. "I will never hide anything from you either."

"That sounds rather ominous, my lord."

"Read it, and you will see."

She eyed the thing but kept her hands in her lap. "That is your personal correspondence, my lord. It would not be right for me to read it."

"You are my wife, Fortuity. Whether you wish to be or not." He unfolded the note and dropped it onto her lap. "Read it so you will not be caught unaware." He snorted with another disgruntled huff. "And for heaven's sake, stop calling me *my lord*. I am your husband, your friend, your Matthew—I am not now nor ever will be *your lord*."

Rather than say anything that would upset him even more, she picked up the letter and read:

My dearest Matthew,

Not only am I older, wiser, and back from the Continent, but I am also widowed. I come to you begging for forgiveness even though I know you might not wish to. If it is any consolation for the pain and humiliation I caused you, please know that I reaped what I sowed and was repaid in full and then some for my selfishness. Rest assured, I have been well and thoroughly punished for my thoughtless behavior.

I would give anything to go back and make a different choice, the choice I should have made all along. You, Matthew. I should have chosen you. I beg you—nay, I beseech you—please give us another chance.

My heart will ever be yours,
Olandra

Fortuity looked up from the letter and met his gaze, almost gasping at the intensity of the pain reflected in his eyes. Even though she had never met the woman or heard her name, she knew who this was: Matthew's greatest love. The one who had left him standing at the altar while she ran off to Gretna Green with a duke. She wanted to crumple the letter, hunt the woman down, and claw her eyes out for causing him so much agony. But a *lady* did not do such things. Life was so bloody unfair sometimes. But then she wondered, was it the timing of the thing that upset him? If they hadn't married, he could have reclaimed his precious Olandra, the widowed Duchess of Esterton.

"I am sorry," she said softly. "If only you had received this a day sooner, you could have been with her rather than me."

He narrowed his eyes at her. "Is that truly what you think I want? You think that is why I showed you that letter?"

"You love her."

"I do not." He refilled his cup with brandy and added a splash to her tea without asking. "Olandra showed me exactly what sort of woman she is, and falling prey to her once was quite enough, thank you. I am not a fool, Fortuity. I remember the lessons I am taught quite well."

She wasn't so sure about sipping the brandy-laced tea. Not when everything within her stormed and raged to hunt down that cruel woman and yank out all her hair. Whenever she was overset, her stomach always reacted. If she cast up her accounts in the parlor, she would never forgive herself. "What will you do? Running into her at parties and balls will be inevitable if she is in search of another husband."

"I will introduce her to my lovely wife, and then tell her to go straight to the devil."

While his answer warmed her heart, she couldn't help but wonder if he truly meant it. After all, this was the woman who had made him swear to never marry. "I daresay that might be considered slightly rude, my…Matthew."

He glared at her and shifted on the settee until their shoulders touched. His scent of sandalwood, citrus, and angry male made her heart flutter faster. "If you address me as *my lord* one more time, I shall kiss you senseless and obliterate your condition of being married in name only."

A heat the likes of which she had never known rushed through her, pooling low in her belly and between her thighs. It made her catch her breath and wet her lips. "Matthew! I…I…"

"You what?"

She cleared her throat. "I daresay we must concentrate on how you intend to respond to your letter." She balled it up and threw it at him, hitting him in the chest with it.

His frown melted, and his broad shoulders relaxed as he gave her a sultry grin. "That letter is not worthy of a response." He retrieved the paper from the floor and tossed it into the hearth. "Good riddance."

"If that was your intention all along, then why did you share it with me?" He had become so confusing of late, keeping her mind whirling and wondering about what motivated his actions. Protecting her heart under such circumstances was becoming increasingly difficult.

"I told you. I will never hide anything from you." He settled back down beside her and took another sip of brandy. "And if I had not shared it with you, you would have been ill prepared when, God forbid, we came across the woman out amongst Society."

"And the tongues will wag. Lending life to the old rumors about what happened between the two of you ages ago."

"Exactly."

The curious ginger kitten took that opportunity to leap from behind the settee, jump into her lap, and bump its head against her arms while purring loudly.

"Well, hello…" She arched a brow at Matthew.

"Abercrombie."

"Such a long name for a kitty," she said as she scratched him behind the ears. "I would have called you Rumbles because of your purring."

"Then he shall hereafter be known as Rumbles." Matthew lifted his cup, then fixed her with a look that made her shiver. "This is *our* home, Fortuity, *your* home. Do as you wish. Do what makes you happy."

A pitiful whine came from underneath the settee. Then a snuffling, snorting thump against the back of her skirts made her giggle. "I wish for you to tell Ignatius he may come out of hiding and join us for tea." Thank heavens for the animals saving her from Matthew's determination to—what? The question made her swallow hard and shy away from the answer. No, they were friends. Nothing more. "Please?"

He rolled his eyes, then leaned forward and snapped his fingers. "Come out, Ignatius. Acting pitiful is a coward's way of manipulation."

The pug wiggled out from under the furniture and bounced into Matthew's outstretched hands. He picked him up and deposited him on the cushions between them. The cat butted his head against the dog's as if the two had successfully colluded to achieve their current positions.

"I believe they plotted against us for this," Fortuity said as she broke a biscuit in two then fed half to the dog, and the other half to the cat.

"I have no doubt of it." But then Matthew went quiet and fixed her with a look that tempted her to squirm. It was only by sheer force of will that she managed to sit still. "I showed you the letter because I never want you to think that I would hide anything from you, nor would I ever wish to hurt you. I care about you, Fortuity, whether or not you choose to believe it."

She ached to believe he meant more than friendship but dared not risk it. Her poor, battered heart simply couldn't take being rejected again. "I appreciate your sharing it with me. I know it could not have been easy."

He bowed his head and scrubbed a hand across his eyes. "In other words, you still do not believe me." He slowly shook his head while staring at the floor, making her ache to comfort him even though she knew she dared not. "You refuse to believe I am happy we are married and cannot imagine any other woman being my wife."

After risking a sip of her brandy-laced tea to stoke her boldness, she set it back on the table, then shifted on the cushions to face him. This argument, this façade of his being the happy new husband, had worn on her as long as she would allow it. "It has been less than a month since you announced quite loudly at Lady Atterley's dinner that you and I were *friends only*. You also informed me we could never be anything more than friends and asked for that to be enough. Moreover, both you and everyone closest to you made it clear as crystal that you had sworn you would walk straight through the gates of hell before you would ever return to the altar to wed. Do you deny the truth of anything I have just stated? Am I remembering any of it incorrectly?"

His jaw flexed, and he dropped his gaze once more. "Sadly, you are not remembering any of those things incorrectly."

She rose to her feet, placed the ginger cat on the cushions next to the pug, then nervously brushed the wrinkles from her skirt. Refusing to allow him to argue further, she went to the bellpull and yanked on it.

Thebson appeared so quickly that she suspected he had been

hovering just beyond the doorway to overhear their conversation. "Yes, my lady?"

"Show me to my room, Thebson, and then please inform Mrs. Greer I shall take my supper in my dressing room." She forced a smile. "The day has wearied me."

The butler glanced at Matthew, still sitting on the settee with his head bowed.

"Is there a problem, Thebson?" she asked, silently asserting herself as mistress of the house.

"No, my lady. Please follow me."

Chapter Ten

I T HAD BEEN an entire month of pure, unadulterated torture.

Matthew stared at the draft of Fortuity's story, unable to concentrate on a single blasted word of it. Fortuity's mouthwatering scent, the heady fragrance of lilacs, books, and a delectable woman who continued to evade him at every turn filled the air of her office. How the devil had he failed to convince her to not only open her heart but her bedchamber as well? They should've been a happily, *consummated* married couple by now. A disgruntled huff escaped him.

She turned from the window streaked with the incessant April showers. "And what does that mean?"

"What?"

"When you blow air like a horse determined to snot on its groom, it cannot be anything good. What do you disagree with about those chapters? You claimed two publishers found the first sample of the book intriguing. Do these not follow up well with what you already gave them?"

He tossed the pages onto the sofa beside him and rubbed his tired, gritty eyes. "I assure you my horse-snotting sound was not directed at your prose."

She arched a brow at him and meandered closer. "Are we fractious today?"

"We are when we are spoken to as if we are a child."

Scooping up the pages he had set aside, she settled down

beside him and tucked her arms in a prim fold high across her middle. He hated it when she did that. It plumped her breasts, causing them to round ever so temptingly above the neckline of her gown. She didn't say a word, just eyed him, waiting for him to open his mouth and make a fool of himself yet again.

His plot to draw out the process of getting her book published so he might spend more time with her was killing him. Literally. He ate little and slept less than that because of his all-consuming need to win his own damn wife. At night, he swore he could hear her breathing in the next room, even though the door separating them remained tightly closed. And her alluring scent came to him wherever he went, taunting him with that which he could not have.

"How many of the changes I suggested did you make?" he asked abruptly.

She raised both eyebrows as if unable to believe he dared to ask that. "I gave you those pages an hour ago. Have you read none of it?"

"How many of the changes I suggested did you make?" he repeated, refusing to admit to anything.

Defiantly tipping her chin higher, she glared straight ahead. "One."

"One?"

She shrugged and made a face. "You were correct about the scones, but how was I to know? Felicity is the one who loves cooking. Not me."

Trying to keep his gaze off the rise and fall of her bosoms with her every breath, he shifted on the sofa to conceal a certain part of his anatomy that had hardened with interest as soon as she settled beside him. "What about the kiss?"

Her sideways glare cut through him. "What about it?"

"We agreed they would kiss by now." He pulled in a deep breath but was careful not to snort it out like a horse. "While I understand you do not wish to mirror John Cleland's *Memoirs of a Woman of Pleasure*, your book, your *romance*, will be more popular if there is a bit of *daring behavior* in it, shall we say? Not so much as to have you arrested for obscenity, as he was, but just enough to titillate your readers." Her increased blush gave him a bit of hope. "Have you read that book yet? As I suggested?" He had purposely given her a copy of the scandalous story about Fanny Hill, hoping to stoke the flames of her desires.

She cleared her throat and stared straight ahead. "I have perused it," she said with a strained squeak.

"And did you find it informative?"

She cleared her throat again. "Quite."

He reached over and plucked the papers out of her hand. "Show me where you added the kiss."

Her glare shifted to him and hardened, matching the irritated flexing of her jaw. "I have yet to add it. Do you not feel more tension between the two is needed before they kiss?"

"No, I do not." He tossed the pages onto the table in front of them. "I think the gentleman should sweep the lady into his arms and kiss her." He moved closer, unable to hold himself back any longer. "How would you write the kiss, my little wren? Describe it to me."

The longing in her eyes betrayed her as she wet her lips. "Since our lady is young and inexperienced, I would describe her as not only excited by his approach but also worried. Perhaps even a little afraid."

He stretched his arm across the back of the sofa and teased his fingertips into the tumble of her silky curls resting on her nape, then grazed the softness of her skin and made her shudder. "Why would she be worried and afraid? She knows him, loves him. Does she not trust him?"

She wet her barely parted lips again. "Perhaps she fears disappointing him with her naïveté."

"Nay," he said softly. "He adores her and is excited that no one else has ever touched her."

"Does he?" she whispered.

"He does." He brushed the backs of his fingers along her

jawline. "Does she long to taste him as he yearns to taste her?"

She closed her eyes and hitched in a nervous breath. "She does indeed." Then her eyes flew open, and she jumped up and hurried back to her post by the window. "I shall try to write the scene now, then you may review it, and tell me your opinion."

Her frown at the papers remaining on the table urged him on. He scooped them up and went to her, but rather than put them in her hand, he held them behind his back. "I know how you feel about research from the drawers full of detailed notes from Society's parties and balls. Do you not believe you would benefit from firsthand research regarding a kiss?"

She backed up a step and bumped into the window ledge. "I have seen couples embrace and kiss."

"Seeing is not the same as feeling," he said, before cupping her cheek and sliding his fingers deeper into her hair. "Do you not wish to *feel*?" He leaned in until the softness of her mouth was almost his. "May I show you?"

"I… Uhm…"

"You *what*, my little wren?"

"I do not think this wise."

"All in the name of research," he whispered as he barely brushed his lips across hers, reveling in their warm softness.

"Research," she repeated as she rested a hand on his chest and touched his cheek with the other. "Research is often essential."

"Indeed, it is." He pressed closer and kissed her gently, giving her time to push him away if she wished. Never would he force anything on her.

To his delight, she didn't push away. Instead, she leaned in and opened to him with an urgency that almost made him groan. He dropped the pages and slipped his arms around her, cradling her ever tighter. Her welcoming mouth, her tongue dancing with his, the way she pressed against him made him reel with the need to lower her to the floor and show her the height and depth of the pleasures they could enjoy together.

She clutched him closer, digging her fingers into his back as if she would rip his clothes away if given half the chance. Then, without warning, she pushed back and turned her face aside. "Matthew," she said in a breathless whisper. "That is quite enough research."

He wanted to throw his head back and roar his frustration to the world, but he didn't. "Fortuity."

With the back of her hand pressed to her mouth, she stole a glance at him, as if afraid of what he might say.

"Please be my wife in every sense of the word. I need you, Fortuity."

Eyes wild and chest heaving, she remained silent, her gaze locked with his.

"You are mine, my little wren, as I am yours. Surely you know by now that I truly love you?"

"You do not mean that," she whispered, her eyes suddenly glistening with tears. "You cannot possibly mean that."

He slowly shook his head, unable to understand why she refused to believe him. "Tell me why you think that. In our month of marriage, have I done anything to make you believe I do not want this union to be real? That I do not wish to be a true husband to you in every sense of the word?"

She pressed her lips together and gave a quick shake of her head, looking away to avoid meeting his gaze.

"I was a damned fool, Fortuity. A lazy, damned fool." He gently turned her face back to his, willing her to hear the words of his heart. "I adored being with you so much that I grew not only complacent but feared if I made the mistake of making myself vulnerable once again that I would regret it." He huffed a soft, mirthless laugh. "If you hurt me, my little wren, I could not survive it, for I have found more joy and contentment with you than I ever knew existed. Baser needs are easy to satisfy, but what you give me is priceless and rare. If I ever lost it, I know it would be my undoing."

She trembled with hitching little gasps. "I should write that down," she whispered. "That was marvelous, *my lord.*"

"Do you remember what I told you I was going to do the next time you addressed me as *my lord?*"

She pressed closer, slid her hands up his chest, and buried her fingers in his hair. With an intense look deep into his eyes, she nodded. "I do indeed, *my lord.*"

He crushed his mouth to hers, backed her up, and pinned her against the wall. Her heartbeat pounded against him through their layers of clothing. After thoroughly plundering her with the promised kiss, he lifted his head. "I am a man of my word."

Running her hands up inside his jacket, then undoing his cravat with amazing speed, she smiled up at him. "I am glad you are a man of your word." She stretched and nibbled kisses along his throat, making him groan. "I read about doing this in one of Serendipity's books she always kept hidden from Mama. Is it true what they said about it?"

"What did they say?" Another groan escaped him as he returned the favor and kissed a trail down the curve of her neck to her shoulder as he made quick work of the buttons and ties at the back of her dress.

"Oh my. It *is* true what they say." The warmth of her breath tickled his throat. "I find it most…stirring."

"Indeed." Struggling to control the urge to rip away her gown, he gently worked it off her shoulders and pushed it to the floor.

"You have me at a disadvantage." She tugged at his jacket while attempting a sternness that failed.

He shed his jacket and waistcoat, then ever so slowly turned her and untied her stays. Her corset soon hit the floor and joined the gown puddled at her feet, leaving her in nothing but her chemise, stockings, and slippers.

"I suppose it is too late to ask this now, but…" She eyed him with her bottom lip caught between her teeth, almost cringing.

"What, my darling?" Gads, if she stopped him now, his bollocks and member would surely incur permanent damage.

"Will you be able to dress me as easily as you have relieved me of my clothes?" She tipped her head at the door and arched her brows higher. "I am not comfortable with the prospect of having to summon Anne to my office to dress me. The servants will know what we..." She bounced a sterner nod at him. "You know what I am saying."

"I do." He stretched and secured the door's latch. "Thank you for reminding me to lock the door, because I do not wish us to be interrupted."

She narrowed her eyes as if threatening to deny him.

"Yes, my darling. I can dress you." He took her by the hand, led her back to the settee, swept her up into his arms, and then gently deposited her upon it. "But let us finish undressing you first. I have longed to enjoy the completeness of your beauty."

"And now I am afraid again," she admitted in a breathless whisper.

The way she looked up at him, so loving, yet so unsure... It was hard to breathe. This time had to be perfect for her. It simply had to be. "Tell me what you fear, so I might slay those demons."

"I fear I will not be...enough."

"Enough?" He leaned forward, kissed her forehead, her nose, then sampled her mouth again tenderly. "You are more than I ever hoped for, my love. You are *enough* and then some."

She reached up and touched his cheek. "I have loved you so very long. I am afraid I shall awaken and discover this to be but a dream."

"You are my dream, my precious wren. The balm to my heart and soul and the answer to all that I have always needed." He gave her a sheepish smile as he removed her slippers. "I was just too damned thickheaded to admit it."

She watched him, her eyes growing ever wider as he slid his hands up her legs and untied the ribbons securing her stockings. "You will tell me what to do, then?"

He laughed. "When have you ever done what I have told you to do?"

"Well..."

He slowly slid her stockings off, tossed them, then bent and kissed the silky skin above her ankle. "Like the richest velvet. Just as I knew it would be." He kissed and tickled his way higher, breathing in her warmth, reveling in the scent of her yearning. "You taste delightful."

"I am not quite sure what to say in response to that," she said, sounding even more breathless. She twitched and made an endearing high-pitched noise as he rubbed his face along her inner thighs and added a sprinkling of kisses against their warm softness. "Oh my. The stubble of your beard. It tickles."

"In a good way or a bad way, my love?"

"A good way," she answered while fisting her hands against her middle.

He stretched over her and nudged a kiss to her knuckles. "Close your eyes and *feel*, Fortuity. This is not research—this is real, for your pleasure."

"If I close my eyes, how will I know if I am supposed to do something?"

"Trust me, my beauty. You will know. Now, close your eyes."

After unleashing a shuddering sigh, she did.

He pushed her chemise higher and gently blew on the V between her thighs.

"Oh my." She wiggled and clenched her fists tighter, making her knuckles whiten.

"Eyes closed, my little wren. Feel."

She answered with a sigh that sounded more like a groan.

He licked her stomach and drew slow circles with the tip of his tongue, moving ever lower with each swipe.

Wiggling beneath him, she bent her knees.

"A wonderful idea, my lovely." He hooked her legs over her shoulders, spreading her legs.

"Surely, you are not going to—"

He interrupted her with a slow, well-aimed swipe of his tongue.

She sucked in a deep breath, then thrilled him with a soft moan.

He licked her again, deeper, slower, exploring her sweetness until she buried her fingers in his hair and clutched his head with both hands. When he slipped a finger into her hot wetness, she shrieked and arched higher, pulling his hair with an urgency that told him, so far, this was a job well done. He ached to take her. It had been such a long, lonely month fantasizing about this pleasure, but he had to take his time and make it right for her. Increasing the rhythm of the combined efforts of his mouth and his fingers, he struggled for control, determined to bring her to the pinnacle of bliss.

"Matthew," she gasped. "Oh, Matthew."

With her every uttering of his name, he pumped his fingers faster while drawing the nubbin of her sex deeper into his mouth.

Her throaty moan turned into a roar as she bucked into his touch and clutched his head harder. He kept her there until her spasms no longer clenched his fingers, then he lifted his head and slid her chemise upward even more.

Gasping for breath, she sat up and whipped it off over her head, then caught hold of him and pulled him in for a kiss, making him stretch across her. He cupped her breast, teasing her hardened nipple between his thumb and forefinger, but he growled in surprise when she pushed him as if demanding he stop.

"Why are you still dressed?" she demanded.

"A fair question." He tore off his shirt, unbuttoned his falls, and kicked off his boots and trousers.

Her eyes widened. "Oh dear. I do not see how this is going to work at all."

"Trust me, my love." Cupping her breasts as he stretched over her, he kissed them each in turn, reveling in their perfection as he knelt between her legs. "I have wanted this so very badly."

"I too," she whispered, while cradling his face between her hands. "But I was so afraid to risk it."

He gazed down at her, drowning in the stormy blue depths of her worried gaze. "You own me, my little wren. Heart and soul, you possess me with a fury I was a fool to deny for so long. Please forgive me."

"As long as you always remember that you possess me as well."

"I will, my love. I swear it."

She ran her hands down his sides and hugged him between her thighs. "I love the way you feel, the way you make me feel, and I am ready for you to show me the rest."

He lowered his head and kissed her with a slow, determined patience that took all his control. Then he nibbled along her jawline and lower, teasing the tip of his tongue along her collarbone as he stroked her nipple with his thumb. As he took it into his mouth and sucked it harder, he slid his hand downward and cupped her buttock, barely grazing his fingertips across her wetness.

She arched upward, cradling his head to her breast and wrapping her legs around him and squeezing.

Unable to wait any longer, he entered her slowly, waiting to bury himself fully to allow her incredible tightness to accommodate him. "Gads, Fortuity, you are exquisite."

"This is so—" She lifted her head and glanced down between them. "Oh my."

He gave her a reassuring kiss and nudged in deeper until the barrier of her maidenhead stopped him.

She bucked upward, then flinched and raked her fingernails down his back and dug them into the cheeks of his buttocks. "More, my husband. Make me *feel* and return me to the bliss of before."

With more control than he ever dreamed he possessed, he claimed her fully, then slid back out and plunged in again.

She moved beneath him, meeting him with every thrust and making those wonderful sounds she had made before. "Oh, Matthew, this is…"

"Yes, my love." He kissed her shoulder, then buried his face in the curve of her neck and pumped harder. The time for conversation had passed.

She squealed and raked her nails down his sides while shuddering wildly.

He drove into her harder. A growling roar tore from his throat as he pounded faster. "Fortuity!" As he bellowed her name, he spilled his seed, pouring into her with such force and fervor that it left him trembling. He collapsed but caught himself on his elbows to keep from crushing her as he gasped for breath.

"Why did we wait so long to do this?" she asked with a breathless laugh.

He would not ruin the moment by reminding her of her stubbornness or her fears. Instead, he kissed her before rising and looking into her eyes. "I have no idea, my love. But I can assure you that we shall not deny ourselves of this pleasure any longer." A moment of determined clarity made its way through the warm sensations thrumming through him with the steady rhythm of a heartbeat. "You shall sleep in *my* bed from now on. Agreed?"

She gave him a wicked grin. "Then what shall we do with my bedchamber that adjoins yours?"

"When the time comes, it will make a proper nursery."

"Oh, it will, will it?"

He nodded, then kissed her forehead and resettled himself more comfortably between her legs.

Her smile grew. "That is becoming quite nice again. None of my research mentioned a man's ability to…uhm…become amorous again with such speed." She frowned. "Is that normal, or does it mean I failed to give you enough pleasure?"

"It means you gave me so much pleasure that you made me greedy for more." He arched a brow. "Is that all right, my love? After all, this is your first time, and I do not wish to make you sore."

"It is more than all right," she answered while rocking her hips to meet his slow, steady thrusts. "Because you have made me greedy for more too."

"Excellent, my love. That is all I needed to hear."

LAZILY DRAPED ACROSS him as if he were extra cushions for the settee, Fortuity smiled as Matthew's steady heartbeat thumped against her cheek. "I can only imagine the conversation around the servants' table downstairs."

His hearty chuckle vibrated through her. "From the whisperings I have managed to overhear, they should be very pleased with us today. I believe they feared we were about to take up separate households due to incompatibility."

"Well, *I* fear we became rather loud. So there should be no doubt in their minds that we are *very* compatible."

He rumbled against her with a heartier laugh and tightened his arms around her. "Yes. Very compatible, indeed. By the way, your removal of my cravat was most impressive for an inexperienced virgin."

She pushed up and propped herself on her elbow. "Are you doubting my purity?"

"I am not," he said with an urgency that revealed his fear of insulting her. "But even old Ablesby takes longer to untie my neckcloths, and he's been my valet for years."

Toying with the dusting of dark hair across his chest, she debated whether to tell him a long-held Broadmere sister secret.

"Is it that dire?" he asked with a leery look, while enticingly running his hand up and down her side.

"You must swear to never tell a soul."

He grinned and palmed her buttock as if checking it for ripeness. "I swear on this delectable arse."

She rolled her eyes. "Papa and Mama were always very strict about us all arriving at the dinner table in a timely manner. *Tardiness is a passive insult,* Papa always said, and Mama insisted it was the height of rudeness."

Matthew frowned. "What has that to do with your talent of whisking off a cravat in the blink of an eye?"

"When we were younger, Chance was even more unbearable than he is now. So, all of us sisters learned how to relieve him of his perfectly tied cravat when it was time to march down to dinner so he would have to return to his rooms and have it sorted. It always made him late, and he got into terrible trouble with Papa, who refused to believe his innocent daughters would know anything about untying a gentleman's neckcloth."

"Poor Chance."

"Poor Chance?" She thumped Matthew on the chest. "He was a thoroughly insufferable jackass to us all—still can be, at times."

Matthew caught her wrist before she could playfully thump him again and pulled her down for a long, slow kiss that left her deliciously breathless.

She drew back from him and teased him with a well-placed wiggle. "You are quite good at that, you know. Of course, I have no other with which to compare you."

"And you never will, my love." In one swift motion, he yanked the velvety throw off the back of the settee, tossed it onto the floor, then rolled them off on top of it. He stretched, grabbed a cushion, and placed it under her head.

"Ever the gentleman," she said as she wound her arms and legs around him and pulled him down where he belonged. The inferno he had awakened within her was ready to be stoked once again.

Propped on his elbows, he gave her a look filled with such caring and concern that her heart threatened to burst with joy. "I try, and as a gentleman, I must ask if *this* is all right?" He nibbled a tender kiss across her mouth, then raised his head again. "I shall never get my fill of you, my love, because you are so exquisite. But I do not wish you to be miserable afterward because you are so very sore. This is a new *activity* for you."

"You make me sound like a horse that has been overridden."

He snorted with laughter, then quickly turned his head to bury his face in his shoulder. Once composed, he gave her as innocent a look as he had ever managed. "I would never compare you to a horse, my love."

She squeezed his taut buttocks just as he'd squeezed hers. With a wicked grin, she wrapped her legs tighter around him and arched upward, aching for him to return her to ecstasy. "I am unsatisfied with that weak apology. I believe you should make it up to me, *my lord.*"

As he filled her and settled into that wonderful rocking motion that thrilled her, he managed a proper nod. "I am yours to command, my love. Ever yours to command."

Chapter Eleven

"IT PAINS ME to see you so very miserable," Fortuity told Blessing while inwardly cringing at the astonishing size of her sister's middle. Mama had never gotten this large when expecting. Or, at least, Fortuity didn't remember her ever becoming so huge. Blessing looked as if she had swallowed half of London. "Is there a possibility there could be more than one in there?"

"How am I to know?" Blessing snapped. "I have neither windows nor magical powers with which to view this demon who threatens to break my ribs whenever he or she is not busily bouncing so hard that I nearly wet myself." She immediately looked abashed. "Forgive me. I am vileness itself. How on earth did Mama ever do this eight times without either killing Papa or forbidding him to touch her ever again?"

"Perhaps once she held the babe and the miserable part had passed, she forgot about it until it was too late, then found herself stricken with it all over again." Fortuity stared, awestruck as her sister's stomach shifted, then rolled as though something within her was testing for weak spots to burst through and escape. "What does that feel like?"

"When the imp hooks its foot under one side of my ribcage and grabs hold of the other side and stretches, it hurts like the bloody devil. But it can be quite magical when the beastie calms to a gentle, rolling swim." Blessing nodded at her. "You will know soon enough."

"Whatever do you mean by that?" Fortuity sat straighter and tugged some of her curls closer around her neck, wondering if Matthew had left some telltale marks along her throat while nuzzling her awake for a delightful morning romp.

Blessing leaned forward as much as her swollen middle allowed. "You are no longer a virgin. Admit it."

"I have no idea what you are talking about."

"Liar."

Fortuity huffed. She had never been able to hide anything from her sisters, especially not Blessing. "How did you know?"

"Easily enough, dear sister. You seem genuinely happy and content for a change." Blessing shifted on the fainting couch, struggling to rearrange the pillows to support her better.

Fortuity jumped to help her, tucking smaller cushions behind her back and larger ones behind her shoulders and under her feet. "Shall I ring for tea? Are you hungry?"

"I am perpetually hungry, but every time I eat, my stomach feels as though I have swallowed live coals, and then I belch like a drunkard at the pub."

Fortuity eyed her, trying not to laugh. "Observed many drunkards at pubs, have we?"

"Oh, just shut your gob, Fortuity, do." Blessing retrieved the handbell that had disappeared among the cushions and rang it as if winding up to throw it. As soon as the butler appeared, she sadly shook her head and unleashed a long-suffering sigh. "Tea again, please, Cadwick, and do not forget extra milk and sugar. And an abundance of cakes and biscuits, of course—along with kippers. The extra-salty ones from the oiliest batch. I have a terrible need for them, it seems."

"Right away, my lady," he said before disappearing to fetch it.

"Extra-salty, oily kippers?" Fortuity shuddered at the thought of eating them with sweet cakes and biscuits. "That poor man must be terrified of you. He didn't even flinch." The butler had to be at his wits' end between the herds of cats that he despised and his mistress's odd requests.

"I am sure poor Cadwick feels as if he has descended into the deepest level of hell." Blessing rubbed the mound of her stomach as though it were a magic lamp, and she was summoning Aladdin's genie from Antoine Galland's *Les Mille et Une Nuit*—or, as Fortuity had enjoyed the English translation, *One Thousand and One Nights*. "Now tell me, when do you intend to inform Chance and Mr. Sutherland the elder that you are happily married, so Gracie can take her place on the chopping block next? Serendipity tells me that Chance is positively unbearable since Mr. Sutherland informed him that your marriage did not satisfy the condition of the will."

"Did Mr. Sutherland ever say what would happen if one of us did not achieve the marital bliss that Mama and Papa wished?"

Blessing shrugged. "It is my understanding that Chance's allowance increases with each happily married sister, but he will not get the entirety of the coffers of his longed-for dukedom until all seven of us achieve such bliss." She gave a wicked smirk. "For my amusement, don't tell Chance about the change in your level of happiness. Let him simmer a while longer. He deserves to suffer after comparing me to the size of a hot air balloon."

Fortuity gasped. "He didn't!"

"He did."

"Then I shan't tell him for at least another week."

Blessing clapped her hands and chortled happily. "I do love sisterly plotting."

Cadwick reappeared with the tea and accouterments, served them both, then hurried back out again.

"I don't believe I have ever seen that man move so quickly," Fortuity said.

Blessing balanced a platter overflowing with biscuits, cakes, and kippers on the shelf of her stomach. "I am rather enjoying that part of his behavior. By the way, Thorne tells me the Duchess of Esterton has slithered her viperous self back into London and been welcomed with open arms. How are you coping with that?"

"Matthew and I are presenting a united front that, according to the latest *on dit*, she finds most infuriating. Especially since he ignored not only the first letter she sent him upon her return to London, but the second and third letters as well."

"Has the woman no pride?" Blessing asked around a mouthful of cake.

"None whatsoever." Fortuity sipped her tea and settled more comfortably in her chair. "In her last letter, she offered to become his mistress. Even went so far as to say that she didn't mind sharing him as long as he kept her in the style to which she was accustomed when her husband lived."

"Apparently, her husband's dying before she could give him an heir has proven to be most detrimental to her purse." Blessing exuded a state of sheer bliss as she shoved an entire kipper dripping with oil into her mouth. With a finger in the air to bid Fortuity to wait while she finished chewing, she took a sip of tea to speed up the process. "Thorne reports that her dearly departed husband's nephew is the new duke and has never been impressed with her or her spending habits. It appears she is quite comfortable requesting advancements on her future allowances because she blows through her coin so readily."

"Well, she is not my problem." Although, if Fortuity was brutally honest with both herself and her sister, the Duchess of Esterton's return to London had set her nerves on edge. Even though Matthew had been quite open about the letters and only given the dowager the most basic level of civility whenever their paths had crossed, she still wished his former infatuation had remained on the Continent and never returned. "But I do have another."

Blessing frowned. "Another problem?"

"Eleanor is returning for a visit." Fortuity wrinkled her nose, not caring in the least that it might be petty for her to do so. "Agnus married the local vicar."

"Agnus Sykesbury? Agnus Sykesbury, who wore nothing but

black for three solid years after her husband died?" Blessing held her forehead as if the prospect of Matthew's cousin's marrying again had sent her mind reeling. "Remind me how long it has been since they were packed off to the country?"

"Less than two months." Fortuity threw up her hands. "I know. I thought it another of Eleanor's lies until we received a separate letter from Agnus bearing her new name."

"Well then, it must be true, because Agnus was always the light to Eleanor's dark." Blessing set her plate aside, scowled down at her loose day gown, then started brushing crumbs off the enormous mound of her stomach. "When is the evil one due to arrive?"

"Today."

Blessing looked up and ratcheted both her brows higher. "Do you wish to stay here for a while? You could tell Matthew you are keeping me company because confinement is already causing me to teeter on the brink of madness."

"Is it?" Concern filled Fortuity.

"No... Well, perhaps somewhat. But everyone's visits help immensely. However, we can use the excuse to your advantage, if need be."

"I cannot in good conscience saddle Matthew with that little chit."

"He can go to the club, and the two of you can meet for heated trysts until evil Eleanor returns to the country."

"I must say, pending motherhood has caused you to become extremely creative." Fortuity rather liked the idea of heated trysts with her husband and felt certain he would too. But sleeping without him by her side would not be pleasant at all, not since she'd become so besotted with the lovely feeling of waking up in his arms.

"And why exactly does Eleanor feel she must return to where she is not wanted simply because her mother married?" Blessing sipped her tea, then frowned down at it. "Would you mind freshening this for me with a bit more milk and sugar?"

Fortuity rose, took her sister's cup to the table, and added copious amounts of milk and sugar. Good heavens, the concoction was already the consistency of syrup, but far be it from her to point that out to Blessing. As she placed the cup and saucer back in her sister's hands, she said, "Eleanor—in her current persona of thinking of everyone but herself—stated that it was only proper she give her mother and the vicar the privacy a newly married couple need."

"You and Ravenglass haven't been married all that long either, at least, not in every sense of the word." Blessing sipped her tea and smiled. "Perfect. Thank you ever so much."

"You are quite welcome, and you are also correct, but not everyone is aware that my stipulation in the marriage contract was recently declared null, and that I am now sharing my husband's bedchamber."

"So what will you do? Poison her?" Blessing peered at Fortuity over the rim of her cup.

"Blessing!"

"Do not deny you hadn't already considered it."

"I do not wish her dead. I simply wish her gone. Forever."

Blessing grinned. "Sounds like dead to me."

"I do not remember you ever being so cutthroat." Fortuity freshened her own tea, wrinkling her nose at the noxious odor rising from the oily kippers. The longer they sat on the table, the fishier they smelled. It was a wonder gulls weren't pecking at the windows to get to them. "Have you always been so murderous?"

Blessing shrugged, then patted her stomach. "The larger I become, the worse I seem to get, but Dr. Tattersol assured Thorne that it was quite normal. Although I have noticed that the irritating physician makes it a point to never turn his back on me."

"I do not blame him." Fortuity returned to her chair. "But to answer your rather interesting question, I have no idea how I shall handle Eleanor. My behavior shall depend upon hers." Her insides were already twisted in knots over the Duchess of

Esterton's return. She did not need the additional worry of Eleanor, especially not when she and Matthew were trying to settle into their roles as a married couple in every sense of the word.

"Do not trust her under any circumstances," Blessing advised.

"That goes without saying, dear sister."

"IF WE MARRIED her off, she would no longer be our problem," Fortuity suggested as they descended the stairs after being informed that Eleanor had arrived and awaited them in the parlor. "Might I suggest Lord *Smellington?*"

Ignatius thundered past them with the four cats in hot pursuit.

Matthew shielded Fortuity between himself and the wall until the animals were well past them and did not appear to be returning. Everyone in the household had learned to traverse any staircase with the greatest of care. With any luck, either the pug or one of the cats would trip Eleanor and cause her to break her neck. If they did, Matthew would see to it that they received the very best of treats for the remainder of their lives. Although he did have Eleanor to thank for forcing him to take Fortuity as his wife. There was that, and he supposed her unintentional assistance should count for something and grant her a little grace.

"Matthew, what do you think? I feel sure the Marquess of Debt would most readily accept her."

"I prefer she marry someone who can support her, my dear. Not someone whom I shall have to support."

"I suppose there is that." Fortuity shifted against him with a heavy sigh.

"I know you do not trust her. We shall be alert and confirm everything she tells either of us." He halted at the bottom of the stairs and pulled her into his arms. "You are my everything,

Fortuity. Know that and never forget it, no matter what comes to pass."

"That sounds rather ominous." A worried pout plumped her tempting lips as she lovingly touched his cheek. "I do not wish for *us* to move backward rather than forward. While we are much better than we were, I still worry—"

"Stop worrying." He treated her to a long, slow kiss that made him wish they were still upstairs, Eleanor be damned. But he supposed duty called, and the longer they left his cousin down there alone, the less they knew about any plots she might be planning. He grudgingly ended the kiss and pressed his forehead to Fortuity's. "I love you, Fortuity. Always. Please know that with every bit of your heart."

"I am trying." She framed his face with her hands and gave him a faint smile. "I have loved you much longer than you have loved me—remember?"

"Not true. I simply failed to realize I loved you because I was a clot-headed fool." He wished they had more time for him to reassure her, and reassure her he would. All the rest of his days, if need be. But for now, he turned and laced her arm through his. "Come, my precious wren, we must go to war now and face the enemy."

"Indeed."

As they entered the parlor, Eleanor rose with a strained smile pasted across her noticeably flushed face. "Cousins, thank you ever so much for allowing me back into your home."

"Temporarily." Matthew wasn't about to let down his guard nor allow Eleanor to believe she could put down roots and torment them for any longer than the month he and Fortuity had granted her.

The chit batted her lashes as if her eyes were suddenly stricken with dust motes. "Of course, my lord. I would never suggest otherwise." She offered Fortuity a hesitant smile and curtsied. "Marriage suits you, my lady. I have never seen you looking so beautiful."

Fortuity accepted the obvious flummery with a curt dip of her chin and a cold "Thank you."

Eleanor's smile faltered. "You would not believe it is Mother, were you to see her now." She shifted her focus back to Matthew. "Marrying the vicar has turned her into a laughing, carefree lady once again."

"I daresay if she is a proper vicar's wife, she will not be carefree for very long." He led Fortuity to the settee and seated himself beside her. "She will often be called upon to assist him in serving his flock."

"I suppose." Eleanor nervously resettled herself in her chair.

"Why are you really here, Eleanor?" Fortuity asked.

Proud of his wife for firing a warning shot, Matthew nodded. "Yes, cousin, tell us. The truth, if you please?"

The dark-haired troublemaker sat there with her mouth ajar, eyeing them both. "I told you in my letter. Mother's happiness is of the utmost importance to me, and time alone with her new husband would surely help them build a more solid foundation."

"Did they send you away as Matthew did after your performance at Lady Burrastone's ball?" Fortuity jutted her chin higher, clearly itching to do battle.

Eleanor stiffened and jerked her attention from Fortuity back to him. "Are you not keeping your wife happy, my lord? I have never known her to be so harsh."

"Answer her," he replied. "What you deem as harshness is merely the forthrightness taught to her by your prior behavior." He reached over and took Fortuity's hand in his own. "In fact, you taught it to us both. Did they send you away, Eleanor? What devil's work did you stir in the country?"

His cousin lowered her gaze. "As I am sure you have already surmised, they thought it was high time I returned to London to find a husband."

"Your mother would not usually send you away," Matthew said, sensing there was more to be told. "The woman constantly made excuses for you. What changed?"

"Mrs. Palmeroy from the parish did not take a liking to me," Eleanor said, her familiar waspishness emerging. "She turned the rest of the gentry against me and even complained to the vicar."

"Your mother wrote that a month's visit to London would be most appreciated and should be adequate. Is she hoping for the parish to calm by then, or is there perhaps a *Mr.* Palmeroy who might be out of harm's way by the time you return?"

When she failed to answer, he knew he'd hit upon the truth. Knowing it would cost him to fund her dowry, taking away coin that rightfully belonged to his future children, Matthew gritted his teeth. Damn the selfish girl. He should've left her to her fate in India.

"Thebson!" he bellowed, flinching when Fortuity jumped. "Forgive me, darling. I did not mean to startle you."

The butler rushed into the room with alarm. "Yes, my lord?"

"Show Miss Sykesbury to her room. Immediately."

The man visibly relaxed, then nodded at Eleanor. "This way, miss."

Fisting her hands until her knuckles turned white, Eleanor glared at Matthew, then jumped up and followed Thebson out of the room.

"She will never change," Fortuity remarked, as though bemoaning terrible weather. "What poor man do you dislike enough to leg-shackle her to, since she is neither an heiress nor in possession of a pleasing demeanor? I wouldn't even wish her on Chance, and my brother often infuriates me." She flinched as though struck with even more unpleasantness that his wicked cousin had caused. "And I suppose we shall have to supply her dowry?"

"I am afraid so. What little her father provided for her was spent after his death, when she and her mother were extricating themselves from his family in India and the arranged marriage with some unfortunate gentleman she decided she did not like."

"And you felt *compelled* to rescue them?"

"Agnus has always been a dear cousin to me, and the only

family I had. Unfortunately, when I rescued them, I did not realize what a spoiled, selfish little chit Eleanor had become." He caught Fortuity's hand and kissed it. "Thank the Almighty I now have you, and with His blessing, we shall have our own family someday."

"You might not think it a blessing if I become like my sister when I get in the family way."

"Oh?"

Fortuity shook her head. "A topic for another day." She nodded at the doorway. "Eleanor is a danger to us, Matthew. A danger to the fragile peace and contentment it took us so long to find. No matter how careful we are, no matter what we do or say, she is a risk we can ill afford. I do not want us ruined by her, nor do I wish the Ravenglass name sullied by her any more than it already has been. Gossip about our sudden nuptials was just fading when the Duchess of Esterton returned to make everyone watch and see how you reacted. And now Eleanor is back." A snorting growl escaped her as she jumped to her feet and took to pacing while wringing her hands. She meandered around the side tables, chairs, and settees scattered throughout the large parlor. "What about the Earl of Alcester? At one time, he was sniffing around my sisters looking for a wife. Is he still an eligible bachelor?"

Matthew shook his head. "Married soon after Thorne and your sister, and already has a potential heir on the way."

"Farnsworth, then? Or Cedarswik? I remember them showing up to court Blessing when they heard the rumor that her dowry was greater than the rest of ours."

"I daresay that neither of those gentlemen would be interested in the dowry I am willing to supply for Eleanor."

Fortuity threw up her hands. "I do not wish us to be saddled with her for the entire month. And if we cannot attach her to some unsuspecting soul, what then? Do we send her back to the countryside to stir more unrest that you will eventually have to deal with whenever we leave London for the summer and retire to the manor house?" Her pacing increased to a frenzied swirling around the room. "I have the stress of stories to finish, a completed story in the hands of a publisher, and your former lady love glaring me down at every tea, ball, and dinner party we attend." She halted and faced him. "The additional irritation of Eleanor is most inconvenient, and I resent Agnus's assumption that her wayward daughter is our problem to resolve."

He went to her, wishing he had a solution for the whole bloody mess. "We could hear from the publisher any day now. They said they wished to review the entirety of the work before they made us an offer."

"Or they might not," she snapped. "What about the other publisher? Would they still be interested?"

"We chose the better of the two. Patience, Fortuity. I warned that nothing in the world of books ever happens quickly. Remember?" He poured them both a glass of Fortuity's favorite brandy, knowing that tea would never do for the seemingly insurmountable issues at hand. "Here. To calm you."

She took the glass and narrowed her eyes at him. "I was calm until I laid eyes on Eleanor. Calm is no longer a state I feel inclined to assume."

"If not for her, we might not have married," he reminded her. As soon as the words left his lips, he wished he hadn't said them. Fortuity looked ready to throw her drink in his face. He could be such a damned fool at times. They would have eventually married as soon as he had stopped behaving like an idiot and admitted to himself that he loved her. "What I meant to say was—"

"You said exactly what you meant to say," she snapped. "Quite clearly." She downed her drink in one gulp, clutched her chest, and wheezed against the heat searing her gullet.

He set aside his drink, took hold of her shoulders, and forced her to look at him. "We would have married, Fortuity. It would have simply taken longer because of my unwillingness to admit that I loved you. I was a cowardly, stubborn fool. Without

Eleanor's trap that forced me to open my eyes, who knows how long it would have taken me to embrace the truth rather than run from it?"

"You see what she does?" Fortuity pulled free and stepped back from him. "Not even here a full hour, and we are already at odds with one another."

"My lord," Thebson said hesitantly, revealing he had overheard their turmoil. He lifted a silver salver higher. It held more than one missive. "A messenger awaits a response to the uppermost envelope. Shall I ask him to leave so that you might reply to it at your leisure?"

"No," Fortuity informed the butler as she hurried over and snatched up both pieces of mail. "Have them wait. Lord Ravenglass shall respond to whomever it is once he has read the message. He will ring for you when ready."

Thebson shifted a leery look to Matthew and arched a scraggly brow.

"Carry on, Thebson." God help the man if Fortuity noticed the butler's hesitation to obey her. As the servant nodded and disappeared into the hallway, Matthew risked moving closer to his displeased wife, hoping to achieve a tenuous harmony at best. "Who awaits our response, my little wren?"

She glanced up at him, her eyes bright and dancing. "The publisher, Matthew. It is the publisher who awaits our response."

"Open it, my love. Hurry!"

Her hands trembled as she carefully unsealed the envelope and removed the letter. As her eyes went wide and her lips parted, Matthew itched to snatch it from her and read it for himself.

"For heaven's sake, what does it say?"

"Seven hundred pounds," she whispered as she looked up from the paper. "They are offering seven hundred pounds for the one novel. That is only a hundred less than Cadell & Davies paid Ann Radcliffe for *The Italian*, making her the highest-paid novelist in the 1790s." She bounced in place, shaking the letter at him.

"And that was not even her first novel. This is my first, and they are offering us seven hundred pounds!"

"Wonderful news!" Joyous laughter exploded from him as he caught her up and spun in place, hugging her tightly as they whirled. "I knew they would love it and make a generous offer. I knew it!"

She clung to him, her laughter flowing over him and thrilling him even more. "It is not the money that thrills me. It's my name on the title page—*written by Lady Fortuity Abarough Ravenglass*. I have waited so very long for this dream to come true."

His heart lurched, and he went still, gently lowering her feet to the floor. "You changed your name on the title page to include Ravenglass?"

She shyly twitched a shrug. "I am your wife. Am I not?" Then a shadow of uncertainty fell across her. "Did you not wish me to use your name? Would you rather no one knew it was your wife writing such romances?"

He hooked a finger under her chin and lifted her face to his. "I am honored you changed the title page to include our family name, and never would I ever be ashamed of you." It troubled him, the speed with which her doubts about him had returned. He had prayed they were past that. Apparently, those prayers had yet to be answered. "I adore you, Fortuity. What will it take to convince you my love for you is genuine? That I do not regret our marriage?"

She eyed him with a seriousness he found most unnerving. "Time, I suppose." She glanced down at the unopened letter she still held, then wilted in front of his very eyes as she handed it to him. "From the Duchess of Esterton. Letter number four."

He took it from her, ripped it in half, and tossed it into the hearth, before taking her by the hand and leading her to the small writing desk in the parlor's corner. "Shall we accept their offer of seven hundred pounds, or do you wish to negotiate for more?"

"Negotiate for more?" she squeaked. "We wouldn't dare. That would be…ungrateful."

"The decision is yours, my love, but make haste. Their messenger is waiting for your reply." He tapped on the writing desk before going to the bellpull and giving it a hard yank.

Thebson immediately appeared in the doorway.

"Champagne, my good man. By the time you return with it, we shall have a response for the waiting messenger."

The butler nodded. "Right away, my lord."

"Champagne, Matthew?" Fortuity paused with her quill in midair.

"Absolutely, my love." He moved behind her and hugged her back against his chest, keeping his arms tight around her waist as he peered over her shoulder. "It is the glorious first of many celebrations of your novels, I am sure." He nibbled at the soft skin beneath her ear and whispered, "After you finish your response for the messenger, shall we take the champagne upstairs to our bedroom?"

"In the middle of the afternoon? During receiving hours?"

"Hang the time," he murmured while continuing a trail of kisses along her neck, then pushed her gown aside to kiss the curve of her shoulder. "I want to celebrate my wife's accomplishment with champagne and more research into what techniques make her moan the loudest and keep her the most breathless." He peered over her shoulder and down at the paper in front of her. "You have yet to write anything, my love. Think of that poor messenger waiting on the steps."

She cleared her throat as she bent forward, dipped her quill into the ink, then started scratching out her reply.

Being ever so careful, so as not to cause her a writing mishap, Matthew slid his hands down to her hips and held her in place as he pressed into the softness of her delectable rump. "Do you feel how ardently I wish to celebrate with you?"

She cleared her throat again and swayed back, wiggling her bum against him. "Indeed, *my lord.*"

"The only thing preventing me from taking you here and now, my tempting vixen, is that you have yet to finish your task."

Still pressed up behind her, he cupped one of her breasts and gently squeezed. "Well, *that* and the champagne should be here soon."

"*My lord,*" she teased in a husky tone that excited him even more, "you are making it most difficult to concentrate and phrase my response properly."

Matthew stepped back just as the butler reached the door, pushing a cart with a bottle of champagne and two glasses. "Do forgive me, Thebson, but might you be able to take that upstairs? My wife and I have decided to retire to our private sitting room to celebrate. If anyone calls, do be good enough to inform them we are not receiving today."

Without so much as blinking in surprise, the servant nodded. "As you wish, my lord."

"Oh, and Thebson…" Fortuity darted across the room and handed the man a note. "Please give this to the awaiting messenger."

"Yes, my lady."

Once the man had disappeared to accomplish his tasks, Matthew swept Fortuity up into his arms and headed toward the stairs. "Come, my lovely wife—we have celebrations and affirmations to attend to."

"Affirmations?"

"Yes, my darling. This afternoon, I intend to love away every doubt about us you have ever entertained."

Chapter Twelve

"Good afternoon, Lady Fortuity," the shopkeeper sang out from behind the counter.

"Good afternoon, Mrs. Mortimore." Fortuity paused a few steps into the bookstore and pulled in a deep breath, reveling in the sweet perfume of exciting new stories waiting to be discovered. "By the way, this is my sister, Lady Grace."

"Good afternoon to you as well, Lady Grace," the kindly matron said.

"Good afternoon." Grace looked around the establishment in wide-eyed wonder. "Serendipity will have nine kinds of fits if she discovers I came here today." She moved past Fortuity and started sorting through the crammed bookshelves.

"Ha!" Mrs. Mortimore disappeared from view with a quiet thud, then emerged from behind the tall counter that concealed her whenever she hopped down off the wooden crate, which elevated her to a height that enabled her to better serve her customers. "Is this the same Lady Serendipity whose most recent order is to be picked up later this week?"

"Indeed, it is," Fortuity said with a wry grin. The eccentric shopkeeper might be tiny in stature, but she was enormous in spirit. Mrs. Mortimore was one of Fortuity's most favorite people in the world, and she considered her a trusted friend.

"'Do as I say and not as I do' Serendipity?" Grace rolled her eyes and returned to browsing through the books. "Such a hypocrite. I should have known."

"You know of the collection of stories she always kept hidden from Mama. Seri could start her own library." Fortuity turned back to Mrs. Mortimore and winked. "Or a bookstore."

The shopkeeper cackled as she tucked her wild, silvery curls back behind her ears. "I shall keep her in mind should I ever decide to retire. Perhaps she might wish to take over?" She motioned them toward a set of shelves at the back of the shop. "My newest volumes are just there. I put them out today. You ladies are the first to see them."

Grace stayed put, engrossed by the contents of the first shelf she'd discovered. Fortuity followed Mrs. Mortimore to the rear of the shop, excited to be the first to peruse the new titles.

"Have you time for tea today, my lady?" Mrs. Mortimore asked her. "I have a lovely new custom blend from Twinings. They made it especially for me, and I am quite besotted with it."

"That would be delightful." Fortuity couldn't think of a better way to escape the woes of this past fortnight's disasters. If they didn't get Eleanor married off soon and discover a way to rip out the Duchess of Esterton's claws, Fortuity held little hope for her sanity and even less for the survival of her marriage.

Matthew couldn't seem to understand why she couldn't extinguish her insecurities as easily as snuffing out a candle. She was sure of herself when it came to her writing or any number of other things, but when it came to knowing with any level of certainty that her husband was really and truly devoted to her? She still failed miserably. Wicked little voices at the back of her mind kept whispering that as soon as the *new* wore off their intimacy, he would tire of her and be ready to move on. After all, he had conquered her and claimed her spoils. Once a man got what he wanted, sometimes he discovered he didn't want it anymore. The thrill was in the hunt. She had once overheard Mama tell that very thing to Papa about one of their acquaintances.

"Lady Fortuity?" Holding a tray with a teapot and cups, Mrs.

Mortimore nodded at the small, round table in a cozy nook stocked with overflowing shelves. "Forgive me for saying so, but you do not seem yourself today."

"That is because a pair of wicked ghosts from her husband's past won't leave her alone," Grace said while slowly working her way along another shelf, then moving on to the next. Keeping her gaze locked on the spot where she had paused, she slid a pile of books onto the table, then returned to the shelf and took back up where she had stopped. "Do you have any books on poisons or issuing curses? That might help her."

"Gracie."

"Do not growl at me. You know it is true, and I distinctly remember your saying you trusted Mrs. Mortimore implicitly."

"Why thank you, Lady Fortuity." The kindness and understanding in Mrs. Mortimore's eyes did little to ease Fortuity's embarrassment. "Sit and pour our tea while I draw the shade. We shall talk as long as it takes."

"Draw the shade?"

"Of course. Since I am the owner, I close whenever I wish— and I now wish it." The shopkeeper didn't bother looking back as she made her way to the door, pulled down the shade with the assistance of a long, hooked rod, then turned the latch and locked it. "Now, we can relax and enjoy our tea uninterrupted."

Grace stacked another pile of books beside the first pile she had selected.

"You mean to purchase all of those?" Fortuity asked, trying to recall the last time she had seen her sister reading.

"They are about dogs."

"Ah." That explained everything. Dogs were Grace's favorite subject. Fortuity added a dollop of milk to Mrs. Mortimore's tea, then handed the saucer and cup to her. "I did not realize your shop's offerings were so wide ranging."

The shopkeeper gave her a sly grin as she lifted her steaming drink for a sip. "Not everyone enjoys the stories many young ladies are excited to read and keep hidden from their mothers."

"Indeed." Fortuity recalled that many of her sisters' scandalous books were still hidden in cupboards and drawers even though Mama had passed away over two years ago. Determined not to allow her spirits to sink any lower, she sampled the tea and held the rich, herbaceous blend on her tongue, breathing in to enjoy the heady new flavor.

Mrs. Mortimore's eyes sparkled. "Delicious, isn't it? Twinings never disappoints."

"It is indeed exquisite." Fortuity relaxed back into the threadbare yet comfortable chair and allowed herself a sigh.

"Poisons, curses, or perhaps a book about hiring assassins?" Grace asked Mrs. Mortimore.

"Gracie!" Fortuity groaned, then turned to the shopkeeper. "Please pay her no mind. She is not nearly as bloodthirsty as she seems."

"She loves her sister and seeks to help her," the matron said. "Quite admirable of her, I think."

Grace gave Fortuity a victorious smirk, then hopped up from the table, returned to the last shelf she'd been pawing through, and fetched another book. "This one is a gothic murder mystery. Perhaps it will give us some ideas."

Fortuity heaved another desolate sigh, wondering what had ever possessed her to bring her sister to her favorite sanctuary.

"Who are these ghosts who dare torment my dearest friend?" Mrs. Mortimore daintily held her teacup between her hands while propping her elbows on the table. She took a sip and kept the drink elevated as if another sip should soon follow.

"My husband's cousin, Miss Eleanor Sykesbury, has returned to London. Staying with us, in fact, while she looks for a husband. I am certain you heard of her when reading about the astonishing speed of my nuptials in the gossip rags."

Mrs. Mortimore narrowed her eyes in a displeased squint. "Yes. I recall the name. From you, actually, when you told me you had taken Lord Ravenglass's name, then insisted I still call you Lady Fortuity."

"So I did." Fortuity felt a momentary flash of guilt. "I am so sorry. It appears I come whining to you whenever I am troubled."

The ever-patient matron lowered her teacup back to its saucer and gently patted Fortuity's arm. "I am honored that you confide in me. That is what genuine friends do."

"Thank you, Mrs. Mortimore. I do cherish you."

"Well, go on. Tell her about the other ghost," Grace prodded without looking up from the book she had propped open against her cup and saucer.

"I believe I already know the identity of the other ghost." The matron rose from her chair and disappeared behind the tall counter at the side of the shop. After an abundance of rustling and disgruntled mumbling, she reappeared with a pamphlet in her hand. After climbing back into her seat, she placed it on the table, then flattened her small, delicate hand on top of it. "This is the latest edition of *On Dit—What a Treat*. There is mention of a widowed duchess—by name—and her determination to win back a certain viscount whom she left standing at the altar some years ago."

Fortuity's heart fell, and her face blazed hot with embarrassment and humiliation. She swallowed hard and forced in a deep breath, held it to a slow count of five, and then let it out. "May I see it, please?"

"Are you certain?" Doubtfulness and concern filled Mrs. Mortimore's tone.

"Yes. Absolutely." Fortuity unfolded the reprehensible sheet and found the paragraph immediately.

Have you ever wondered which is stronger? Old love or new? Or is the new love not really love at all but a simple act of honor? We know what the Duchess of Esterton hopes, since she has not only sent innumerable correspondences to her dashing viscount's home but also allows her lovesick gaze to follow him wherever he goes. She may be a widow, but he is not. Could it be, though, that he is in the market for a mistress? We all know how dreadfully dull marriages of convenience can be. Undoubt-

edly, Her Grace would happily comply with whatever her dear raven requests.

Fortuity handed the pamphlet to her sister, knowing Grace would wish to read it.

"That woman's self-worth must be lower than the gutter." Grace tossed the despicable sheet to the table and wrinkled her nose as if it stank.

"What do you mean?" Fortuity asked.

"She had to have given them those details," Grace said. "How else would they know she had sent *innumerable* correspondences to your Matthew?"

"Perhaps they guessed? Hoping to strike a nerve?" And strike a nerve they had. Fortuity felt like crawling into a hole and sobbing.

"When they guess at things they are usually more vague," Mrs. Mortimore said. "According to what you are saying, the details of that drivel are too accurate. Of course, anyone could observe her watching your husband, but knowledge about the correspondence is different. They purchased that information, either from the widow herself or someone else. Who else would know about the letters?"

"Only my family and the servants." Fortuity knew none of her sisters would ever take part in such a heartless attack. That only left the servants. "But I thought they liked me." A sense of despondency as heavy as lead filled her.

"Who?" Mrs. Mortimore asked.

"Matthew's servants." Fortuity wrung her hands together, slowly shaking her head. "Mrs. Greer helped us care for Mama before I recommended her for the housekeeper's position after Mama passed. The others seem happy enough with me. I cannot think of a single one with whom I have had a cross word."

"Perhaps one of them needed money," the shopkeeper suggested. "Desperate circumstances often force people to do desperate things."

Fortuity glared at the pamphlet on the table. "I am so tired of all the stares, the whispers, the covert glances at every dinner party, every ball, even at the theatre and modiste. One would think I ran a brothel in the middle of Mayfair."

"Unfortunately, there is little you can do other than hold your head up and stare them down," Mrs. Mortimore said. "There is no fighting the tattling tongues of the *ton*."

"Perhaps not." Fortuity snatched up the pamphlet. "But I must at least learn if my household is secure. If it was not the widow who gave them this information, what if this person decides they need more coin? Who knows what else they might attempt to sell? They might even decide to make things up and sell them lies."

Mrs. Mortimore thoughtfully tipped her head to one side. "There is always that possibility."

"How do you intend to discover your betrayer?" Grace asked. "Any you ask will simply deny any part in it and claim innocence."

"I know I can trust Mrs. Greer. She was such an angel with Mama." Fortuity wished she could say that of the others. They all seemed nice enough, and their work was exemplary, but she simply hadn't known them as long as she'd known the servants back at Broadmere House.

"I have always thought Thebson an odd sort." Grace wrinkled her nose. "But as bumbling and unorganized as he is, do you truly believe he could not only orchestrate but conceal such a betrayal?"

"Perhaps his bumbling is an act?" Mrs. Mortimore suggested.

"No one could put on an act that convincing," Fortuity said while mentally crossing the butler off the list of possibilities. "But he is the one who not only received the letters at the door but also delivered them to Matthew."

"Did Matthew open them in front of him? Did the man know what the letters held or who they were from?" Grace asked.

Fortuity frowned, trying to remember. "No. Matthew didn't

open any of them in front of him, and as far as I can recall, Thebson only mentioned a messenger waiting for a response on the first letter. But that does not necessarily mean he knew the duchess was the sender." She held up the pamphlet to Mrs. Mortimore. "May I have this copy, please? I need it to confront my staff."

"Of course, my lady." The matron refreshed her tea, then gave a curt nod. "And if there is anything else I may do to help with this unpleasantness, I beg of you, do not hesitate to ask."

"This sanctuary you provide helps me more than you could ever know," Fortuity told her. "I am most grateful for your friendship and your understanding ear."

Mrs. Mortimore accepted the praise and thankfulness with a graceful nod. "It is my honor, my lady. Now, do finish your tea before it grows cold."

Fortuity obediently took another sip, knowing she would need the tea's fortification for the next activity on this afternoon's agenda: interrogating her staff.

"You do not have to come inside and help," Fortuity said. "It could become unpleasant." She dreaded what she was about to do, dreaded it with a fury.

Grace gave her a defiant look as they climbed Ravenglass Townhouse's front steps. "No one betrays one of my sisters and escapes my wrath. No one."

"Very well, then." Fortuity glanced back at George, Broadmere House's head footman, standing beside the carriage bearing the Broadmere ducal crest. "Guard Lady Grace's books well, George. You know how she can be."

The handsome young man grinned, then gave them a proper bow. "With my life, Lady Ravenglass."

As they entered the townhouse, Thebson failed to greet

them, but Ignatius the pug and Rumbles the ginger cat made up for his absence. The enthusiastic animals bounced around them, vying for attention.

"You need more dogs," Grace said as she scratched the wiggling canine behind his ears. "Poor Ignatius is outnumbered."

Fortuity rubbed the loudly purring orange tabby under his chin. "Rumbles here acts more like a dog than a cat. That evens the odds somewhat."

Mrs. Greer came around the corner and clapped her hands. "All right, you two. Off with you to the kitchen. Cook has you a treat, and those other three are already at it. You best hurry or there'll be none left for you."

Appearing to understand every word, the pug and the cat took off down the hallway.

"And how are you this fine day, Lady Grace?" Mrs. Greer asked with her usual cheerfulness.

"That remains to be seen, I am afraid." Grace gave Fortuity a pointed look.

"Oh dear." The housekeeper turned to Fortuity with an expectant tip of her head. "My lady?"

Fortuity picked at the cat hair on her gown, loathing what she was about to do. "Mrs. Greer, could you please assemble everyone, including Mr. Ablesby, Mr. Turnmaster, and the stable lads? I would like to speak to the entire household regarding a most dire matter."

"Everyone as well as the valet, head groom, and the lads?" The housekeeper's eyes went wide, and she clucked like a fretting hen. "Must be a dire matter, indeed."

"Indeed, it is." Fortuity swallowed hard and squared her shoulders, determined to see this through. "Please gather them in the dining room, then come and fetch me from my office."

"At once, my lady." Mrs. Greer toddled off, still making fretting noises and shaking her head.

"I hate this," Fortuity told her sister as they entered her office to wait. "I hate this with everything in me."

"You have no choice. You have to be able to trust your staff. Don't accuse them. Just read the insulting drivel to them, and I shall help you by watching their reactions."

"What if they fail to react?"

Grace scowled at Fortuity as if she thought her a mindless ninny. "Of course they will react. How could they not? And whoever doesn't react may be your culprit." She moved to the window, fingered the draperies aside, and peered out. "By the way, where is your husband?"

"I am not sure." Fortuity held her head, massaging her temples and wishing the ever-increasing ache would cease its pounding. There was no time for a megrim today, and this confrontation, a thing she never did well, would only fuel it with a vengeance. "Matthew told me, but I have forgotten. We had words this morning."

"From your expression, I take it the words were not pleasant ones?"

"His patience has worn thin with my insecurities regarding our relationship." Fortuity gave up on trying to ease her throbbing head and pressed both hands to her aching heart. "He does not understand why I cannot ignore all the furor that Eleanor and the dowager duchess create." She slowly shook her head. "I wish I could ignore them, and all the trouble they stir, but I simply cannot." She pulled the folded gossip rag from her reticule and sadly stared down at it. "How can I, Gracie? They are trying to steal away that which I longed for and feared I would never have."

Grace hurried over and gave her a reassuring hug. "But you do have it. That is what you must always keep in mind, and fight them. Do not fight Matthew and push him away. That is what they are trying to force you to do. Do not let them steal your joy and win."

"I am trying to be strong." Fortuity pulled in a deep breath and released it with a heavy sigh. "There is simply so much to lose."

"You are not going to lose anything. We will not allow it. Be like Mama. Would she allow anyone to take Papa from her?" Grace jerked her head downward in a determined nod. "You have always shown great strength, Tutie. I know it is wearing thin, but remember, you have the advantage. You are Matthew's wife."

A light tap on the door interrupted them.

"Yes?" Fortuity braced herself, sensing it was time.

Mrs. Greer opened the door wide enough to peep inside. "Everyone is in the dining room, my lady. Just as you asked."

"Thank you, Mrs. Greer. I shall be right there."

The housekeeper nodded and closed the door.

Fortuity tossed her reticule onto her desk, along with the light shawl she had worn to protect her from the coolness of the spring day. She never wore hats. Hated them, in fact. But she tugged off her gloves and deposited them into the pile with the rest of her things, refusing to wear them in her own home. One of the maids would take them up to Anne so she could get them sorted. She turned and noticed Grace had shed her outerwear as well and draped her things over a nearby chair.

"Ready?" Fortuity asked her sister, already seeing the answer in Grace's snapping eyes.

Grace nodded. "Absolutely."

"Very well, then." With the dreadful gossip rag in hand, Fortuity led the way to the dining room.

Mrs. Greer had assembled every servant in Ravenglass's employ and had them lined up as though they were about to be marched off to the gallows. Some in the somber group were quite pale. Others twitched in place, nervously shifting and resettling their stance.

Fortuity cleared her throat and held up the tattered pamphlet. "I do not know if any of you are aware of this despicable publication, but this particular edition contains an extremely unsavory paragraph about Lord Ravenglass. Anything that besmirches him also besmirches me, and this most definitely does."

She cleared her throat again and read the terrible thing aloud, proud that her voice remained strong and didn't quiver a single time. Once finished, she slowly refolded the pamphlet into the small wad she'd carried in her reticule, then lifted her head and studied each and every servant, noting their expressions of shock and some even of horror. Mrs. Greer had turned an alarming shade of red and held her fists clenched so tightly that her knuckles glowed a bright white.

"I am not accusing any of you," Fortuity said, hoping she sounded sincere, "but the part about the correspondences concerns me. How would this publication come by such information?" She paused, hoping Grace was having better luck than she was at deciphering their expressions. "If not given to this rag by the dowager duchess herself, how would they know she had sent several messages here to Lord Ravenglass?"

Mrs. Greer stepped forward and whirled about, prowling up and down the line of servants like a warring general. "If any of you betrayed her ladyship and his lordship, I shall have your guts for garters!" She shook her fist at them. "Confess now, so we can call the vicar to pray over whatever is left after I finish with you." She halted in front of the butler and jabbed a plump finger in his face. "You! Thebson! You would be the one to deliver whatever letters came here. Only you would know how many and who they were from."

The old man sputtered and spat and, for the first time since Fortuity had met him, actually showed some emotion. "I would never!" he said in a loud, bellowing voice that was surprisingly strong for one his age. "I have been with Lord Ravenglass since he was born. Never would I betray him." He pointed a shaking finger at Fortuity. "Nor would I do anything to harm or sadden our fine mistress. Her ladyship deserves only the very best of our honor, respect, and protection."

The rest of the servants agreed with vigorous nods. One of the stable lads stepped forward and said, "We would never tell private things about this house, your ladyship. You and his lordship treat us good and pay us well. 'Twould be a sorry cove, indeed, who did such a cutthroat thing."

They all seemed so sincere, so sympathetic, and angry about the cruel gossip. Fortuity glanced at Grace—who waved her closer.

"I do not think it was any of them," she whispered. "It must have come from the duchess."

"I feel the same," Fortuity said just as quietly. She turned back to the dedicated group of people. "Thank you all so much. I appreciate everything you do for his lordship and myself. Again, I was not accusing any of you, but you needed to know that someone somewhere is handing over information about our household. If any of you see anything suspicious, please bring it to my attention. Thank you for meeting here today. You may return to your duties."

Mrs. Greer shooed them out of the room as if herding sheep. As she reached the servants' door that led to the kitchen, she turned and gave Fortuity an apologetic bow. "I am more than a little sorry about that ugliness, my lady. Very sorry, indeed."

"Thank you, Mrs. Greer. I know you are."

"What is going on here?" Matthew asked from the doorway of the dining room, his cloak in the crook of his arm.

"I'll be going now," Grace announced. She curtsied to Matthew. "Brother." Then she scurried around him and disappeared.

"Fortuity?"

His befuddled yet displeased expression made Fortuity wish she had handled things in a timelier fashion. She had never intended to show him the horrid sheet of gossip. But it appeared there was no helping it now. "Gracie and I visited Mrs. Mortimore's bookshop today, and she showed me this." She handed him the tightly folded wad of paper.

He frowned down at it as he gingerly unfolded the thing, as if it held a poisonous viper. "And this is?"

"*On Dit—What a Treat,*" she said. "One of the more popular gossip rags in London."

With a shake of his head, he heaved a great sigh. "I suppose there is something in here about us?"

"About you, mainly. I am only implied."

"Where?" His voice had gone to that dull, dreaded tone he recently took on whenever their conversations shifted to her insecurities about their marriage and feelings for one another.

She echoed his heavy sigh but stood her ground with her hands folded in front of her. "Midway down the first page. The paragraph discussing the Duchess of Esterton's hopes."

His eyes narrowed, and the muscles in his jaw rippled as he read the offensive piece. Then, ever so slowly, he crumpled it into a ball and hurled it at the hearth. He stared at it as the flames took hold and ate into the paper, then he turned back to her, his eyes filled with pain. "You were questioning the staff to see if there was a betrayer among them?"

"Yes."

"And what did you discover?"

"I do not believe any of them handed over the information about the duchess's letters. They all were as incensed as I about the gossip sheet and what it held. Gracie watched their reactions and came to the same conclusion. Our staff can be trusted."

"Why would the duchess do such a thing?" He raked his hand through his hair. "Does she not realize how foolish, how terribly pathetic, this paints her?"

"That is why I questioned our staff. I could not imagine why anyone would purposely portray themselves in such a poor light. Has your Olandra suffered from low self-worth in the past?"

His glare hardened on her as he ever so slightly bared his teeth. "She is not *my* Olandra, dear wife. You are the only woman I consider *mine*. Why do you find that so impossible to accept?"

"Did you not once tell me you did not feel for me what you had felt for her?" Fortuity refused to cry in front of him. No matter how badly her eyes burned to release the unshed tears that made her pounding head hurt even worse. "Do you recall that conversation?"

"As I recall, I said it was not the same. That does not mean that I do not love and cherish you." Once again, he combed his fingers through his dark hair, making the thick, rich locks stand on end. "You are my world, Fortuity. My entire world. I beg you to know the depth of my love for you and find comfort and peace in it."

She turned away and held her head, closing her eyes as she dug her thumbs into her temples and tried to rub the pain away. She hated all this turmoil, absolutely hated it. "What I know for certain is that I weary of the humiliation heaped upon me everywhere we go because of Eleanor and Olandra's evil machinations and manipulation of Polite Society's opinions."

He wrapped his arms around her and pulled her back against his chest. Once she would've luxuriated in his embrace, but now all she had the strength to deal with was this bloody throbbing in her head. She had reached her limits for the day, for the foreseeable future, really. She had reached her limits about everything.

"You are not well," he said as he gently turned her to face him. Without another word, he swept her up into his arms and cradled her like a babe.

"What are you doing?" A groan escaped her as she buried her face into the perfect folds of his cravat.

"I am taking you to bed, to rest and be pampered. I am certain our Mrs. Greer will have a tonic to help you feel better and return the color to your lovely cheeks."

She swallowed hard, suddenly finding herself dangerously nauseated. "Do not sway me, Matthew. Everything inside me is threatening to come back out." She squinted her eyes tightly shut and focused on taking slow, deep, relaxing breaths.

"Mrs. Greer! Anne!"

"Matthew! I beg you, do not shout, or I shall spew all over you."

"We are nearly there, my love. Hold fast." He kicked open the door to their private suite, crossed the sitting room, then kicked open the bedchamber door. "Where the devil are those women? Do they not realize they are needed?"

"Just get me to the bed. All I need is a bit of a lie-down to be rid of this silliness."

He lowered her into the pillows, not even bothering to turn back the counterpane. After ripping off his jacket and spreading it across her, he gently brushed her hair back from her face and kissed her forehead. "I shall return with those blasted women, so you might know some relief."

She curled into a tighter ball beneath his coat and breathed in his familiar scent of sandalwood that clung to its fibers. It steadied her. It was almost as if she was still in his arms.

"Do not bellow at them," she said as loudly as she dared as he went to leave the room.

"I will not bellow at them."

"Liar," she mumbled to herself. But his protectiveness made her smile.

Chapter Thirteen

"M RS. GREER! ANNE! Where the devil are you?" Matthew charged down the hallway, immediately forgetting his promise to Fortuity that he wouldn't bellow. "Where the bloody hell has everyone got to?"

"Your lordship—here! I am here." Anne popped out of the servants' stairwell with several of Fortuity's gowns in her arms. "Is aught amiss?"

"Yes, aught is amiss. My wife is gravely ill. Fetch Mrs. Greer immediately so the two of you can bring her some ease."

"Oh my goodness. Yes, my lord. Immediately." Anne dipped a hurried curtsy, then took off running with the clothing still clutched to her chest.

Matthew debated whether to return to Fortuity or hunt down Thebson and send for every physician in London. As he stood at the top of the stairs, trying to make up his mind, Eleanor emerged from her rooms.

"Whatever could be wrong, cousin?" she asked, with a little too much interest for his liking.

He glared at her. "I am in no mood, Eleanor. Either return to your rooms or go elsewhere. I have neither the time nor the patience for you today."

"As you wish, my lord." After an indulgent tip of her head and a graceful curtsy, she floated down the staircase and disappeared toward the parlor.

He scowled after her long after she was no longer in view, noting she had neither appeared shocked nor displeased at his directness. The chit was up to something, again. He would wager his best bottle of brandy on it. Perhaps she was the one behind the humiliating entry in the tattle sheet. That would make more sense than Olandra selling it to the publication and bringing embarrassment to herself. Also, rather than avidly pursuing the most eligible gentlemen at every soiree, Eleanor had situated herself amongst the cackling hens known for their cruelty and penchant for tormenting the weakest members of the *ton*. It had been well over a fortnight since his cousin's arrival, and she was no closer to courting a husband than the day she showed up on their doorstep. He would speak to Thebson and Mrs. Greer about Eleanor's mingling with those of the household. He had warned them once she was not to be trusted. With this most recent debacle, it bore repeating.

He turned to rejoin Fortuity when a rapid thudding from the staircase made him look back. *About bloody time.* Mrs. Greer, Anne, and the maid, Mary Louise, hurried toward him.

Huffing and puffing from the exertion, Mrs. Greer clutched her chest, trying to catch her breath while she spoke. "Her ladyship? Ill?"

"A terrible pounding in her head, and she fears she is about to cast up her accounts." He herded them down the hallway toward the master suite. "She is on the bed. On top of the counterpane. There was no time to strip it back. I covered her with my coat to keep her warm. Pray, tell me you can help her."

The housekeeper gave him an understanding dip of her plump chin. "It sounds like one of her terrible megrims. They often struck her when I helped tend to her mother." She narrowed her eyes, pinning him with an accusing squint. "They usually come on when she has been overset with worries longer than she can tolerate. Much like a covered pot boiling over because the fire burns too hotly." Before he could defend himself, she turned to Mary Louise and handed her a key from the ring pinned to the starched white apron lashed around her ample waist. "Fetch up a kettle of hot water, a sturdy cup and spoon, and the three bottles from the highest shelf in my apothecary. And do not fail to lock the door back upon your exit."

"Yes, Mrs. Greer." The maid took off at a hard run.

The housekeeper nodded at Anne. "You fetch her softest night rail, and the lavender and peppermint oils I gave you for her toiletries in the dressing room."

Anne skittered away as quickly as the other maid.

Mrs. Greer turned back to Matthew and shooed him off as if he were a trespassing goose. "Go away, my lord. She needs darkness, quiet, and nothing to remind her of the trying day she has endured." The matron's face reddened with a fierce scowl. "Are you aware of that hideous publication? That is what caused our dear lady's illness."

"I am aware of it, and I fear you are correct about it making her poorly." Although, if he were to be honest, he felt sure he had a hand in Fortuity's misery as well. He could have been a damn sight more understanding with her at breakfast.

"Daren't you worry about her, my lord," Mrs. Greer said over her shoulder. "She will be fine soon enough."

"Swear to it, Mrs. Greer. I cannot bear the thought of losing her." And he meant that more than he had ever meant anything before. He couldn't tolerate the possibility of life without Fortuity.

Pausing with her hand on the door latch, the housekeeper smiled back at him. "She will be fine, my lord. Mark my words." She disappeared into the room, quietly muttering to herself as she was wont to do.

"I need a drink," he told the cats winding in and out around his ankles. He loped down the stairs and was greeted at the bottom by Ignatius. The dog plopped down on his square behind, cast a glance at the parlor door, and growled.

"Too true, old man." Matthew didn't trust himself with another unpleasant confrontation with Eleanor, not in his current frame of mind. "Come, Ignatius. We shall take refuge in our lady's sanctuary."

The faithful dog followed him into Fortuity's office and jumped onto the low cushioned bench in front of the corner window that Fortuity had placed there specifically for him and the cats. Matthew went straight to the amply stocked cabinet of spirits he had ordered installed in the office in case he and his lady love decided to lock the door and make good use of the settee once again.

After pouring himself a glass of port, he went to the other window and eyed the view of Chesterfield Street but didn't see a bit of it. All he saw was his beloved wife: pale, her forehead peppered in a cold sweat, gulping air and holding it to keep from being ill. Damn and blast this sorry mess of rumors and gossip and the misery they caused her.

A soft knock on the door interrupted his inner turmoil. "Yes?" he said without pulling his gaze from the sunny day outside.

"A parcel has arrived, my lord," Thebson said from the doorway.

"A parcel?" Matthew still didn't turn from the window. He preferred to sulk in solitude with the softly snorting dog and his drink. "And the sender is?"

"Minerva Press, my lord."

Minerva Press was the publisher printing Fortuity's stories. Matthew hurried to the doorway and accepted the carefully wrapped package that was the perfect size for a single copy of her book. "Thank you, Thebson. That will be all."

"Very good, my lord." The man nodded and closed the door, leaving Matthew to himself with what surely had to be Fortuity's copy of her first of many books. This would most definitely make her feel better after the terrible day she'd had. He tucked it under his arm, tore out of her office, and vaulted up the stairs, his excitement growing with every step. She would be so very thrilled when she saw her name on the cover. His heart threatened to burst with love and pride. She had worked so hard for this, and now she could hold her dream in her hands.

He slowed when he reached their suite and quietly crept inside just as Mrs. Greer and Anne emerged from the bedroom. "Is she asleep?" he whispered, hoping they would tell him no.

Mrs. Greer fixed him with a stern look that *almost* backed him up a step. "No, my lord, but she does not need to be disturbed."

He held up the parcel. "Her dream has come true. I am certain this is a copy of her book. It is from her publisher. I thought that might brighten her day and help her feel at least a little better. Would you not agree?"

Both the housekeeper and Anne beamed at him with the widest of smiles.

"Do go in, my lord," Mrs. Greer said. "What a fine way to make her feel better." She held up a finger. "Mind you, the light hurts her eyes a bit, so I turned down the flame on her lamp. Just warn her before you adjust the wick and brighten it."

"I will." As excited as a lad escaping his lessons for the day, Matthew eased into the bedroom. "Fortuity," he said in a loud whisper. "You have received a parcel, my love. A package I feel certain you will wish to open immediately."

She lay on her side, holding her head and shielding her eyes from what little light filtered into the room from between the closed draperies and the lowered flame of the oil lamp. "A parcel?" she replied weakly. "I am really not up to parcels right now."

"It is from your publisher." Surely that would tempt her.

Her deep sigh echoed through the dimly lit room like a lonely wraith rising from its grave. "Are you certain, Matthew? I do not feel well at all."

"I am positive, my love. Minerva Press is stamped in great, bold letters on the wrappings."

"Adjust the light," she said with another heavy sigh. "But forgive me for not sitting upright. My head will surely split in two if I rise even a little."

After turning up the flame, he eased down onto the side of

the bed beside her, taking great care not to jostle her. "Shall I cut the twine for you?"

"Yes, please."

With the aid of the wick trimmer for the night candle, he snipped the twine, then placed the loosely wrapped book in her hands. It was only right that she be the first to see the physical reality of her dream.

Squinting against the light, she pulled the brown paper wrapping away. The joyous smile Matthew expected never came. Instead, she puckered her brow with the slightest frown. Abruptly, she shoved the book back at him and rolled away from the light.

"Fortuity?"

"Take it away," she bit out with a short hitching sob. "It is not my story—but yours."

"What?" He turned the leather-bound book and read the gold lettering beneath the title she had so carefully chosen: *Written by Lord Matthew Ravenglass*. Hands trembling, he opened the cover to the title page, then bared his teeth. It also stated he was the author. "I shall go to the publisher this very moment and have this heinous oversight corrected. All copies will be pulled and reprinted. I swear it."

"It does not matter," she said in a despondent whisper. "Dreams are for children." She buried her face in her pillow and wailed with heartbreaking fury.

"Fortuity—" He touched her shoulder, but she shrugged him away.

"Just go, Matthew. Leave me and never return. You heap sorrow upon me from every direction."

"I did not do this, Fortuity. Surely you know that."

She rolled to the edge of the bed, grabbed the basin off the table, and retched into it. Sobbing as she finished heaving, she shook her head. "Leave me! Now!"

"I will fix this," he swore as he backed toward the door. "I promise you."

"Get out!" Her agony-filled shriek ripped through him.

"What in heaven's name—" Mrs. Greer charged into the room, then hurried to the side of the bed. "Bless my dear lady. Bless your poor, aching soul." She gave Matthew an angry scowl, then glared at the door, giving him a clear and urgent dismissal.

He tore out of the room, realizing too late that his coat remained behind. "Ablesby!"

"Yes, my lord?" The valet stepped out into the hallway from Matthew's adjoining dressing room.

"I need a coat. I am going out immediately."

"Right away, my lord."

Ablesby dashed back into the dressing room and quickly reappeared with the items needed. "Here you are, my lord. Do you require your cloak? The day has become considerably warmer."

"No. My frustration will keep me heated enough, thank you." Matthew dashed back down the stairs, bellowing, "Thebson! Thomas! My coach! Immediately!"

He would make this right for Fortuity even if he had to throttle A.K. Newman with his bare hands. How on earth had they made such a grave error when only Fortuity's name had been on everything submitted? He found it inconceivable.

"Thomas and Mr. Turnmaster shall be around with the coach momentarily, my lord," Thebson said as he offered Matthew his hat and gloves. "Mr. Turnmaster prepared it when informed of her ladyship's illness in case additional help was needed. I do hope our lady has not taken a turn for the worse?"

Matthew found reassurance in the butler's genuine concern. "She is not well, Thebson, not well at all, but it is my intention to get things sorted, so she will soon feel better."

"I indeed hope so, my lord. Godspeed to you."

Thomas the footman burst in through the front door, then came up short and tried to adopt a composed demeanor. "Beg pardon, my lord. Carriage is ready. Mr. Turnmaster wasted no time."

"Indeed, he did not." Matthew followed the footman out and climbed into the carriage.

"Where to, my lord?" Mr. Turnmaster asked.

"Thirty-three Leadenhall Street, and make haste as much as possible in this London traffic," Matthew replied. Perhaps he should've ridden his horse rather than bothered with the carriage. Damn this sorry day. It had turned him into a mindless fool.

"'Twill be done, my lord."

As the carriage lurched into motion, Matthew stared down at the book, still unable to believe the error. Fortuity's abject disappointment and heartbreak played over and over in his mind. *Gads alive!* Why the devil had he not unwrapped the bloody thing and looked at it before carrying it up to her? "I am the greatest sort of idiot."

All he had wanted to do was make her feel better and share in her joy when she realized her dream. But instead, he had broken her heart and torn her soul asunder. He had absolutely crushed her. "This will be made right," he said with a low growl as he stared out the window. "This is *her* book, and all shall know it."

The ride through the crowded London streets seemed interminable. When they finally reached Minerva Press, Matthew leapt from the coach before it rolled to a complete stop and marched into the establishment, letting the door bang shut behind him.

"Might I be helping you, sir?" asked the startled clerk from behind the counter.

"Lord Ravenglass to see Mr. Newman. Immediately."

"I... Uhm... Yes. I see. One moment, my lord." The lad bobbed a polite nod, then rushed down a narrow hallway to the right of the counter.

Matthew rocked up onto the balls of his feet as if preparing to spar at Gentleman Jackson's club. He felt like sparring and would not regret doing so if he did not get satisfaction regarding the reprinting of the book.

"Lord Ravenglass." Arthur King Newman, the partner who

had taken over upon the retirement of William Lane, the founder of Minerva Press in 1773, hurried to open the swinging door that led to the hallway beside the counter. "Do come back to my office, my lord. My clerk seems to think something is amiss. Surely he is incorrect."

"He is not incorrect," Matthew said as he charged down the hall and into the only office walled off from the printing and binding operations. He paused long enough to allow Newman to close the door, then charged toward him brandishing the misprinted book. "Would you care to explain why I am listed as the author of this work, and my wife is not?"

"I beg your pardon, my lord?" The gentleman appeared not only confused but thoroughly shocked. He dodged to one side, caught hold of the book, and backed away with it clutched to his chest. "Forgive me, but did she not apprise you of her decision?"

"*Her* decision?"

The publisher tapped on the book's cover. "She requested that you be listed as the author, so a wider range of readers would accept the book. Quite a wise marketing decision, if you ask me. Upon reading her letter, I heartily agreed, and ensured that the change was made before the copies went to print."

Matthew stared at the man, his roiling emotions making it difficult to fully comprehend what the publisher claimed. "Lady Ravenglass asked that her name be removed and rather than state the author as anonymous, she requested you use *my* name?"

Newman nodded but remained close to the door. He looked ready to make a hasty exit to save his sorry hide.

Cowardice rolled off the man in steady waves, but Matthew sensed he was telling the truth. Newman was too afraid to lie—a wise decision on his part.

"Show me this letter," Matthew said through clenched teeth.

"Of course, my lord." Newman sidled his way along the wall of the small room, ensuring he faced Matthew at all times until he was behind his desk. While shooting quick, nervous glances Matthew's way, he opened the top drawer of the tall cabinet in the corner and removed a folder. He placed it on his desk, then backed away and nodded at it. "It is the most recent document, my lord. There to the front."

What a bloody coward. Matthew opened the file and stared down at the letter written on Fortuity's favorite stationery. He read it, then flipped it over. What a poor fraud, but it had served its nefarious purpose. Not only was it not written in Fortuity's hand, but neither did it bear her former Broadmere seal nor the Ravenglass seal, which his beloved wife always took great pride in using, rather than simply tucking a letter within its own folds and sealing it with a plain wax wafer.

He tossed the forgery back onto the desk. "My wife did not write that letter."

Newman's coloring diminished considerably, and he appeared to clutch the book tightly to his chest. "Are you quite certain, my lord?" Perhaps she simply wished to surprise you."

Matthew slammed his fist on top of the offensive paper. "That is not her hand. Compare it to the manuscript, you bloody oaf, and see it with your own eyes."

The man opened and closed his mouth like a fish yanked from the water. He alternately stared at the letter on the desk, then eyed Matthew.

"Do it, man!" Ready to lunge over the desk and shake the fool until his teeth rattled loose, Matthew fought for control as he pounded his fist on the letter again. "See for your bloody self."

Newman hurried to nod and turned back to the same cabinet, opening the bottom drawer this time and drawing out a thick sheaf of papers tied together with the same sort of twine that had sealed the parcel bearing the completed copy of the book. He cut away the strings, shuffled through a few of the sheets, and studied them alongside the fake letter. "It appears you are quite correct, my lord," he said quietly before looking up and adding, "I am so very sorry."

"Repair this." Teetering on the brink of uncontrollable rage, Matthew bared his teeth. "Immediately."

The publisher lifted his trembling hands with a pitiful shrug. "How, my lord? Copies were delivered to libraries and every bookshop in London and beyond earlier this week. Your copy was inadvertently sent late, and for that, I most heartily apologize. Some have surely already found their way into reader's hands." He sadly shook his head. "I fear the damage is done. If we were to attempt to collect every copy sent out, reprint the book, and reissue it, word of the cruel scheme would get out and be the talk of the *ton*, possibly causing your wife's future works irreparable harm. All we can do now to save her reputation as a talented writer is claim this book was a marketing ploy to introduce her work without the bias against female authors overshadowing it."

Matthew sagged down into the nearest chair and dropped his head into his hands. Heaven help him, what a bloody mess. The soundness of Newman's logic was not lost on him, but how in the devil would he ever explain it to his beloved Fortuity? Eleanor and Olandra's escapades had already worn her patience and good nature to the snapping point—made her physically ill, in fact. He lifted his head and glared at that damnable letter. There was only one individual who could have done this. He rose from the chair, picked up the forgery, and studied it one last time before folding it and tucking it away inside his waistcoat.

With a glare he knew would terrorize the publisher, he said, "In future, all of my wife's books shall bear her name: *Lady Fortuity Abarough Ravenglass*. Is that understood?"

Newman nodded. "Understood, my lord. And if perchance any letters are received requesting changes, no changes will be made before personally confirming the adjustments with yourself and your wife."

"Very good, Mr. Newman." Without waiting for additional pleasantries from the publisher, Matthew charged out of the office and into his coach. "Home, Mr. Turnmaster, and once there, keep the carriage ready. We will have need of it within the hour."

"As you wish, my lord."

As soon as they reached the townhouse, Matthew loped up the steps and headed straight for his office, not pausing for a word to any servants or animals. Rage had his blood roaring in his ears. The closer he drew to the proof he sought and intended to use for sentencing the culprit, the harder his heart pounded.

He yanked open the bottom drawer of his desk, dug through an orderly stack of letters, then selected one of them and spread it open in front of him. He pulled out the letter that had been sent to the publisher and compared the two. Just as he'd thought. The handwriting was, without a doubt, the same.

Rather than bellow with rage and shatter the quiet of the townhouse, he yanked on the bellpull, then returned to his chair behind his desk.

Thebson appeared at the doorway almost immediately. "Yes, my lord?"

"Escort Miss Sykesbury to my office. Immediately." Matthew fisted his hands so tightly that his knuckles popped. "And inform her maid to pack her belongings, under the supervision of one our maids. Miss Sykesbury will depart for Bombay on the East India Company's next ship. Hastings owes me a favor." He scratched out a quick note on his formal stationery, sealed it with the Ravenglass insignia, and gave it to the butler. "Have Thomas deliver this to their port office at once."

Thebson nodded. "Yes, my lord."

Matthew leaned back in his chair, grazing his fingertips across the stubble of his chin as he glared at the closed office door. His cousin Agnus would not be pleased, but so be it. It was time her daughter Eleanor reaped what she sowed and returned to where he should have left her when she had written requesting sanctuary from the marriage her father's family had arranged. The Sykesburys could bloody well have their granddaughter back now to do with whatever they wished. May God have mercy on their souls and shield them from Eleanor's evil.

Eleanor burst into his office without knocking, the color

riding high on her cheeks. "What has come over you, cousin? I am not returning to Bombay."

He glared at her, knowing that his silent scowl would infuriate her even more.

"You promised Mama to help me find a husband here in London."

"And how have you thanked me for that courtesy, Eleanor? How have you shown your appreciation for your rescue not only from my enraged parish in the country but also from India?"

She tossed her dark head and squared her shoulders, scowling at him as if sizing him up for battle.

Good. He was ready for a battle.

"Mama and I have expressed our gratitude many times," she said while jutting her chin higher.

"Yes. I suppose you have." He leaned forward. "You placed me in a compromising situation with a dear lady that ended in a marriage she is still attempting to adjust to. You sell information to the gossip sheets to make her adjustment to the marriage even more difficult, and then you ruin her lifelong dream by forging a letter to her publisher and changing the authorship of her book. Your definition of gratitude needs correcting, dear cousin, and correct it I bloody well shall."

Eyes flashing with hatred, her lovely mouth curled into an ugly sneer. "I meant for you to use that *compromising situation* to force the Duke of Broadmere to marry me, you fool! But instead, you leg-shackled yourself as meekly as a lamb led to the slaughter." She stormed closer. "Have you no cunning? No sense of survival? Not only could you have been rid of me and my spineless mother, but you could have remained a bachelor to bed whomever you wished."

"I consider the duke a friend. Never would I have saddled him with the likes of you."

She shook with rage, fisting her hands at her sides. "I am not going back to India."

"You will either go willingly, as a free woman to the

Sykesburys of Bombay, or you will go in shackles as a prisoner charged with forgery and whatever else I decide the authorities might find interesting."

"You cannot do this to me."

"I already have."

Tears welled in her eyes and overflowed, streaming down her cheeks. "This will kill Mama. You know that. You know how much she loves me. She would never wish me trapped in a marriage so far from her."

"She will either overcome it or die with it. The choice is hers, and I am certain her new husband will help her rise above her turmoil." He slowly rose out of his chair but kept the desk between them for her protection. "Did you truly believe I would allow you to continue your torment of my beloved wife?"

"You do not love her. You said so yourself. Said she was nothing but a friend." She dove toward the desk and tried to grab the proof of her forgery, but he snatched it out of her reach. "We are blood, you and I," she sobbed. "You cannot do this to me."

"As far as I am concerned, my only family is Fortuity and our future children." He yanked on the bellpull.

Thebson and Thomas both came to the door.

"Ask Mr. Turnmaster to deliver Miss Sykesbury and her maid to the port. Thomas, you go along and assist him. If Miss Sykesbury does not behave like a genteel lady and go willingly, hand her over to the authorities and ask them to come and speak with me." Matthew put the letters in his center desk drawer and locked it.

"Come along now, miss," Thebson said.

Young Thomas stood beside him, looking ready to drag her away if need be.

Eleanor stood taller and fixed Matthew with a haughty glare. "I will never forgive you for this."

"I can live with that." He waved her away. "Godspeed to you, cousin."

Chapter Fourteen

STANDING IN THE doorway, Matthew watched the carriage carry Eleanor away. He should have done this long ago. In fact, he should never have enabled the wicked woman into his home in the first place.

After blowing out a heavy sigh, he went back inside, ambled through the entry hall, and eyed the staircase. Fortuity needed to be told about the forgery and Eleanor's departure. While he hoped the latter would bring her some comfort, he knew in his heart that the ruination of what should have been the joyous occasion of her publishing debut would take quite some time for her to get over. Especially since her name would not grace a cover or title page until her next book.

Mrs. Greer appeared at the top of the stairs, her usually cheerful demeanor darker and sadder than he had ever seen it. Alarm shot through him, making him rush to meet her. "Pray, do not tell me her condition has worsened?"

The usually jolly matron avoided his gaze and wet her mouth as if struggling to coax the words free. "Nothing has happened to her ladyship, my lord. She is much better, in fact."

"But?"

"It would be better if you spoke to her."

"You say she is *better*. Is she fully recovered?"

"The herbal I blended has lessened her megrim greatly." The housekeeper kept her eyes downcast. "I must hie myself to my apothecary now and blend some more for when she may next need it. Excuse me, my lord."

An ominous thrum of dread filled him, growing stronger with every step he took toward their private suite. As soon as he opened the door, his heart fell.

Anne was checking the straps on a pair of trunks. When she looked up and set eyes on him, she backed away and curtsied. "My lord."

"What is going on here?" he asked, forcing himself to speak in a quiet, reasonable tone.

"I am going to stay with Blessing." Fortuity stepped into the room. Dark shadows, purplish black smudges of unwellness, plagued her troubled eyes, and her pallor concerned him. "It is for the best," she added softly, as if that explained everything and made it all right.

She was leaving him. Everything had become too much for her.

"Please stay," he whispered.

"Do not make this more difficult, Matthew, I beg you."

Anguish moved him a step closer. He had to make her understand. "It was Eleanor who put my name on your book. She forged a letter to your publisher, writing it as if it were you." He yanked the thing out of his pocket that he'd retrieved from his desk and held it for her to take. "I have sent her back to Bombay. She will never torment us again."

Fortuity glanced at the letter in his hand but didn't move to take it. "I see." She turned to Anne as if the movement pained her. "Do we have everything packed?"

The maid nodded, then edged back toward the bedroom. "I shall check for anything we may have overlooked."

"Thank you." Fortuity watched her leave them as if wishing she could follow.

"You do not have to go now," Matthew insisted, drawing her attention back to him. He shook the paper and stepped even closer. "Look at this letter. You will see. If you wish, I shall take you to Mr. Newman so he can assure you this will never happen again. He promised that any future last-minute adjustments would be personally confirmed with you."

She shifted with a heavy sigh and touched her forehead. "I notice you did not mention the recovery and correction of the books, so I must surmise that is not going to happen."

"Mr. Newman fears it would trigger gossip about Eleanor's scheme and harm your reputation as a writer. It could cast a pall over your future books, one they might not be able to overcome."

She huffed a sad laugh while still rubbing her head. "There will be no future books, Matthew. I am done. With everything. Writing. Marriage. The *ton*. I shall help my sisters with their offspring and find comfort in their joy."

Dread closed icy fingers around his heart and squeezed until his blood pounded in his ears. "You cannot do this, Fortuity. Please do not leave me. I beg you."

"I must, Matthew. But do not worry about any gossip. Everyone will be told I am helping my sister during her confinement. I will do nothing to draw any additional speculation down upon the Ravenglass name. After Blessing's confinement ends, I shall think of another lie to feed to the *ton*."

"Hang the gossip and the speculation." He closed the remaining distance between them, dismayed when she took a step back to avoid his touch. "Please, Fortuity. I know this has been difficult, but surely you know that none of this is my fault? None of it was of my doing."

The sadness and resignation in her eyes cut off his ability to breathe. She moved to the bedroom door and called out to Anne, "Please fetch my shawl. I wish to be on our way."

"Yes, my lady."

"Fortuity." He shook his head and held out both hands. "Why are you doing this?"

"I need peace," she said, her strained whisper crackling with emotion. "And while nothing is directly your fault, everything has to do with you." She shrugged. "Perhaps we are cursed to be star-crossed lovers. I do not know. All I know for certain is I need peace for my own survival." Her sad smile cut through him. "I have always been a creature of the shadows, a wallflower content to hide among the draperies and watch the lives of others. Becoming the tongue waggers' focus has made me unwell. I am done, Matthew. This is the only way I know of to fight back and save my sanity."

"By running and hiding."

She accepted her shawl from Anne and draped it around her shoulders before meeting his gaze. "Yes. By running and hiding."

As she walked past him, he caught her arm and pulled her close. "I cannot live without you," he rasped, staring into her eyes and willing her to feel his pain. "You are…everything to me."

She turned her face away. "I must do this."

"At least promise me it is not permanent," he begged. "Promise me you will consider coming back once you are better." Desperation overwhelmed him. She could not toss him aside, not after all they had shared. "What if you carry our child?"

She squinted at him the way she had when the light hurt her eyes. "I do not carry our child." She gently but firmly pulled free and hurried from the room. Anne rushed to follow her.

Bernard, one of the lesser footmen, waited at the door to collect the trunk. "My lord?"

Matthew stepped aside and waved him in without a word. He grappled with the choices of throwing back his head and roaring, and rushing downstairs, grabbing her up, and locking her in their rooms until she promised to stay. But then she would hate him for failing to understand her need to remove herself from the storm for a while. At least, he prayed it was for a little while. He would do everything in his power to get her to come back home, to be his wife, and grant him all the rest of her days to prove to her how much he loved her.

"Tutie, I am so very sorry." Propped in bed amid a multitude of pillows, Blessing stretched out her open arms. "Come here, my poor, brokenhearted pet."

Fortuity tried not to crumple into a weepy mess but failed. She clambered onto the bed and dove into her sister's embrace, clinging like a drowning soul adrift in a stormy sea. "Everything is so awful," she wailed between jags of hard sobbing.

"I know." Blessing stroked her hair and gently rocked from side to side, as she had often done when they were children, and nightmares or thunder had frightened Fortuity.

"Mama would be so ashamed of me." Fortuity sniffed while pressing the back of her hand to her infernal nose that insisted on dribbling whenever she cried. "Do you happen to have a handkerchief?"

"Here, pet." Blessing fished a square of linen out from among the pillows and pushed it into her sister's hands. "And Mama would not be ashamed of you. She taught us to do whatever was required for our own wellbeing. You needed an escape, and from what little you have told me, that is perfectly understandable."

Fortuity pushed herself up from Blessing's embrace and blew her nose with a very unladylike snort. "The problem is Matthew did not actually *do* any of those horrible things. They simply evolved from those two awful women from his past determined to use him for their own selfish means." She hiccupped a shuddering breath and dissolved into more tears. "He kept asking me to ignore them and all the humiliation they caused, but I just couldn't anymore. I just couldn't. And he simply couldn't understand that no matter where I went, the stares and whispers followed." She noticed her ink-stained fingers and mourned her broken dream with another high-pitched howl. "And his name is on *my* book. Everyone will think he wrote it."

"Your name will be on the next book," Blessing said, speaking louder to drown out Fortuity's wails.

"There will be no next book. That dream is gone." Fortuity scooted back against the headboard and hugged her knees. "I am going to find a hole to crawl into and never emerge again."

"I see." Blessing rocked from side to side while flailing her arms among the pillows. "Give a whale a hand, will you? My bum is sore from sitting like this. I need a bit of a shift."

"Forgive me, Essie." Fortuity helped her sister move to a different position and rearranged the pillows to support her better. "Here you are, as miserable as can be, and I have shown up on your doorstep a whimpering ninny."

"I told you to come here anytime." Blessing huffed out a groan, then wiggled and flexed her back again. "No. This will not do either. Help me to my feet. I shall walk the floor a while."

Clambering off the bed, Fortuity grabbed her sister's hands and pulled. After much grunting and scooting, she leveraged Blessing to a standing position. Her sister's state of unrest made her forget her own misery. "Is the baby coming, perhaps? Remember what Papa said about how Mama got when Merry was born?"

Blessing waved away the possibility and waddled over to the window. "I am not really in pain. It is simply difficult to find a comfortable position in which I can breathe and not be all achy." She wrinkled her nose. "The accoucheur was quite detailed about what sort of agony to expect." She shuddered. "He also described the mess that comes when my waters let go. The monthly nurse was also unpleasantly specific when she visited for us to get acquainted."

"I should not have come here to burden you. I should have been staunch and courageous like you and Mama and stuck it out." Fortuity unleashed a despondent sigh. If she told Anne to repack everything she was currently unpacking, the poor maid would probably think her mad. "What is wrong with me?"

Blessing frowned at her. "You have never been the hysterical sort before. Is it possible you are with child?"

"No. I got my courses last week."

Blessing waddled closer and peered at her with sisterly concern. "Is that yet another thing upsetting you? You realize it sometimes takes time to be blessed with a baby?"

Fortuity pulled in a deep breath and held it to the count of five, reminding herself not to be curt. None of this was Blessing's fault, and her sister had always been there whenever she needed her. She counted off on her fingers as she clarified why she was so unbearably overset. "Eleanor's defiance and betrayal in my own home upsets me. Olandra's greedy determination and blatantly obvious maneuvering to get Matthew into her bed upsets me. Matthew's inability to comprehend how I could possibly be ill at ease about either of those bloody hedge whores upsets me most of all." Fortuity threw up her hands, then clutched her fists to her chest. "And *my* book, the heart of my dreams, does not bear *my* name! *That* infuriates and saddens me beyond all comprehension."

With a thoughtful nod, Blessing returned to her slow waddling around the room. "Well, then. We are clear now on what has upset you." She rubbed her lower back as she walked. "The question is: what do you intend to do about those things?"

"The devil if I know." Fortuity settled onto the cushioned bench at the foot of the bed. She rubbed her tired, gritty eyes that burned from too much crying. "Matthew was overwrought about my leaving."

"Well, that is a good thing." Blessing took another lap, then paused and gazed out the window overlooking the street below. "He is also sitting outside in his carriage." She propped her hands on the sill and leaned forward, squinting. "Or, at least, I believe that is him. Did you not send your coach back to the townhouse?"

Fortuity joined her at the window. "I did." She eyed the vehicle parked across the street from the Knightwood residence. "That is either him or one of the servants." A frustrated snort escaped her as she shook her head. "Gossip is one of the things that chased me out of my own home. Is he trying to create even more exciting morsels for the tongue-tattlers to gobble up?"

With her hands still planted on the ledge of the windowsill, Blessing rocked back, groaning quietly as she stretched. "The tongue-tattlers will simply think you and he came to welcome the baby."

Fortuity tore her gaze from the carriage below and eyed her sister more closely. "Is it time to send for the accoucheur and his nurse?"

Blessing bowed her head and rocked in place, stretching her back again. "Quite possibly."

"Get back in bed." Fortuity took hold of her sister's arm and gently tugged.

"I will not." Blessing smacked her away. "When I lean like this and stretch, it eases the pain in my lower back."

"I thought you said you were not in pain?" Panic rising, Fortuity rushed to the door and yanked on the bellpull several times to summon the entire household, if need be. "You said there was no pain."

"It is an ache. A sort of cramping, not *pain*, exactly." Blessing scowled at her. "When did you become such a nervous, flighty creature? Stop it, this minute. We come from a large family of strong women. Act like it."

Fortuity bit her tongue to keep from calling her sister a snappish little chit. Blessing was about to give birth. She had every right to be more fractious and overbearing than usual. Fortuity yanked on the bellpull again. "Did you give all your staff the day off?"

Meggie, Blessing's lady's maid, rushed in from the adjoining dressing room. "Yes, my lady? Are you all right?"

"It might be time," Blessing said with another groan, "to send for the accoucheur. Do not alert Lord Knightwood just yet. I believe he had meetings all day, and there is no reason to interrupt him until we know for certain that little Starpeeper has decided that today is the day to meet us."

"Yes, my lady." Meggie paused in the doorway. "Is there anything else you desire that might bring you comfort while I do as you ask?"

"My sister is here." Blessing smiled at Fortuity, making her worry that she might not be up to the task. "She will take excellent care of me until you return."

"Very good, my lady." The maid rushed off to do her mistress's bidding.

Fortuity fell in step beside her sister, and they returned to pacing the circumference of the room. "You realize I was only four years old and toddled alongside Mama when she gave us Merry. There is little else I know to do?"

"Talk to me," Blessing said. "Keep me from worrying."

"And what shall we speak of?"

"Whether you shall return to your husband or crawl into that hole you mentioned earlier and live out your life as some sort of burrowing animal."

"You think I am being oversensitive. That I have overreacted."

"I did not say that."

"You did not have to."

"Be that as it may..." Blessing paused, clamped her mouth tightly shut, and squeezed Fortuity's hand with an impressive amount of strength.

Fortuity watched her, praying the babe wouldn't drop out and land on the floor between her sister's feet. "Should you not return to your bed?"

"I do not want to be in that bed!"

"Fine. I was simply concerned about my new little niece or nephew landing on their head between your feet."

Blessing gave her a murderous glare. "I will know when the babe is coming out."

"I would hope so." Fortuity wrapped an arm around her sister and helped her continue pacing. "I still say you think I overreacted."

Blessing rolled her eyes and shook her head. "Since you failed to assault, poison, or murder the two hedge whores or your husband, you did not overreact." She caught hold of the bedpost, bent forward, and stretched as she had done at the windowsill. "Why does my lower back hurt so? Should the pain not be confined to where the child comes out?"

"You are asking the wrong person, as I have neither had a child nor done any research on the birthing process." On impulse, Fortuity balled up her fists and rubbed her sister's back, working her knuckles hard into Blessing's poor, knotted muscles. "Is that better or worse?"

Blessing rumbled with a long, low groan. "You are an angel, and may live here forever if you wish."

"I shall take that as a positive sign that this helps." Fortuity continued massaging until Blessing straightened and started pacing again.

"Save your strength for the next pain," she said. "Now tell me, what do you intend to do, since you appear to be second-guessing your hasty departure from your home?"

"I don't know. Pride forbids me to return the same day I left, doesn't it?"

"Pride can be a very troublesome thing in a marriage." Blessing stretched from side to side while resting her hands on her hips. "I have done the research on that."

"What are you suggesting?" Fortuity glanced back at the bedroom door, wishing that someone who knew what to do during this delicate situation would show up to help.

"When the troops arrive to help me relocate little Starpeeper from my belly to my arms, go down there and talk to your husband." She tapped on the windowpane. "He is standing outside the carriage now, looking much like a puppy that has been kicked out of the house for chewing on the furniture."

Fortuity blew out a groaning huff as she went to the window and looked for herself. There he was. Hat in hand. Standing beside the coach with such a mournful expression one would think he had just been widowed. "Oh dear heavens. Have you ever seen anything more pitiful?"

"Yes," Blessing said. "You."

Fortuity narrowed her eyes. "You will not be bringing forth this child forever, dear sister, and I have a very long memory when it comes to insults."

Blessing smiled. "That sounds better. It is about time my brave sister who fights for what she wants returned. Now go down there and drag your fool of a husband either into the carriage or our sitting room so the two of you can have a conversation without the world watching."

"I shall go down there when your people arrive. You should not be left alone at a time like this."

"Lady Knightwood, do be good enough to return to your bed," said a bespectacled man as he breezed into the room without knocking.

A brusque woman dressed in black marched around him and took hold of Blessing's arm. "Allow me to help you, my lady."

"She does not wish to be in the bed," Fortuity said while holding her sister's other arm. "Walking has given her some ease."

Both the accoucheur and the nurse glared at her as if shocked she had contradicted them.

Blessing yanked her arm free of the nurse's hold and patted Fortuity. "Go to your task, pet. I can handle these two."

"Are you certain?" Fortuity eyed the gentleman and his nurse, ready to defend her sister's wants if need be. That was the way of sisters. They picked and fussed at each other, but if an outsider threatened one of them, they banded together until the bitter end.

Through another strained groan, Blessing managed a graceful nod and an evil wink.

"Very well, then," Fortuity told her as she made her way to the door. "I shall attend to my business and wait for the delightful announcement of your precious Starpeeper's arrival."

"Starpeeper?" the stern-faced nurse repeated. "Is that to be the child's name?"

"If I wish it," Blessing said with a warning growl as she returned to waddling around the room.

Fortuity held her breath to keep from laughing as she went into the hallway. The accoucheur and his nurse had no idea whom they were dealing with. But then a somber thought about the dangerous task ahead made her turn back, open the door, and call out, "I love you, Essie."

"I love you, Tutie." Blessing blew her a kiss and waved her onward.

Fortuity softly closed the door, then bowed her head while still holding tightly to the latch. "Please keep her and the babe safe," she quietly prayed. Then she stepped away and hurried down the hallway, meeting an army of maids bearing extra linens, steaming kettles, and additional basins.

As she descended the stairs, she dodged innumerable cats and wondered how they would get along with the newest addition to the family. Thorne's mother—little Starpeeper's soon-to-be grandmother, Lady Roslynn—loved her kitties and had fostered a deep adoration of them in Blessing as well. Fortuity laughed softly, and now four former Knightwood felines resided at Ravenglass. It appeared that Lady Roslynn and her ever-expanding cat army were taking over the world—or, at the very least, London.

When she reached the bottom of the stairs, Fortuity noticed Cadwick standing beside the front door, peering out the tall, narrow window beside it.

"Is he still out there?" she asked the butler.

The poor man jumped and faced her with a startled clearing of his throat. "Lord Ravenglass appears to be waiting on the other side of the street, my lady."

"Very good. I shall fetch him."

"Do you require your parasol or hat, my lady? Or perhaps a shawl?"

"No, thank you. I will be returning with him posthaste."

The butler bowed, then opened the door for her.

Not giving a whit that she'd not donned her gloves or any of the socially expected accessories when one stepped outside the house, Fortuity caught up her skirts and darted down the steps and across the street as if she were a young girl running through a field of wildflowers.

Matthew stared at her with his mouth ajar and his dark brows ratcheting ever higher. "Fortuity?"

After a quick glance to ensure they were alone on the street, she faked a smile just in case someone watched from the windows and hooked her arm through his. "You must come inside this instant. What in heaven's name do you think you are doing out here?"

He remained rooted to the spot with the strength of the cantankerous mule that had lived at the Broadmere country manor when she was a child. "I intend to sit out here until you come home."

"Come inside," she said through clenched teeth, the forced smile making her cheeks ache. "And we shall discuss it." Thankfully, that got him moving, but his stormy expression remained. "And the baby is coming. So, we shall be here until little Starpeeper arrives."

"I noticed the gentleman and a rather somber woman had arrived, and prayed nothing was wrong."

"I hope nothing goes wrong." Fortuity kept hold of his arm as they climbed the front steps and entered the wide front door together. "Babies are a joy, but it is a dangerous time for both the mother and the child."

She led him into the parlor, then released him. "Thorne has yet to return from wherever his meetings were held, but I am sure once he arrives, he will be most grateful to find you here for support."

"I am here for you." His steely gaze captured her, making her catch her breath. "I cannot bear Ravenglass Townhouse without you in it, and I am not the only one. When I left, Ignatius was howling, and two of those infernal cats were roaming the hauls caterwauling at the top of their lungs."

After a yank of the bellpull, she nervously paced closer to the door to watch for Cadwick. "It sounds as if the only reason you wish me to return is for peace and quiet."

"You know better than that."

Cadwick appeared with impeccable timing. "Yes, my lady?"

"Tea, please, and brandy."

The butler nodded and disappeared.

Stoking her courage, she faced her unhappy husband, her precious Matthew. "I did not leave to torment you or the animals. The thievery of my book was the tipping point. I had to escape for a little while. Speak to someone who would hear me as I needed to be heard."

He resettled his footing and dropped his gaze, looking well and truly ashamed. "I am sorry that I was not more understanding about the pain and torment of the gossip." He rolled his shoulders in a frustrated shrug. "Men do not worry so much about the tongue waggers, or at least, I never have. But Mrs. Greer helped me realize how different it is for ladies."

Fortuity couldn't help but smile. "Are you all right?"

"I beg your pardon?"

"Mrs. Greer's explanations can sometimes be fierce."

He scrubbed his jaw while squinting one eye shut. "Let us just say it was very enlightening." He deflated with a heavy sigh. "And then the book—damn and blast it all, Fortuity. I will never forgive myself for allowing that conniving chit to hurt you that way."

"But you sent Eleanor away, yes?" She had been so upset and her head had still pounded, so she wasn't sure if that was what he had told her or if it was merely her own wishful thinking.

"Back to her father's family in Bombay. The only way she will ever return to England is if they ship her back or she marries someone rich enough to bring her here. I have washed my hands of her and notified Agnus of that fact as well."

Fortuity found herself breathing easier. "Good." She ached to run into his arms, but just couldn't bring herself to do so. Granted, she had *somewhat* overreacted by fleeing, but he had as much as patted her on the head and told her to stop being so silly about Eleanor and Olandra. At least now he realized that her issues with Eleanor were well founded. Battling with her pride and stubbornness, she stared at the floor, not entirely sure what else to say.

"I know this book cannot be changed, but future—"

She turned away and held up a hand to interrupt him. "I am not entirely certain there will be any future books." That disappointment was still too fresh, too raw.

"I love your stories, Fortuity. They give me a glimpse into your soul. Even if you decide never to publish again, will you please continue writing them for me?"

A lump of emotions made her throat ache. She swallowed hard to be rid of it. Still not facing him, she kept her gaze locked on the floor. "I cannot promise that."

The heat of him behind her made her close her eyes and breathe in his nearness. *Please hold me,* her heart begged, but she bit her lip to keep the words inside. There was still the matter of Olandra. Would he continue to think her silly about that too?

"I love you, Fortuity," he whispered, "and I will never brush off your worries or take your uneasiness about anything lightly ever again. I swear it. Please come home."

She couldn't bear it any longer. Whirling about, she wrapped her arms around his neck and held on tight. "I love you too, Matthew. I am so very sorry for this uproar."

He crushed her closer and buried his face against her neck. "Thank God Almighty," he said in a rasping whisper. "I feared I had lost you."

"No!" Thorne gave an anguished cry from the parlor's doorway. "My Blessing? Our babe?"

Chapter Fifteen

"Thorne, no!" Fortuity sprang away from Matthew. "Last I saw her, Blessing was growling at the nurse and accoucheur, and little Starpeeper was causing her a great deal of discomfort, as is expected."

"Praise God Almighty." Thorne sagged against the door.

"Forgive us for giving you such a fright," Matthew said, regretting his friend's sudden pallor. He offered Fortuity an apologetic smile. "I was a fool and nearly lost my precious wife. But thankfully, she has granted me a second chance to do better."

Thorne gave him a damning look as he straightened and entered the parlor. "Yes. My wife made mention of Fortuity's unhappiness over the past few weeks. Several times, in fact. Consider yourself lucky, old man. The only thing that kept her from storming Ravenglass Townhouse and boxing your ears was her unwieldy condition. These Broadmere sisters protect one another fiercely."

Matthew hugged Fortuity to his side, needing the feel of her against him. Breathing her in and relaxing in the warm, familiar sweetness of her lilac scent, he couldn't resist pressing a kiss to her temple. "You have no idea how lucky I consider myself, and I will not make the same mistake again."

Cadwick and a footman entered with tea, a decanter of brandy, and an additional decanter of spirits and glasses. "My lord," the butler said to Thorne, "I took the liberty of bringing your favorite port as well. I thought you might require it under the circumstances."

"Well done, Cadwick." Nervously pacing the room, Thorne kept glancing at the ceiling. "How long do these things usually take?" he asked Fortuity.

Matthew also wanted to know, since he sincerely hoped to be in the same situation as Thorne one day in the near future. "Yes, with so many siblings, do you remember?"

Fortuity caught the corner of her bottom lip between her teeth and shrugged. "I am afraid I cannot recall. Merry is the youngest, and I was only four years old when she came along. I vaguely remember all of us walking with Mama round and round her bedchamber, but then the midwife shooed us out, and we sat with Papa in the parlor. Seri or Chance would know better than I. They were six and seven at the time."

"Good heavens," Matthew said, "I never realized the lot of you are like stair steps, one right after the other."

"Yes. Each of us is only a year apart from the next one."

As an only child, Matthew couldn't imagine a house filled with so many children at the same time. His parents had despised each other so much that once his mother had fulfilled the requirement of producing an heir, they had rarely occupied the same residence. "However long it takes, we shall stay and keep you company," he assured Thorne.

Fortuity poured a cup of tea, then paused with the teapot hovering over another cup and saucer. "Spirits or tea?"

"Not tea," Thorne said, "thank you."

"I shall pour for us, my love. Enjoy your tea." Matthew used the pair of glasses that the butler had so thoughtfully provided along with the decanters.

The way she smiled and meandered over to gaze out the window as she sipped her tea gave him pause.

"Excuse me, old man." He handed an overflowing glass of port to Thorne, then joined his wife at the window. "Fortuity? Are you all right? Are we not...better than we were?"

Frowning, she shifted with a deep inhale, then exhaled with a heavy sigh. "I worry for her," she whispered after stealing a glance back at Thorne, who was once again staring at the ceiling. "I sent up a quick prayer. Do you think the Almighty heard me?"

"I am sure He did." He brushed her golden curls back from her cheek and tucked them behind her ear. "We must hold fast to positive thoughts and look forward to meeting the newest little Knightwood. A house filled with love and light should greet the little one."

She smiled while looking out the window once more. "Little Starpeeper Knightwood. I shall miss that name whenever she or he is christened with a more appropriate one." She shifted and rested a hand on his chest, then started plucking at the folds of his cravat, a thing she did whenever struggling to find the proper words for whatever she wished to say. "After the baby's christening, might we go to the country manor house rather than wait until late June or July? The city tires me of late. I long for the quiet of the country."

"Is this about the continuing issue with the shameless Olandra or the debacle with your book that just entered the world?"

"Both, I suppose." She twitched an unhappy shrug. "Gossip is sure to heat up even more when the *ton* discovers you are an author of romance."

"If anyone inquires about my name on your book, I will simply tell them what Mr. Newman suggested."

"Which was?"

"We did it as a marketing ploy to avoid the bias against stories written by women. Once readers fall in love with your work, they won't care that you are a lady. They will simply want your next novel." He cupped her face in his hand, then slid his fingers deeper into the silkiness of her hair. "And I have an idea about how to deal with Olandra, if she insists upon sending more notes and publicly eyeing me like a jilted lover."

Hopefulness shone in Fortuity's eyes like a candle piercing the dreariest night. "What will you do?"

"It is a surprise, my love." He chuckled. "I am almost certain you will approve."

"I hear a multitude of thumps and slamming doors," Thorne complained while circling the parlor and scowling upward. "What in heaven's name is happening up there, and why is no one informing me of anything?"

"They are caring for your wife and child," Matthew said, then glanced at Fortuity to make sure he had the right of it. Her amused look and slight nod encouraged him. "As soon as anything is certain, someone will come and fetch you. At least"—he stole another look at Fortuity—"I would assume so."

"I am sure they will," she confirmed. "Their concern at the moment is Blessing and little Starpeeper."

"I suppose that makes sense." Thorne blew out a great gust of air, then drained his glass.

An enormous black-and-white cat traipsed into the parlor and took a seat in front of Thorne as if granting him a royal audience before sweeping the room with her bored, golden-eyed gaze and flipping her tail.

"The baby is coming, Hera," Thorne told the cat. "You cannot be in the room at the moment. Go to Mother's room and keep her company." He watched the cat amble off. "Perhaps I should speak with her and let her know what is happening. She hasn't been the same since her fall."

"Holding her grandchild will bring her around." At least, Matthew hoped it would. During his last visit, Lady Roslynn hadn't recalled who he was, and confusion had clouded her dancing eyes. But she always remembered the names of each of her many cats. That gave them all hope she would somehow regain her strength and her memory.

"Shall I help her into her chair and wheel her in here so she can wait with us?" Fortuity asked.

"Gads, no." Thorne gave a hard shake of his head. "Her maid accidentally rolled it over one of the cats' tails, and now Mother thinks it is the throne of Satan. It was all I could do to keep her from firing the poor woman over it."

"She loves her cats fiercely," Matthew said. "But does that not make her bedridden?"

"Occasionally, she allows our footman, Mr. Donnelly, to carry her into the garden or the parlor and settle her on a pillowed chair." He grinned. "Mr. Donnelly has a way with the ladies, and Mother is not immune to his charm."

A sudden flush of worried possessiveness made Matthew turn to Fortuity. "You are to have no dealings with Mr. Donnelly, wife. You are mine."

Her faint smile blossomed, and a rosy happiness colored her cheeks. "Mr. Donnelly could never hold a candle to you, husband."

"Good." He kissed her cheek, lingering a little longer to let her know he needed her ever so badly.

A baby's lusty wail filtered down to them, making them all go still.

Easing out into the hall, Thorne looked back at them and smiled. "Listen. Is that not a strong, healthy cry?"

"It is, indeed." Matthew caught Fortuity up in a tight hug. "We have a new little niece or nephew."

She squeezed him just as tightly, laughing. "Oh my goodness. Listen to that furious roar. Little Starpeeper wants all of London to know he or she is here."

Thorne nodded at the stairs. "Here comes Mrs. Hartcastle. She looks happy."

"Praise God Almighty," Fortuity said as she and Matthew joined him in the hall.

The housekeeper clapped her hands as she reached the bottom of the stairs. "You have a fine, healthy daughter, my lord. She and her ladyship are well and will be ready to see you momentarily. There's a bit of tidying up left to do."

"A daughter," Thorne repeated, looking suitably awestruck. "Little Starpeeper is a girl!"

Matthew clapped him on the back. "Congratulations, old

man! Well done, indeed."

"A little niece." Fortuity hugged her brother-in-law. "I cannot wait to meet her."

Mrs. Hartcastle started back up the stairs. "I shall fetch you all as soon as her ladyship is ready. She wanted everyone to know that all was well."

Grabbing hold of the banister, Thorne sagged down to sit on the steps and dropped his head into his hands.

"Help him," Fortuity whispered while nudging Matthew toward her brother-in-law.

Matthew hurried to sit beside his friend and wrapped an arm around his shoulders. "Are you all right, old man?"

Thorne lifted his head. "I was so afraid for her. So afraid I would lose her." He slowly shook his head, his voice cracking. "I am nothing without her. Blessing is my heart and soul."

Matthew looked up at Fortuity and locked eyes with her. "I understand completely, my friend. Fortuity is the same for me."

She caught her hands to her chest, and her eyes shone with the sheen of tears. Her reaction pleased him immensely. He needed her to know that he loved her more than life itself, more than anything in the world.

I love you, he mouthed.

I love you as well, she mouthed back.

He breathed easier now, and the throbbing tension in his shoulders eased. All would be well now. He refused to accept otherwise.

"SHE IS SO perfect," Fortuity whispered as she cuddled the babe closer. Dragging her gaze from the sleeping infant, she smiled at her sister. "And what is little Lady Starpeeper's official name, may I ask?"

With a weary yet happy sigh, Blessing tickled her daughter's chubby cheek, making the sweet cherub twitch and pucker the plump bow of her tiny pink lips. "Aurora Cassia. Aurora for the Roman goddess of the dawn who rides her chariot across the sky each morning announcing the arrival of the sun and proclaiming renewal." She cupped her baby's velvety head that shone in the candlelight with an ether-like dusting of silvery golden hair. "And, of course, Cassia after Mama. I like to think she is looking down on us now and smiling. Hopefully, she will watch over her precious granddaughter, and somehow guide her as she has always guided us."

"I am sure she will. Can you not just see her hugging Papa with joy?" Fortuity kissed the baby's forehead and breathed her in, closing her eyes at the indescribable *baby* scent that made her long for a child of her own. *One day,* she promised herself, gently rocking from side to side. One day, she and Matthew would know this joyous miracle of new life.

"And what of your assigned task? Did you do as you promised?" Blessing smiled as she settled more comfortably against the fresh pile of pillows behind her. "You seem a great deal more relaxed than before."

"Anne is packing, and you shan't have to worry about a houseguest during your lying in." Fortuity gently settled the infant into the cradle beside the bed, then poured her sister a fresh cup of tea laced with one of Mrs. Greer's recommended tonics. "Here you are. Drink this before you sleep. I am sure when I return home, Mrs. Greer will ask if you took the tonic she sent over for when the baby came."

Blessing hazarded a sip as if fearing the liquid held poison, then gave a happy nod. "Hmm... Not nearly as offensive as I expected. You know how some of her remedies tend to be." She took another drink, then balanced the cup between her hands. "And you also know you are welcome to stay here as long as you wish. You are not a houseguest. You are my sister."

Fortuity perched on the edge of the bed beside her. "I appreciate the offer, but my place is at home." She couldn't deny that she still harbored a bit of uneasiness. Or to put it more aptly, pure rage when it came to her book being published under her husband's name instead of hers. But she would stop being a ninny and push through this. After all, as Blessing had pointed out, they came from a long line of strong women. She would be strong too and deal with the matter with intelligence rather than emotion. She reached over and gently squeezed Blessing's arm. "However, I shall visit often for an exorbitant amount of cuddles."

Blessing laughed. "With so many aunties, little Aurora won't be wanting for cuddles." Her mirth faded, and she shook a finger at Fortuity. "As soon as I am able, I shall help you deal with the dreadful Miss Sykesbury and the Duchess of Disgrace."

"About that—" Fortuity said louder than she intended. She cringed and peeped into the cradle to ensure she hadn't awakened the baby. "I failed to tell you earlier because I couldn't remember for certain if it was true, but Matthew sent Eleanor back to India. Permanently."

"Good on Matthew." Blessing nodded her approval. "And what of Her Grace? How do the two of you intend to deal with the shameless Olandra? Just continue ignoring her until she wearies of being such a nuisance?"

Fortuity shrugged. "Matthew assures me he has a plan but wishes it to be a surprise."

"Interesting," Blessing said. "I hope he waits until after my lying in has ended. I want to watch."

A light tapping on the door interrupted them. "My lady?"

Blessing wrinkled her nose. "There is that horrid monthly nurse, Mrs. Flackney, returning with Mrs. Bretherton so I can speak with her again."

"Who is Mrs. Bretherton?"

"A wet nurse whom I am not entirely certain I like. That is why I wished to speak with her again. Our initial meeting was less than satisfactory. If her disposition has not improved, I refuse to allow her anywhere near my child. After all, I nursed Aurora perfectly well when they put her to my breast. Just look how contented she is. When I decide I need a wet nurse, it will be a woman I can trust with my precious baby." Blessing huffed and glared at the door. "I am sure whatever I decide will shock Mrs. Flackney, since she behaves as if every word that falls from her lips comes straight from the Almighty Himself, and I should accept it without so much as a whimper."

The tapping on the door repeated, a little louder this time. "My lady?"

Fortuity rose. "Do you wish to see them now, or shall I send them away?"

Blessing pushed herself higher among the pillows as if ready to declare war upon whoever dared to interrupt them. "Let the wretches enter at their own risk."

Fortuity went to the door and opened it. As her sister had predicted, the scowling Mrs. Flackney stood there with a stern-faced woman at her side. "The baby is sleeping, so do be quiet," Fortuity told them, delighting in how their eyes widened in surprise at her curt instruction.

Both ladies offered her a somewhat irritated nod, then entered without so much as a peep.

"Go to your husband, sister," Blessing said with a calculating smile that assured Fortuity she had the situation well in hand.

"I shall return tomorrow," Fortuity promised. "Send for me if you need me sooner."

"I will, pet."

Fortuity couldn't help but smile as she left the room and softly closed the door behind her. Before going downstairs to Matthew, she returned to her room to check on good-natured Anne, who hadn't batted an eye when Fortuity had asked her to repack everything she had just unpacked because they would be returning home. They nearly collided as the loyal maid opened the door to exit the room just as Fortuity reached for the latch to enter.

Anne hopped back and caught a hand to her chest. "Goodness, my lady. I was coming to tell you that Mr. Donnelly just carried your trunks down to the wagon. All is ready whenever you are."

"Thank you so much, Anne. I am sure Lord Ravenglass is ready to leave. Follow me down and let Cadwick know to fetch my shawl."

Anne held out her gloves. "I know you do not like them, my lady, but since you are going outside…"

A frustrated sigh escaped Fortuity before she could stop it. She despised gloves and thought them silly unless the weather was freezing or one was attending an elaborate ball that demanded full-length gloves to accentuate one's arms. She tugged them on and gave her maid a curt nod. "There. My mother would thank you."

Anne merely smiled and politely bowed her head.

Fortuity cast a last glance down the hallway toward her sister's room and sent up a silent *thank you* to the Almighty yet again for the safe delivery of little Aurora. She swept down the stairs, with Anne trailing behind her.

Matthew awaited her, looking as if he could barely restrain himself from pulling her into his arms. A warm flush of longing washed across her, settling her uncertainties about whether this was the right thing to do. Yes. It was the right thing to do. She belonged with the man she loved, and she would learn to ignore the *ton*'s stinging barbs. Somehow. At least she would do her level best.

"Are you ready to return home?" she asked him.

His face lit up, effectively answering her without uttering a word. With a lopsided smile, he offered his arm. "Indeed, I am, my love. We can return for your things later."

"Anne already had Mr. Donnelly take my trunks to the wagon. We are ready as soon as she fetches my shawl from Cadwick." She leaned to peer into the parlor. "How is Thorne? Bursting with pride, I suppose?"

"Absolutely. He is in with Lady Roslynn at the moment." Matthew sadly shook his head. "He hoped to convince her to use her bath chair once again so they might carry her upstairs to see the baby. If that won't do, I believe he intends to locate a sedan chair and see if she will trust that, since it has no wheels that would harm her cats."

"Poor Lady Roslynn. She is such a kind soul. I do hope the cloudiness of her mind clears so she can enjoy little Aurora."

"Aurora?" Matthew smiled. "So we shan't be calling our new niece Lady Starpeeper?"

"Aurora for the Roman goddess of the dawn and Cassia for Mama. But I am sure if we occasionally call her Lady Starpeeper, no one will mind." She hugged herself at the memory of holding the sweet child. "She is such a precious baby. Holding her made me eager for one of my own."

With a smoldering glance, Matthew moved closer and pressed his mouth close to her ear. "As soon as we reach home, we can do our best to satisfy that eagerness, my love."

A shiver of heat shot through her, making her catch her breath.

"Your shawl, my lady," Anne said as she emerged from a side room with the garment held ready to drape around Fortuity's shoulders. "And Mr. Donnelly said I would be most welcome to ride with him on the wagon to prevent me from overcrowding the carriage with you and his lordship."

"Did he now?" Fortuity noted the high coloring on Anne's cheeks but granted her the grace of not calling her a liar. After all, the maid was patient as the day was long, and always took the best care of her. She only hoped she wouldn't lose her to the charming Mr. Donnelly. "That was very considerate of him. Please give him our thanks."

With her gaze lowered, Anne bobbed a quick curtsy. "I will, my lady. If that be all, Mr. Donnelly and I shall set out immediately, so I might get to the unpacking and have everything sorted by the time you arrive."

"Thank you, Anne." After the maid hurried off, Fortuity turned and narrowed her eyes at Matthew. "I heard you snickering."

"Snickering? Me? Surely you are mistaken." He caught her close and nibbled at the spot under her ear that was always her undoing. "I am merely overjoyed to have my wonderful wife back in my arms where she belongs. And I am even happier to learn that I shall have you all to myself during our long carriage ride home."

"Long carriage ride?" she managed to say in a breathless whisper as he drew her earlobe into his mouth. "Home is but a few streets over."

He stepped back and smiled at her, then looped her arm through his and escorted her out to their awaiting carriage. "It is amazing how long it can take to cross Mayfair when one sets one's mind to it."

She shivered in anticipation as she seated herself inside and noticed it took him a bit longer to join her. She couldn't hear what he told the driver, but her cheeks burned as she imagined what he might be saying. Surely, he wouldn't tell the man to take a tour of London, so they might have ample time to enjoy a heated reunion in the carriage?

She shivered again and fanned herself, finding the idea not without merit.

He climbed inside without uttering a word, pulled down all the shades, then took her into his arms and crushed his mouth to hers. The fast pounding of her heart made her blood roar in her ears as she arched into him and clung to him just as tightly. Perhaps misunderstandings were not such a bad thing after all if they ended like this.

A moan escaped her as he kissed his way down her jawline to her throat, then pushed even lower while fondling her breast. "So many dreadful layers between us," she said, then bit her lip. "Oh my, I should not have said that."

He rucked up her gown, grazed his hand up her thigh, and cupped her bottom before lifting his head and smiling down at her. "Indeed, you should have said it, my love, because I could not agree more."

"Surely we should wait until we get home." But she arched into his touch as his fingers swept between her thighs and touched where she needed him most. "Or perhaps not."

"I choose *perhaps not.*" He nuzzled her breast through her gown as he slid his fingers inside her. "It is my intention to enjoy you now and yet again whenever we arrive home."

"Whenever we arrive home?" she repeated with a breathless groan, finding it increasingly difficult to form an intelligent response. All she wanted to do was *feel*, revel in the ever-increasing bliss storming within her.

"I instructed Mr. Turnmaster to drive around until I gave him the signal to turn toward home."

"How fortunate." She slid lower in the seat, wrapping her legs around Matthew where he knelt on the floor between the seats. "I need you, Matthew, so very badly." She bucked as his talented fingers dipped faster and his thumb rubbed the spot that drove her insane. "Oh my! Do not let me shout and startle the horses."

He swallowed her cries with a deep kiss that crested the ecstasy and made it shudder through her even harder. Whirling with the delicious, hot waves crashing across her, she vaguely noticed him fumbling with his falls. Then he grabbed her by the hips and buried himself inside her. "I am a greedy man, my love. I had to have you."

"Good, because I am greedy too." The rocking of the coach and the bumps in the road made his plundering of her all the more effective. She clutched the sides of his waistcoat and yanked him toward her, encouraging him to rut harder and faster. She clenched her teeth and locked her jaws to keep from shrieking with pleasure and telling all of London that she was shattering into blissful bits of euphoria.

Matthew rumbled with a low, strained growl, then threw back his head and roared as he emptied into her.

She clapped a hand over her mouth. Why? She had no idea.

She wasn't the one who had just bellowed like an enraged beast while touring the crowded streets of London.

As he sagged over her, he started laughing.

"Matthew," she whispered. "What will Mr. Turnmaster think?"

"It is a little late for whispering, my love," he said, chuckling as he nuzzled kisses along her throat. "And I do not give a damn what Mr. Turnmaster or anyone else thinks. You are all that matters to me and making love to you makes me whole again." He lifted her, spun about, and plopped down into the seat, settling her astraddle him. "Hmm… I rather like this position too. Shall we allow your Anne plenty of time to unpack your things?"

"Indeed." She wrapped her arms around his neck and rewarded him with an impassioned kiss for such a splendid suggestion.

Chapter Sixteen

FEELING SMUG ABOUT the possibilities tonight's ball held, Matthew handed Fortuity up into the carriage. "There you are, my love. Have I told you how positively breathtaking you are tonight?"

She cut a sideways glance at him, narrowing her eyes with suspicion. "As a matter of fact, you have. Twice before, actually. What are you up to now?"

"Can a man not admire his wife's beauty? Repeatedly?"

"When he is genuine—yes. When he is distracted by whatever nefarious doings he has plotted with my sister—no."

"I would never plot anything nefarious, nor would Lady Blessing. Effectiveness is our goal, nothing more."

"Effectiveness?"

"For us."

She scowled, then puckered her tempting lips into the most adorable pout he had ever witnessed. "I repeat my earlier question: what are you up to? What is this plot the two of you have hatched? I would like to be prepared."

"There is nothing for which you need to prepare, and I am simply looking forward to an enjoyable night out with my wife."

"Liar."

"Is that kind?"

"No. It is truthful."

She didn't sound angry, so he hazarded a smile and patted his waistcoat that held the key element for the trap. "Rest easy, my love. If tonight goes as planned, the Duchess of Esterton will worry us no more, nor will the *ton* continue laying odds on your meek acceptance of a roving husband or your refusal to ever allow me back into your bed."

"What do you intend to do?

"You shall see soon enough."

She snorted a very unladylike huff. "I believe you are enjoying this."

"I am indeed, my lady. That woman has caused us untold misery, and it is time for it to end." He took her gloved hand in his and frowned down at it. "I hate gloves. They bar me from the enticing feel of your bare skin against mine."

"I do not care for them either. But one does not go to a ball without one's gloves." She rolled her eyes and made a face. "Or so Mama always used to say and now Anne ensures I remember." She leaned into him and offered up her mouth along with a suggestive nudge against his chest. "A kiss would help me endure the sacrifices I am forced to make for propriety."

He happily complied, groaning at the sweet taste of her and drawing upon every strength he possessed to break the connection and lift his head. "Such a wicked temptress, you are, my love, making me yearn to stay home rather than attend another of Lady Atterley's infamous balls."

Fortuity gave an equally put-upon sigh. "I would rather stay home as well, but Blessing is so looking forward to seeing the results of this scheme the two of you devised, since you were good enough to wait until after her churching and Aurora's christening to launch it." She nudged him in the ribs this time. "I cannot believe you plotted with my sister rather than me."

"Thorne begged me to because your Blessing was not at all pleased about being barred from overseeing the construction of her new observatory for the four weeks of her lying in. Plotting the duchess's downfall served as a distraction to maintain peace in the Knightwood household."

"Well…I did get the pleasure of enjoying little Aurora's company while the two of you worked out the details of your nefarious plan."

"I told you, it is not nefarious. Only effective. Or should be."

The thrill of the hunt surged through him as the carriage rolled to a stop, and Lady Atterley's footman opened its door and let down the steps. Matthew alit, then helped Fortuity disembark. She truly was lovely this evening, bedecked in her gown of lavender that shimmered with silvery threading embroidered in an elegant trail of ivy that swirled around her as if she were the queen of the fae. But it was more than just the gown. An unexplainable glow emanated from her, as if something magical glimmered within her.

He halted her before they continued up the steps. "You steal my breath away, Fortuity. Please know this is not just the idle babbling of distraction. You are my world—now and forever—and the strength and depth of my love for you sometimes frightens the blazes out of me. I would be lost without you."

Her lips parted with a surprised but silent *oh*, and a sheen of happy tears glistened in her eyes. She rested a hand on his cheek and tiptoed for a tender kiss. "I love you with a fury as well," she whispered.

A polite clearing of a throat behind them interrupted the moment.

Matthew glanced back at Lord and Lady Billersford. "Do forgive me. I am completely besotted with my wife and sometimes forget my surroundings."

Crusty old Billersford nodded and affected an understanding smile that he obviously did not mean. As he and his wife stepped around them, Matthew overheard Lady Billersford curtly question her husband, "Why do you never say things like that about me?"

Fortuity pressed her fingers to her lips, her shoulders quivering with amusement. "You have done it now, Matthew, gotten that stodgy old goat on the bad side of his wife. They shall not have a pleasant evening now."

"I very much doubt if they were going to have a pleasant evening to begin with." He tucked her arm through his and kissed her cheek. "I know public displays of affection are frowned upon, but if they dislike it, they can either look away or go straight to the devil. I love my wife and do not intend to hide it."

"You are in rare form this evening."

"I have merely found my feet as a devoted husband." And he had. He couldn't imagine life without Fortuity beside him. "Come, my darling. Stay close. Lady Atterley's ball appears to be quite the crush."

"Indeed, it does."

Matthew scanned the crowded ballroom from the top of the grand staircase that led down into it. "Your brother and most of your sisters are already in place beside the terrace doors. Do you see Knightwood and Blessing?"

"*Already in place beside the terrace doors?* Have you enlisted my entire family in this escapade?" Fortuity looked all around, then pointed across the way. "Essie and Thorne are there, making their way over to join the rest."

"Good, and Blessing suggested we gather as many as possible. It appears she has been quite busy in that regard." A sense of satisfaction filled him. This ploy would take control of what Olandra felt was her power: the manipulative and damaging gossip of the *ton*. "Several are following Knightwood and your sister. Her recruitment has been quite successful."

Fortuity clutched his arm tighter as they descended the steps and slowly made their way through the crowd surrounding the dance floor. "A hint of what is to happen would be most appreciated," she murmured for his ears alone.

"We are taking control and *acting*, my love, rather than *reacting*."

She glared at him.

He didn't wish to make her nervous, but if he took the time to explain, the ploy might fail. Instead, he made a show of whirling her out onto the floor to get her across the room to her siblings even quicker. "Our first dance was a waltz. Remember?"

"I might recall that," she said, with a slight snippiness to her tone.

"I need you to trust me, my love. Can you do that?"

She gave him a pained look. "Do I have a choice?"

"You always have a choice," he said as he spun them closer to the Broadmere family. "And I hope you always choose me." Thankfully, that melted her. She relaxed in his arms and relinquished her worries with a patronizing smile.

"You know I always choose you."

The music ended at the perfect moment, enabling them to halt in front of the Broadmeres. "Your Grace," Matthew said to Fortuity's brother as he handed her over. "Thank you for your assistance this evening."

"It is always my pleasure to take on my sister's enemies," the duke said, then smiled and glanced at the rest of the sisters. "We may often squabble among ourselves, but the Broadmeres always defend our own. Our forces are at your service."

Matthew bowed to Fortuity, then kissed her hand again. "Stay with your family. They know what to do."

"But—"

He shook his head. "Trust me, my love."

She looked up at him and gave a resigned sigh. "Godspeed to you, Matthew."

He waited until the Broadmeres, Knightwood, and the friends they had gathered all filed outside through the terrace doors leading to Lady Atterley's impressive garden, the place where many a searing scandal had started, and where Olandra's machinations would end. He rubbed his hands together and eyed the crowd. Time to invite the guest of honor to the scheme.

Olandra, the dowager duchess, was easy to find. Not only did her annoying laugh drown out any amount of conversation or music, but her coppery red hair shone like a beacon. She loved a crowd and fed on attention and ratafia, which, if she drank enough of it, increased both the pitch and volume of her laughter. What the devil had ever made him think he loved that woman?

"My lord." She curtsied low as he approached, her overly bright eyes attesting to the number of glasses of ratafia she had already consumed. "How are you this fine evening?"

"Quite well, Your Grace." With the slightest tip of his head, he glanced in the direction of the terrace doors. "However, I feel the need for some fresh air. The room has grown unbearably warm."

"Indeed, it has." Olandra snapped open her fan and unabashedly waved it in front of her ample bosom, which was about to spill out over her neckline. "Would your wife mind if I joined you?" she asked loudly with a covert glance around to ensure everyone overheard her.

"I am sure my wife would not mind at all." Matthew couldn't refrain from smiling. Fortuity would indeed be delighted when she witnessed what he and Blessing had planned for Olandra.

As they made their way through the crowd and stepped out onto the terrace, Olandra preened like the proudest of peahens. "I am glad my latest message to you finally drew your attention," she said in a low, sultry tone while leaning closer. "Your tastes have changed, my lord. Now, I know it takes a more brazen approach to draw your attention."

"Brazenness always draws attention," he said, trying not to recoil from her touch as they made their way deeper into the east side of the garden toward the known privacy of the half-circle of columns and statuary. "But one must be careful about the attention one draws."

"Oh my. That sounds wonderfully wicked."

He brought them to a halt and reached inside his waistcoat for the most recent note she'd dared to send. "I must say, it was quite bold of you to pelt my townhouse with so many pleas since your arrival in London." He held up the folded bit of parchment bearing her seal. "Have you no shame, Your Grace?"

She frowned at him, blinking as though dust had blown into

her eyes. "Shame?" She tittered with a nervous laugh. "As I said in all my previous notes, I never forgave myself for making the wrong choice." She moved toward him, her frown becoming an astonished scowl when he stepped back from her. "You loved me, Matthew. I should never have thrown that away."

"I lusted after you then, Your Grace. No more. No less. And that foolishness on my part has long since passed. You will cease this harassment that I have decided should be laid bare for all to witness." He glanced around the perimeter of the clearing and gave a curt nod.

The Broadmere siblings, Knightwood, and a great many more guests than had previously been led outside by Blessing stepped out of the shadows. He held out the note to his smiling sister-in-law. "Would you be so good as to read this aloud for everyone's enjoyment, although, I must warn you, this one is particularly scandalous and some might even find it offensive."

"My pleasure, dear brother." Blessing held the note higher to better catch the light of the torches.

Olandra dove and tried to snatch it away, but Blessing dodged her, then started reading in a loud, clear voice that carried quite well.

My dearest Matthew (yes, I still call you dearest even though you have proven to be most stubborn in your faithfulness to that bland little wife of yours),

Since you refuse to respond to my correspondences, perhaps something a bit more salacious might interest you—

"Shut your mouth, you vile creature!" Olandra charged toward Blessing again, but Knightwood caught her by the wrist and dragged her back. "This is all a lie!" Olandra screeched while trying to yank free. "A wicked contrivance. Why would you shame me this way, Matthew?"

Matthew gave Blessing's husband an appreciative nod. "Pray, keep our guest of honor in place, Knightwood."

"Happily," Knightwood told him, before turning to Olandra. "And you may shut *your* mouth, Your Grace, and never threaten my wife again or rue the day you were born."

"Thank you, dearest," Blessing told Knightwood, then turned back to the crowd. "Shall I continue, dear friends? I must warn you, the contents are quite—"

Shouts for her to *read on* interrupted her.

Blessing gave a theatrical bow and read,

Lord Fetterill and Lord Alcester host the most scrumptious of pleasure parties. After all, with their wives confined by the family way, they must find other means of satisfying their voracious appetites. Join me, my darling. Threesomes, foursomes, and every contrived fantasy is most wonderfully explored at these exclusive events. I promise you will not regret leaving the boredom of your marriage bed to join me in their garden of fleshly delights, full of willing—

"How could you do this to me?" Olandra screamed at Matthew. "You loved me enough to ask me to marry you! I had you first!"

"You are an abhorrence, Olandra, and you never *had* me the way my Fortuity has." Matthew went to his precious lady love, took her hand, and drew her into his arms. "I love my wife more than I ever dreamed I could love anyone," he said while losing himself in her blue-eyed gaze, "and I will do whatever it takes to keep her happy and in love with me."

"I love you, Matthew," Fortuity said, "more than you will ever know."

The gathered onlookers clapped and hurrahed as he kissed her with every ounce of tenderness he possessed for her.

Olandra's enraged shriek split the air. "I hate you all!"

"Well, drat," Thorne said with a hearty laugh. "Her Grace appears to have escaped."

"Oh my," Fortuity said as they abruptly ended their kiss and she turned toward the sound. "The Duchess of Esterton will surely do herself harm, running like that."

With her skirts clutched in her hands, the dowager duchess raced across the garden, up the steps, and disappeared into the house.

Matthew turned Fortuity to face him. "Now, everyone knows the truth, my love, the complete and utter truth."

"Again, I love you," she said ever so softly. "That is the complete and utter truth."

"I love you more," he replied before gathering her even closer and bending his head to enjoy more of her sweet kisses. Lady Atterley's ball could be damned. He had his Fortuity—that was all he would ever need.

Epilogue

Ravenglass Manor
Lake District, England
July 1821

LEANING BACK AGAINST the mighty oak with Matthew reclining on the mossy ground with his head in her lap, Fortuity struggled to keep her drooping eyelids open. Sunlight filtered down through the leaves, dappling the ground with mesmerizing patches of dancing brightness. The repetitious *gurrumphing* of bullfrogs in the nearby pond, the lilting lullaby of birds, and the lazy, droning buzz of bees floating from flower to flower made the warm summer day a study in pure relaxation. Ignatius the pug lounged beside them, belly up, his wheezing snores joining in on nature's cacophony of song.

She idly combed her fingers through Matthew's thick hair, finding the silky feel of it as comforting and sleep inducing as everything else about the day. She was so very happy.

Just today, she had received several letters forwarded to her by Minerva Press, her publisher, in London. Letters from those enraptured by her book—the book bearing Matthew's name but turned into a tantalizing mystery that readers couldn't resist. The brilliant marketing ploy: a dare for them to discover the real author of the scintillating romance, the lady hinted at in the flyers sent to every bookstore and library that had received copies of her precious book. Of course, they easily discovered it was her, but best of all, they adored her story and clamored for more—as did the publisher.

So, she had set to the task of polishing her backlog of manuscripts, bringing them as close to perfection as possible in order to send them to the editor well before next spring, when her priorities would realign because of a very precious matter.

A contented sigh slipped free of her.

With his hands resting on his chest, Matthew smiled but didn't bother opening his eyes. "I do hope that was a happy sigh."

"Indeed, it was. I am happier than happy could be."

He chuckled. "Your brother is also happy you convinced Mr. Sutherland that our marriage satisfied the conditions of the will so his allowance could increase by another fourteen percent. That thoroughbred he gifted us is quite impressive. Mr. Turnmaster is delighted with the bloodline and eager to introduce him to a few select mares."

"Chance is incorrigible and champing at the bit to come into the full of his inheritance." With a lazy laugh, she shook her head. "Poor Gracie will be next on the marriage chopping block, I suppose. I think Chance has finally given up on marrying everyone off in the same Season." She smoothed a fingertip along the sleek line of one of Matthew's dark brows. "He means well, though. Deep down, he wants all of us happy."

Matthew caught her bare hand in his and kissed it. "Still no gloves, my lady? And here we are outside and finished with our berry picking? Your Anne will be beside herself at the scandal."

"Anne must accept that while we are in the country, I intend to enjoy a more relaxed following of proprieties."

"I like the sound of that."

"As do I." She leaned forward and nibbled the lightest of kisses across his warm lips. "You taste of the berries we picked."

"I had to sample them to ensure they were good."

"They are indeed good."

He pulled her down for another sampling, pausing just before her lips met his. "Then you should kiss me again, and again."

She gave him a teasing shake of her head. "All in good time. There is something I want to discuss first."

"Oh?" The leeriness in his tone matched the immediate wariness in his eyes.

"It is nothing serious. I merely noted that our home here in the country does not appear to have a nursery."

He stared at her, going still as though turned to stone. "The townhouse in London does not have a nursery either," he said ever so slowly.

"No, it does not. I had noticed that as well." She gifted him with a thoughtful look, enjoying his torture immensely. "I suppose the townhouse's floor plan needs to be updated first, since we shall require a nursery next spring. The nursery here would not be needed until we leave London for the summer."

"You are certain?" He rose and crouched beside her as if ready to leap like a frog.

"Mrs. Greer assures me I am not imagining things. The Ravenglass line is expanding—as I will too. Although, hopefully, I will not enjoy the magnitude Blessing achieved when little Lady Aurora was on the way."

"A baby," he whispered, hesitantly touching her cheek, as if afraid she might shatter before his very eyes.

"*Our* baby," she gently corrected him, her heart soaring. "Little Quill Ravenglass until we are more formally introduced."

Matthew took her into his arms and gently tilted her face up to his. "Quill Ravenglass. I rather like that. Perhaps we should consider keeping it once we meet our precious child."

She touched his cheek, loving the way his day's growth of stubble tickled her palm. "Quill is not a proper name for a lady. I think it sounds more male than female. *Quill* would be for a son. Do you not agree?"

"If we are blessed with a daughter," he said, brushing his lips across hers as he spoke, "we could call her Seshat."

"Seshat?" she whispered, lacing her fingers into his hair and tugging him closer for another kiss. "What does it mean?" she asked once their kiss ended.

"The one who writes. Seshat was the Egyptian goddess of libraries and written accounts, protector of books and knowledge. She was the scribe of the gods."

The vastness of Matthew's knowledge still astounded her even though she had always known him to be an insatiable reader. "How is it you are so brilliant?"

"I am a slow learner, actually," he confessed with a sheepish grin. Ever so gently, he swept a stray curl off her cheek and tucked it behind her ear. "Look how long it took me to realize that the other half of my soul was right in front of me, waiting to be joined with my heart."

She pressed a finger to his lips and shook her head. "That was the past. What matters now is that we are joined." An elated giggle bubbled free of her. "And our union is fruitful and growing."

"A baby," he said. "Quill Seshat Ravenglass, until we meet him or her, of course."

Then all levity left him so quickly it filled her with concern. "My love? What is it?"

"I cannot bear the thought of possibly losing you," he admitted in a rasping whisper. "What if—"

She silenced him by pressing a finger to his lips again. "No. We do not dabble in the dangers of *what if*. We consider ourselves blessed beyond our wildest imaginings and strive to teach our children the same."

His smile returned. "*Children?* How many?"

As she pulled him down for another kiss, she decided it was high time to talk less and enjoy each other more. "I shall let you know when to stop. Trust me."

"I trust you implicitly, my love. Do with me what you will."

"I fully intend to."

THE END

About the Author

If you enjoyed FORTUITY'S ARRANGEMENT, please consider leaving a review on the site where you purchased your copy, or a reader site such as Goodreads, or BookBub.

If you'd like to receive my newsletter, here's the link to sign up: maevegreyson.com/contact.html#newsletter

I love to hear from readers! Drop me a line at maevegreyson@gmail.com

Or visit me on Facebook: facebook.com/AuthorMaeveGreyson

Join my Facebook Group – Maeve's Corner: facebook.com/groups/MaevesCorner

I'm also on Instagram: maevegreyson

My website: https://maevegreyson.com

Feel free to ask questions or leave some Reader Buzz on bingebooks.com/author/maeve-greyson

Goodreads: goodreads.com/maevegreyson

Follow me on these sites to get notifications about new releases, sales, and special deals:

Amazon:
amazon.com/Maeve-Greyson/e/B004PE9T9U

BookBub:
bookbub.com/authors/maeve-greyson

Many thanks and may your life always be filled with good books!
Maeve